PRAISE FOR THE RADIUM AGE SERIES

"New editions of a host of under-discussed classics of the genre."
—*Reactor Magazine*

"Neglected classics of early 20th-century sci-fi in spiffily designed paperback editions."
—*Financial Times*

"An entertaining, engrossing glimpse into the profound and innovative literature of the early twentieth century."
—*Foreword*

"Shows that 'proto-sf' was being published much more widely, alongside other kinds of fiction, before it emerged as a genre."
—*BSFA Review*

"An excellent start at showcasing the strange wonders offered by the Radium Age."
—*Shelf Awareness*

"Lovingly curated . . . The series' freedom from genre purism lets us see how a specific set of anxieties—channeled through dystopias, Lovecraftian horror, arch social satire, and adventure tales—spurred literary experimentation and the bending of conventions."
—*Los Angeles Review of Books*

"A huge effort to help define a new era of science fiction."
—*Transfer Orbit*

"Admirable . . . and highly recommended."
—*Washington Post*

"Long live the Radium Age."
—*Los Angeles Times*

THE GREATEST ADVENTURE

THE GREATEST ADVENTURE

John Taine

introduction by S. L. Huang

THE MIT PRESS
CAMBRIDGE, MASSACHUSETTS
LONDON, ENGLAND

This book was set in Arnhem Pro and PF DIN Text Pro by New Best-set Typesetters Ltd. Printed and bound in the United States of America.

Library of Congress Cataloging-in-Publication Data

Names: Taine, John, 1883–1960, author. | Huang, S. L., writer of introduction.
Title: The greatest adventure / John Taine ; Introduction by S. L. Huang.
Description: Cambridge, Massachusetts : The MIT Press, 2025. | Series:
    Radium Age
Identifiers: LCCN 2024019220 (print) | LCCN 2024019221 (ebook) |
    ISBN 9780262551427 (paperback) | ISBN 9780262381864 (epub) |
    ISBN 9780262381871 (pdf)
Subjects: LCGFT: Science fiction. | Novels.
Classification: LCC PS3503.E4323 G74 2025 (print) | LCC PS3503.E4323 (ebook)
LC record available at https://lccn.loc.gov/2024019220
LC ebook record available at https://lccn.loc.gov/2024019221

10 9 8 7 6 5 4 3 2 1

CONTENTS

Contents

Do we really know science fiction? There were the scientific romance years that stretched from the mid-nineteenth century to circa 1900. And there was the genre's so-called golden age, from circa 1935 through the early 1960s. But between those periods, and overshadowed by them, was an era that has bequeathed us such tropes as the robot (berserk or benevolent), the tyrannical superman, the dystopia, the unfathomable extraterrestrial, the sinister telepath, and the eco-catastrophe. In 2009, writing for the sf blog io9.com at the invitation of Annalee Newitz and Charlie Jane Anders, I became fascinated with the period during which the sf genre as we know it emerged. Inspired by the exactly contemporaneous career of Marie Curie, who shared a Nobel Prize for her discovery of radium in 1903, only to die of radiation-induced leukemia in 1934, I eventually dubbed this three-decade interregnum the "Radium Age."

Curie's development of the theory of radioactivity, which led to the extraordinary, terrifying, awe-inspiring insight that the atom is, at least in part, a state of energy constantly in movement, is an apt metaphor for the twentieth century's first three decades. These years were marked by rising sociocultural strife across various fronts: the founding of the women's suffrage movement, the National Association for the Advancement of Colored People, socialist currents within the labor movement, anticolonial and revolutionary upheaval around the world . . . as well as the associated strengthening of reactionary movements that supported, for example, racial segregation, immigration restriction, eugenics, and sexist policies.

Science—as a system of knowledge, a mode of experimenting, and a method of reasoning—accelerated the pace of change during these years in ways simultaneously liberating and terrifying. As sf author and historian Brian Stableford points out in his 1989 essay "The Plausibility of the Impossible," the universe we discovered by means of the scientific method in the early twentieth century defies common sense: "We are haunted by a sense of the impossibility of ultimately making sense of things." By playing host to certain far-out notions—time travel, faster-than-light travel, and ESP, for example—that we have every reason to judge impossible, science fiction serves as an "instrument of negotiation," Stableford suggests, with which we strive to accomplish "the difficult diplomacy of existence in a scientifically knowable but essentially unimaginable world." This is no less true today than during the Radium Age.

The social, cultural, political, and technological upheavals of the 1900–1935 period are reflected in the proto-sf writings of authors such as Olaf Stapledon, William Hope Hodgson, Muriel Jaeger, Karel Čapek, G. K. Chesterton, Cicely Hamilton, W. E. B. Du Bois, Yevgeny Zamyatin, E. V. Odle, Arthur Conan Doyle, Mikhail Bulgakov,

Pauline Hopkins, Stanisław Ignacy Witkiewicz, Aldous Huxley, Gustave Le Rouge, A. Merritt, Rudyard Kipling, Rose Macaulay, J. D. Beresford, J. J. Connington, S. Fowler Wright, Jack London, Thea von Harbou, and Edgar Rice Burroughs, not to mention the late-period but still incredibly prolific H. G. Wells himself. More cynical than its Victorian precursor yet less hard-boiled than the sf that followed, in the writings of these visionaries we find acerbic social commentary, shock tactics, and also a sense of frustrated idealism—and reactionary cynicism, too—regarding humankind's trajectory.

The MIT Press's Radium Age series represents a much-needed evolution of my own efforts to champion the best proto-sf novels and stories from 1900 to 1935 among scholars already engaged in the fields of utopian and speculative fiction studies, as well as general readers interested in science, technology, history, and thrills and chills. By reissuing literary productions from a time period that hasn't received sufficient attention for its contribution to the emergence of science fiction as a recognizable form—one that exists and has meaning in relation to its own traditions and innovations, as well as within a broader ecosystem of literary genres, each of which, as John Rieder notes in *Science Fiction and the Mass Cultural Genre System* (2017), is itself a product of overlapping "communities of practice"—we hope not only to draw attention to key overlooked works but perhaps also to influence the way scholars and sf fans alike think about this crucial yet neglected and misunderstood moment in the emergence of the sf genre.

John W. Campbell and other Cold War–era sf editors and propagandists dubbed a select group of writers and story types from the pulp era to be the golden age of science fiction. In doing so, they helped fix in the popular imagination a too-narrow understanding of what the sf genre can offer. (In his introduction to the 1974 collection *Before the Golden Age*, for example, Isaac Asimov notes that although it may have possessed a certain exuberance, in general sf from before the mid-1930s moment when Campbell assumed editorship of *Astounding Stories* "seems, to anyone who has experienced the Campbell Revolution, to be clumsy, primitive, naive.") By returning to an international tradition of scientific speculation via fiction from after the Poe–Verne–Wells era and before sf's Golden Age, the Radium Age series will demonstrate—contra Asimov et al.—the breadth, richness, and diversity of the literary works that were responding to a vertiginous historical period, and how they helped innovate a nascent genre (which wouldn't be named until the mid-1920s, by Hugo Gernsback, founder of *Amazing Stories* and namesake of the Hugo Awards) as a mode of speculative imagining.

The MIT Press's Noah J. Springer and I are grateful to the sf writers and scholars who have agreed to serve as this series' advisory board. Aided by their guidance, we'll endeavor to surface a rich variety of texts, along with introductions by a diverse group of sf scholars, sf writers, and others that will situate these remarkable, entertaining, forgotten works within their own social, political, and scientific contexts, while drawing out contemporary parallels.

We hope that reading Radium Age writings, published in times as volatile as our own, will serve to remind us that our own era's seemingly natural, eternal, and inevitable social, economic, and cultural forms and norms are—like Madame Curie's atom—forever in flux.

INTRODUCTION: SCIENCE WONDER STORIES

S. L. Huang

Eric Temple Bell was a California Institute of Technology mathematician and writer of "popular mathematics" books who also became a prolific contributor to the genre then known as *scientifiction*. Starting in 1919 and using the pen name John Taine, Bell wrote rapidly during his summer vacations. In addition to *The Greatest Adventure*, by 1932 he would crank out the Radium Age proto-sf novels *The Purple Sapphire* (1924), *The Gold Tooth* (1927), *Quayle's Invention* (1927), *Green Fire* (1928), *The Iron Star* (1930), *White Lily* (1930), *Seeds of Life* (1931), and *The Time Stream* (1931–1932). He published an additional six novels during the sf golden age, the last—*G.O.G. 666*, a Cold War fable about a Russia-created biological monstrosity—in 1954.

Bell's stories were by no means confined to his fiction. Nearly every account he gave of his own life, from official biographical profiles to outlines of his childhood that he shared with his wife and son, would later turn out to be riddled with fanciful details. Even Constance Reid, whose 1993 biography is titled *The Search for E. T. Bell*, was forced to concede defeat on many aspects of that search. Despite having dug through countless archives, in the end Reid couldn't answer any number of tantalizing questions, such as: Why did Bell conceal his childhood in San Jose?

Why did he lie about his family's fish-curing industry back in his birthplace of Scotland? What was he doing when he disappeared in 1901? How did his abusive father die, and why weren't the records filed properly? How did Bell lose part of his thumb? And so on.

Bell's fabulizing doesn't appear to have been motivated by cruelty or the intent to scam anyone. By all reports, he was a kind and well-liked person, if quick-tempered and excitable. He loved art, cats, and the natural beauty of Southern California—which his poetry depicted as a paradise. (He took his poetry much more seriously than his science fiction, forever frustrated at how difficult it was to find a publisher for it.) He enjoyed rich, meaningful friendships, most importantly with his wife Jessie "Toby" Bell, a fiercely independent and intellectual woman whom he greatly respected.

Bell is best remembered today less for his science fiction or his pioneering work in number theory and combinatorial mathematics (though Bell series, Bell numbers, and Bell polynomials were named in his honor), than for his popular mathematics books, particularly 1937's *Men of Mathematics*. A successful effort to popularize the life stories and legacies of mathematicians from Eudoxus and Archimedes to Poincaré and Cantor, this collection of essays is penned with the same dramatic gusto that the author brought to the monster-filled action scenes of his fiction. It would inspire some impressionable young readers—including John Forbes Nash Jr., Julia Robinson, and Freeman Dyson—to become mathematicians themselves. Another popular math book of his, *The Last*

Problem, would inspire Andrew Wiles to prove Fermat's Last Theorem in 1994.

Perhaps it will be no surprise, however, that Bell liberally embroidered his nonfiction with highly apocryphal stories. His tale-telling was damaging, in some cases. Later biographers of Sofya Kovalevskaya in particular have every reason to be infuriated at how his inaccurate portrayal of the Russian mathematician's life and legacy would become cemented in the popular view. It's almost as if Bell looked at everything through the lens of how to tell a good story and wasn't going to let a piddly thing like the truth interfere with that.

When I started writing science fiction, I was given some tongue-in-cheek advice: "Write only the good parts." That is, simply skip anything you—and thus the reader—might find boring. Bell's proto-sf novel *The Greatest Adventure* embodies this humorous maxim. It seems a book intended to be composed entirely of "good parts," packed to capacity with imagination, adventure, and scientific curiosity.

The Greatest Adventure was published in book form in 1929 by E. P. Dutton and retroactively serialized, in 1944, by the pulp magazine *Famous Fantastic Mysteries*. The novel's breakneck plot—which I will endeavor not to spoil too much of in this introduction—demonstrates just how greatly its author loved to spin a good yarn. And it's peppered with gleeful references to Bell's own life and interests.

In a way, Bell's fiction style is amusingly reflective of his mathematics. Many of Bell's more than two hundred mathematical papers were written in a highly eccentric fashion, to the point that mathematicians both then and now have had difficulty understanding them. As a result, it's not uncommon for a mathematician to "discover" a result that Bell proved long ago. Much to his annoyance, this ongoing phenomenon began when Bell was still alive!

Take the eponymic "Bell series," which are formal power series used to study arithmetic functions. They were introduced in Bell's very first published mathematics paper . . . which is poorly organized and replete with incomplete statements, and which was published in an obscure journal by Bell's own inexplicable choice. Those few mathematicians who've taken the trouble to tease the paper apart have been impressed with its variety of wide-ranging results—most of which have been re-proven since. It was only thanks to Tom Apostol, a younger Caltech colleague of Bell's who took the trouble to puzzle through the paper, that the series were belatedly named after Bell.

One clue to understanding both Bell's mathematical and literary efforts—as well as his surprising lack of legacy in math, given the breakthroughs he made—is how strongly and frequently he pursued innovative *methods* rather than specific *results*. A shockingly broad-ranging and creative thinker who published prolifically in a range of mathematical subfields (though always returning to number theory), Bell was enamored with finding inventive ways to do math. He gamboled joyfully from one new idea to another—the "good parts" version, let's call it—of mathematical research.

Knowing all this makes *The Greatest Adventure*—despite its flaws—all the more charming. Its explorer-biologist protagonist Eric Lane, like Bell's other scientist protagonists, is fervent and even heroic in his drive to be the first to discover the startlingly new and unknown, in this case, an Antarctic monstrosity that bears evidence of ancient genetic engineering. (Bell was friends across departments with chemists, biologists, and other Caltech scientists whose brains he unashamedly picked.) Though he might have failed to find a publisher for his poetry, Bell's evocative language is put to good use here, and his utter lack of restraint only improves the ride. Even the book's abrupt ending tickles my fancy—the author, having apparently run out of "good parts," simply shuts the narrative down.

Bell may not have led an Antarctic expedition, but aspects of his real-life passions and experiences appear all over the narrative. For example, he lived through the famously severe San Francisco earthquake of 1906, and the terror experienced by his book's characters as they undergo a similar disaster is vivid. Bell and his family also loved cats; Lane and his daughter Edith love cats too. Bell was obsessed with the natural beauty of San Jose; his characters wax on about California orange groves as their yearned-for ideal. I began to wonder whether other plot points might be based on Bell's own experiences, or experiences he'd heard about from one of his many friends. After all, I caught real-world references to James Clerk Maxwell and the La Brea Tar Pits that other readers might assume are fantastical. Were Bell's descriptions of, say, a ship buffeted by an undersea oil geyser equally based in some kind of truth, or a completely unresearched invention? Bell is so effective at combining knowledge with wild imagination that it becomes difficult to tell! One wonders if he thought the same way about the tale-telling across the rest of his life.

The Greatest Adventure cannot be called a polished or profound work of literature. Instead, it is a pulpy roller-coaster ride in which unabashed geeking-out about fanciful research and discovery is interweaved with heart-stopping, adrenaline-filled scenarios of life and death. As a writer whose novels might be described in a similar way, I must confess: I loved it.

Before reading a book from the 1920s, I made sure to gird myself against any less-than-progressive attitudes or characterizations. I was pleased and surprised to walk away from the book impressed with how little I detected the racism or sexism of its time. That was, unfortunately, a viewpoint that would shortly become more complicated.

Let's first take a closer look at the book's main female character: Dr. Lane's eighteen-year-old daughter, Edith. Although the lack of women in the story is disappointing—a trait it sadly shares with most other proto-sf stories from the early twentieth century—Edith herself is terrific. She's a woman whose proficiency and competence are at least the equal of any man's. A scientist! An ace pilot who can outfly everyone else on the expedition! A bold adventurer who not only succeeds in the brutal exposure training for Antarctica but who is perfectly capable of stabbing a monster in the eye! What's more, in a book that's somewhat light on characterization generally speaking, Edith's character is as fully developed as anyone else's.

None of this is particularly surprising, given what we know about Bell. As mentioned above, he was an admirer and staunch ally of his highly intelligent and unconventional wife, Toby. He supported her ambitions and interests in ways nontraditional for the time, from matching wits with her in rowdy debates to living apart for a year so she could finish a degree program at Columbia. Toby would later earn her own bachelor's degree in mathematics and advance enough in the field to produce some publishable research. Bell seems to have viewed his life with her as a full and rich partnership, never regarding her independence or opinions as any less important than his own.

Bell had a number of other significant friendships with women, as well. Many of them, like Grace Hubble, wife of astronomer Edwin Powell Hubble, ran in the same Caltech circles he and Toby did. Bell seems to have respected these women as his intellectual equals.

Still, *The Greatest Adventure* is by no means free of sexism. The story's male characters fall prey to paternalistic assumptions about Edith—and these assumptions go unquestioned by the narrative. Edith is the one likeliest to experience difficulties with some survivalist aspect or other, despite the fact that one of the male characters struggles physically; this is a point of his character (he'd rather be indoors with his books). Worse, Edith's very presence on the expedition seems to require explanation:

She's the daughter of the trip leader, and the friend (and light love interest) of another scientist. The male members of the team, by contrast, don't require such justification.

This, too, seems in line with who Bell was. Despite his friendship with and egalitarian respect for the women in his own life, he doesn't ever seem to have felt called upon to take a stand against the era's sexism. This is perhaps most evident in his book of mathematician biographies, *Men of Mathematics*. Though we cannot fault him for the title (which was his publisher's insistence, over Bell's objections), his poor accounting of Kovalevskaya's life was his own doing, and even among the exaggerations and falsehoods in his accounts of the other mathematicians, the sexist assumptions embedded in hers are particularly shameful. Also, although the book mentions the mathematicians Emmy Noether and Sophie Germain in the chapter on Carl Friedrich Gauss, I find it shocking that Bell doesn't give them greater consideration. Noether, after all, was one of Bell's own contemporaries and admired by everyone from Einstein on down, and Bell's obsession with nineteenth-century number theory would certainly have familiarized him with Germain's work.

On balance, Bell's popularization of mathematics still strikes me as a useful effort. Math pedagogy has long fought severe issues with students suffering from insecurity or intimidation, and efforts to demystify the field can have particularly valuable impacts for young women, given society's reprehensibly heavier discouragement. Despite its flaws, Bell's book did inspire across genders. But he could have done better.

S. L. Huang

Before reading it, I had heard that some of Bell's other stories feature more on-page racism than does *The Greatest Adventure*. I had intended to mention here that this book thankfully shows none of those tendencies. However, I discovered close to publication that I'd read an edition from which the publisher had elected to excise potentially offensive passages without making any note of the abridgement. Though a comparatively small percentage of the book, those passages did include some ugly assumptions and two racial slurs, which readers will have to trip over in the full text.

How much would those very short passages have affected my initial enjoyment of the novel? It's difficult to say. When I began reading I was on guard against the attitudes of a century ago, and some of my unalloyed delight in the book was that I felt I had been able to let that guard down. Bell's writing had other flaws, to be sure, but none that required those sorts of caveats.

In fact, it's a testament to how carried away I was by this novel that I was so disappointed to learn about those excised pieces. I think I still would have enjoyed it—but perhaps in a way that remained more conscious of the man behind the words, reminded that he was not an uncomplicated or unflawed person.

After all, I not only loved the book, but I can freely admit that I may have been over-identifying with Bell himself. I so strongly share his fierce desire to spread the joy of my nerdy mathematical obsessions with readers, and to do so with a brash disregard for anything but the science-and-action "good parts." It's a nice thing to be able to lose one's objectivity sometimes . . . but always hard when reality brings it back to earth with a crash.

I still feel a strong affection toward *The Greatest Adventure*. I still find Bell's life and career fascinating. Perhaps, just as with Bell's other tale-telling, it's not a bad thing to know the truth of the matter, and for such affection and fascination to become a little more tempered.

Less magical, but more real.

I hope you can enjoy this book for what it truthfully is: a madcap adventure story, replete with scientific joy, in which you'll occasionally have to ignore prejudices of the time and the man it came from.

1 BIRD OR REPTILE?

Undoubtedly Dr. Eric Lane was a man to be envied. With ordinary luck he might yet look forward to thirty-five years of the keenest pleasure a highly intelligent and healthy man can experience, the discovery of natural laws and their application to the good of his fellow men.

Although today was his fortieth birthday he felt not a day over eighteen. He smiled as the thought occurred to him, for it reminded him of his daughter Edith. She was just the age that he felt. "We're a pair of kids," he laughed, looking fondly at the white and gold porcelain image of a sleepy tomcat, which she had deposited on his worktable as a birthday offering. Their appreciation of cats was but one among scores of likings which they shared in perfect understanding. Edith's gift of sympathy no doubt was responsible for her father's continued widowerhood. Not once in the ten years since his wife's death had Dr. Lane thought of marrying. His wife had been like Edith, quick to understand when he left the thought but half expressed, and tactfully willing to let him think in silence for days when the mood was on him. Her early death had broken him for a year or two, but with Edith and his work to live for he had gradually taken a grip on himself and set his face to the future.

"I wonder what she is doing," he mused, dwelling affectionately on the sleepy cat of her offering. As if in answer to his unspoken thought the study door opened noiselessly two inches. An appraising brown eye took in the situation.

"Come in," he called. "I'm not working. Your precious cat makes me long to sleep."

Edith entered. "Have you everything you want?" she asked, ready to withdraw at the slightest symptom of work on her father's part.

"Everything," he replied with a smile, "but you. Come in and stay a bit. Birthdays come only once a year."

Edith joined him by the worktable with its litter of microscopes and queer looking specimens pallid in their neatly stoppered alcohol jars.

"Do you know," he said, "it sometimes scares me a little?"

"What scares you, dear?" she queried, for once at a loss.

"Why, that I do have everything I want."

"Well, why shouldn't you? Surely you have earned it."

"So have thousands of other men. Yet they have nothing while I have everything."

"Oh," she laughed, "it isn't so bad as all that. You are not a billionaire. Nor do you want the whole earth as some of the others do, and cry when they can't get it."

"Still," he persisted, "there are thousands of men as able as I am who slave all their lives and have nothing but a bare living to show for all their labor."

He strolled over to the French windows and stood gazing absently at the clear spring beauty of San Francisco Bay and the tawny Marin hills on the farther shore. With all the world to choose from he had selected this spot as his abiding place, high upon Telegraph Hill overlooking San Francisco and the whole sublime sweep of the harbor. Often he would stand at this window for an hour at a time, lost in thought, only half consciously watching the swift white ferry boats rounding Goat Island with the clock-like precision of mechanical toys.

In all weathers the colorful panorama of bay, city and steep hills had a stimulating yet soothing effect on his mind. Although much of his work with the strangely diseased things of the sea was not beautiful, the ever changing beauty of his outlook seemed to infuse him with inexhaustible energy for the repellant drudgery which is the necessary foundation of any scientific advance. The warm spring breeze rustling the leaves of the young eucalyptus by the open window brought him back to the present and his surroundings.

"Yes," he continued, "there is young Drake, for instance, twenty-nine and as poor as a crow. When I was his age I had been a millionaire several times over for almost six years. Yet Drake has a fundamentally better mind than I have. He simply did not have my chance. That is all."

"But suppose he had been given your chance," Edith protested, "could he have taken it?"

"No," her father replied thoughtfully. "There's not a grain of business sense in him. Still, for all that, I maintain that his head is better than mine."

"Then why doesn't he use it?" There was just a tinge of scorn in Edith's retort. Her father glanced up at her face in surprise.

"I thought you and Drake were great pals," he said.

"We are," she admitted readily enough. "But the sheer futility of his everlasting inscriptions rather gets on my nerves. I do wish he would turn his brains to something less trivial."

"How do you know his work is so useless?" the Doctor parried.

"Oh, if you are going to begin one of your scientific attacks on me," she laughed, "I'll retire at once to my humble corner. I'm routed. But can't you see," she protested earnestly, "that all his deciphering of outlandish inscriptions cannot make an atom of difference, one way or the other, to human beings today? What does it matter how a half-civilized race, extinct centuries ago, predicted eclipses of the moon? And who on earth cares whether they counted by twenties instead of by tens as we do? Will it make life more endurable for any human being to know how those dead and forgotten people disposed of their corpses?"

"Perhaps," the Doctor hazarded with a smile, "you would prefer to see our young friend Drake turning his unique talents to the unsolved problem of infant colics?"

"It would be more useful," she flashed.

"But consider," her father demurred, "what would become of the Mexican and Guatemalan inscriptions in the meantime. Who would ever read them, fully and satisfactorily? If Drake can't do it, nobody can. After his brilliant success with the Bolivian puzzles he is almost certain to make short work of the rest."

"Yes," Edith admitted. "And if he does, what then?"

"Why, my dear, he will have saved numberless future generations of young Drakes from wasting their lives on a useless piece of tomfoolery."

She laughed. "I knew when we began that you would corner me. Still, I'm morally right, because you slipped out by the back door. That isn't what you really think of Drake's work."

"It isn't, angel child," he admitted. "You must look at life in a broader way. The conquest of disease and the discovery of the origin of life are not even half the problem. As the old fellows used to say, the whole is one, and you can't change the smallest part in any place without altering the entire fabric everywhere. Drake's Bolivian hieroglyphics are just as vital a part of science as are the obscure fish parasites that I mess with in the hope of learning something about cancer. And I shouldn't wonder," he concluded half seriously, "if some day Drake's work gives us a clue to the central problem."

"And shows us what life is?" she laughed. "When it does, I'll eat that."

She pointed to a particularly loathsome reptile in a glass jar. It was one of the Doctor's favorites, as the tumor to which it had succumbed appeared to be something unique in the history of disease.

"You will eat it without salt or pepper?" he stipulated.

"Absolutely," she agreed.

"Very well then. We shall see."

Edith turned to go. "Shall I send up anyone who comes with a real specimen?"

"Only if it looks pretty good."

"Pretty bad, you mean. All right, I'll inspect the horror and use my judgment."

With a last smile she was gone as noiselessly as she had come. She had her work, and the Doctor his. Her morning would be begun in a short conference with the Chinese servants, short because both she and they were efficient and wasted no words. Then she might work for an hour or two among her flowers in the English garden, which was her pride, before settling down to the serious business of the day. This consisted of systematic reading directed by her father. At her own request he had mapped out a course of study and experiment which would enable her to understand something of what he was attempting to do. For two hours every evening a young doctor just from the University eked out his meagre practice helping her over the rough places in the day's work. In this way she made rapid and substantial progress. She never bothered her father with difficulties that any competent teacher could set right.

During the sunny part of the day she studied under the pepper trees by the gate, to be ready to receive and pay the Italian and Japanese fishermen who brought the curiosities of their catches to her father. All up and down the Pacific Coast, and even to Hawaii and far-off Japan, Dr. Lane of San Francisco was a celebrity among the fishermen and sailors. They knew him only distantly and impersonally as a deluded crank eager to pay one dollar apiece for curiously diseased and otherwise unsaleable fish. For weird monstrosities from the deep-sea levels he had been known to give as high as ten dollars each. What he did with all these abominations they never inquired. Sufficient unto their ignorance was the price thereof.

Occasionally some ambitious sailor would offer Edith his ingenious masterpiece of months of painstaking work in the forecastle. This usually took the form of a fantastic kelp and cocoanut mermaid, or an elaborately contrived sea-serpent of fish-bladders and sea-weeds. One such offering convinced him that he had been wasting his time. Edith recognized the subtle distinction between abandoned nature and the highest art at the first glance. If the fraud was sufficiently horrible and otherwise pleasing she would buy it for her own collection, intending, as she told her father when he protested at her growing collection of freaks, some day to write a monograph on marine diseases of the imagination.

Left to himself the Doctor returned to the open window. Spring fever was upon him. Work and all its paraphernalia appeared as an insult to nature. Accordingly he yielded himself to the soft influences of the warm breeze and the flashing blue and silver glory of the bay. Standing there he let the memories of a busy lifetime stream through his mind and out to the future with all its promise of great things to be.

Ever since his school days he had been bitten by the ambition to trace life to its secret source and lay bare its mystery. To create life, or at least to control and direct it when once created, that was the great problem. Then, when he had begun to learn something of systematic biology, he had seen the utter hopelessness of a direct attack. Wasting no time he had turned his energies elsewhere, to humbler things, in order that he might, if lucky, surprise the enemy unaware. For he realized that a wholesale creation of a fully living organism by artificial means was probably centuries beyond the capabilities of science, and his was too high an intelligence to waste itself on unsolvable riddles. If in laborious investigations of lesser problems he might catch a glimpse of the goal he would be happy, provided only that his search was not otherwise fruitless and bore abundant good to humanity in the alleviation of pain and preventable misery. But he would not waste his gifts on crass impossibilities.

His course at first had been hard and indirect. Forced by poverty to work his way through school and college, he had come early to a wisdom far beyond his years. With absolute clarity he had seen that freedom from worry over money matters is the first essential for genuinely creative scientific work. While constantly harassed by poverty he had been powerless to concentrate his abilities on any problem worth the solving. He therefore decided in his second college year to swerve aside temporarily from his ambition and make money. To the regret of his instructors he abruptly threw up the study of medicine and changed over to geology.

The new science was congenial. At many points it touched the past story of life if not the present. Putting every ounce of brain and energy into the work, he mastered the geology of coal and oil formations and graduated easily at the top of his class.

He was now twenty. The day after graduation he shipped as a coal passer on a steamer bound for China. Arrived there, ignorant though he was of the language, he disappeared into the interior.

His subsequent career is one of the classics of mining engineering. In eighteen months he had located one of the richest anthracite fields in the history of coal. Moreover he had obtained from the Chinese government certain concessions which, if worked, would make him one of the hundred richest white men in the world. All he had to do was to stay on the ground and let his prize develop. Capital would come almost unasked.

It was here that he showed the stuff he was made of. Instead of degenerating into a money-making machine he placed all his rights in the hands of an English company. Within six weeks he had sold out for ten million dollars cash all of his interest which, if nursed with ordinary business acumen, would have netted him a hundred million before he died. But he had no time to squander in making money. The most precious years of his life were slipping through his hands, and he was still but half educated for the work he had set himself.

While idling about Shanghai waiting to close up his business he met and married the English girl who for eight years made him a flawlessly happy man.

Having invested his fortune in government bonds he forgot it and proceeded with his wife to Vienna to finish his medical education. That accomplished, he left wife and infant daughter with his mother, and took a year's holiday with half a dozen friends exploring the southernmost extremity of Patagonia in a fossil hunting expedition.

The fossils aroused his purely biological interests. On returning to civilization he again went with his wife to Europe. There he specialized for two years in the great centres of pure biology. At twenty-seven, on returning to America, he felt himself fitted to begin useful work.

Resolutely putting from his mind the fantastic hope of discovering the origin of life, he concentrated his powers on the difficult problems of cell growth. Thus gradually and naturally was he led to the study of cancer, on which he had now been engaged for about ten years, publishing little but learning much, if only in a negative way. Always, subconsciously, at the back of his mind loomed up the greater problem. In his reading and in his experimental investigations he let slip no chance of following out the slightest clue. These excursions into the unpractical sometimes cost him weeks of precious time. Yet he never regretted them, for the least profitable yielded two or three definite facts worth the having.

With singular detachment he had kept his mind free from speculative theories. He followed neither Driesch nor Loeb. To him vitalism and mechanism, as judged by their positive achievements, were equally impotent to describe life. One side philosophized without experiment, while the other, experimenting blindly without reason, contented itself with a vague reference to electricity as the probable source of all living phenomena.

Profound technicalities like the intriguing "polarity" and "heliotropism" that seemed to the unthinking to "explain" so much while in fact they explained nothing but their authors' taste in names, left him cold. All this might be the first step, but surely it was no more. With the rapidly changing fashions in science and the influx of men of genius into biology, ten years might see polarity displaced by some newer fetish equally noncommittal. In the meantime he would remain neutral.

The door opened softly and Edith appeared.

"Oh," she said, "you're not working. I'll bring him up, then."

"Bring who up?"

But Edith had vanished. Presently she reappeared, ushering in a gray-bearded stranger, evidently a seafarer. The newcomer carried a tar-soaked box about four feet long and ten inches square.

"This is Captain Anderson," she said. "He insisted on showing you what he has brought himself."

"Pleased to meet you, Captain," said the Doctor, advancing to shake hands with his visitor. "Won't you sit down?"

"After you have seen what's in here."

Captain Anderson produced a huge clasp knife and proceeded methodically to pry off the lid of his long box. As he worked crystals of rock salt spilled out over the table and floor. The mess seemed to trouble him not at all. Evidently he had great faith in the soothing efficacy of his pickled monster, whatever it might be.

At last the cover was off and the closely packed salt invitingly ready to be scooped out by the handful. The Captain used both hands. Then, reaching in, he got the deceased monstrosity by what had been its neck, gave it a vigorous shake to free it from the last crystals of salt, and asked complacently,

"Isn't he a little peach?"

Edith, case-hardened as she was to monstrosities, could not repress a gasp and a shudder of repulsion. Lane looked paralyzed.

"Good Lord," he exclaimed, "what is it? Bird or reptile?"

2 CAPTAIN ANDERSON'S STORY

The Doctor and Edith stood dumb before Captain Anderson's dried monster. Its elaborate hideousness, unlike that of any living thing, held them with a perverse fascination. Neither bird, reptile nor fish, it was an incredible mongrel of all three. The serpent-like, heavily scaled belly contradicted the bat-like wings with their short, bristly feathers; while the exaggerated beak, crammed full of cruel yellow teeth, revealed by the hard backward snarl of the horny lips, refuted the monstrosity's claims to be considered a bird. Flattened against its withered flanks were two lizard hands armed with ugly claws, to one of which still adhered the dried scales of the last fish the creature had devoured.

A skeptic at first glance would have declared the creature an impossible fraud perpetrated by some over-imaginative sailor in his misused leisure. But Dr. Lane, also at the first glance, thought he knew better.

"It's only a baby of its kind," he said. "The parents have been dead millions of years. This is the one perfect specimen in existence." The Doctor thought he knew what he was talking about.

"Then there are others like it?" Captain Anderson asked, somewhat crestfallen.

"No, only their fossilized bones and the impressions of a few feathers in the rocks that were mud when these things flew. The most perfect impression was found in a mine in Bulgaria about four years ago. But it was only a mark on the stone—not a shadow to this beauty. Where on earth did you get it?"

"In the South Polar seas."

"Frozen into the ice?" the Doctor hazarded. He recalled instantly the reputed discoveries of long extinct mastodons in Alaska, Northern Siberia and elsewhere, their meat as fresh as on the day the giants were trapped on the ice floes hundreds of centuries ago.

"No," the Captain replied. "This thing was still warm when we picked it up. It could not have been dead more than fifteen minutes."

"But how on earth—"

"First let me ask you one or two questions. What is it?"

"I don't know," the Doctor confessed doubtfully. "At first I thought it might be the missing link between the reptiles and the birds—a half-way creature something like a pterodactyl and not quite an archæopteryx. The last is the ancestor of all the birds. We know only its fossil remains. Then I thought—but, here, see for yourself."

Dr. Lane strode over to the bookshelves and selected a large green portfolio. "Put your beast on the table and compare it with this," he said, exhibiting a photographic reproduction of the famous Bulgarian fossil. "Now, isn't yours like this?"

"In the main, yes. But that snake-bird in the mud had no scales on its belly," the Captain objected.

"So much the better for yours. Either this is a forefather of the known reptilian ancestor of the birds or it is a distinctly new species."

"Now for my second question," the Captain continued. "What is this thing worth?"

"That depends upon whom you ask to buy it. A fishmonger down the street might give you ten cents for it as a curiosity. Then again the American Museum of Natural History would offer you, I imagine, whatever it could afford. For this specimen is priceless."

"Very well. I'm only an ex-mining engineer and an old whaler. I know next to nothing about such things and must take your word for the value of this. Now, my last question. How much will you give me for it?"

Dr. Lane hesitated, but only for a second.

"Nothing," he replied.

"Then that's settled," the Captain retorted, restoring his despised monstrosity to its coffin.

"Hold on a minute, Captain. By itself your wonderful find is of little or no value to me. I care only for diseased things. This is perfectly sound. A museum is the proper place for it after the right men have worked out its anatomy in detail. When I said that I would give you nothing for it I meant what I said. But I will give you a considerable sum if you take me to the exact spot where you found this thing, as you said, still warm."

The Captain desisted in his efforts to scoop up all the salt spilled in his first exuberant haste.

"When you say a considerable sum what do you mean?"

"Name what you think right and I'll see."

"Ten thousand dollars?"

"It is not too much. I would offer even more under certain conditions."

"For instance?"

"That you could show me where to find a living specimen like this one you found so recently dead. Can you do that?"

"Let me be above board with you from the beginning, Dr. Lane. I can't."

"Why not?"

"Because we picked this up in the sea a hundred and twenty miles from the nearest land."

"It had fallen into the water from exhaustion and been drowned?"

"I guess not. In fact I know that it never flew the hundred and twenty miles from the land. For I saw it roll up from below directly under the stern of our ship."

"Did it leap out like a salmon? If so, that was a queer performance for a creature built like this."

"No, it boiled out, dead as a dummy."

The doctor regarded the grizzled whale pirate with rather more than a touch of suspicion.

"If I had not seen this thing with my own eyes," he remarked, "I should disbelieve your whole story."

"You haven't heard it yet," the Captain dryly rejoined. "Before I tell it will you agree either to pay me ten thousand dollars for it or to keep still about it after I leave this house?"

"That's fair enough. I agree."

"And this young lady?" the Captain queried, with an interrogative glance at Edith.

"My daughter Edith, Captain Anderson. Pardon me for not having introduced you before."

"Oh, we had a fine row in the garden," Edith laughed, "before I came up. I agree too, Captain Anderson, if you will let me stay and listen. Only please cover up the hideous thing before you begin. I shall have nightmares for a month as it is."

With a laugh the Captain replaced the cover of his box. But the Doctor, after a moment's hesitation removed it, telling Edith she might turn her back if the creature's beauty overpowered her.

"I want to have a good long look at this thing," he said. "It isn't what I thought it might be. Well, Captain, how did you happen to come to me with your find?"

"It was on the mate's advice. One of my men, it seems, once got five dollars from your daughter for a fake mermaid. I thought," he added with a malicious glint in his steel gray eyes, "she might be willing to give me ten for a real one."

"You may be sure, Captain Anderson," Edith retorted indignantly, "that I knew perfectly well what I was buying. And if I gave your man five dollars for a wretched fake worth fifty cents it was because the poor fellow looked half-clothed and underfed. Really, Captain Anderson, you should treat your men better."

"He can't have been one of mine. The only thing my men suffer from is a lack of rum."

"That's fortunate," the Doctor interposed. "Otherwise they might pass by feathered reptiles as mere creations of a rummy imagination."

"True," the Captain agreed. "As a matter of fact all my men know of you and your hobby. I was only trying to get a rise out of your daughter for what she did to me in the garden. We're quits now."

"Are you sure?" Edith asked with exasperating calm.

"Not so sure as I was a second ago," the honest Captain admitted. "No wonder your father lets you do the buying. Now, Dr. Lane," he continued with a change in tone, "as I said in the beginning I want this whole business to be open and aboveboard. So I should like you to know that one of the main reasons for my troubling you at all is the fact that you are a rich man with barrels of money to spend on your hobbies. I have known of you for years. They still talk of your big coal strike over in China. Now a man who knows as much as you do about coal should be able to appreciate the value of oil."

"To a certain extent," the Doctor smiled. "I have sense enough to let wildcatting alone."

"I haven't. And that, in a word, is why I'm here. Unless I can persuade you for once to invest heavily in oil I shall have to take my queer fish elsewhere."

"Perhaps I can afford to throw ten thousand dollars down your oil well to feed the fish at the bottom. Go ahead and see if you can sell me."

"Then here goes. Don't call me a liar until I've finished. I shall tell you only enough to let you see for yourself whether you want to come in or stay out and forget all about me and my queer fowl.

"I was educated as a mining engineer, but gave up my profession to follow the sea. For the past twenty years I have been master and part owner of a whaling vessel.

"About eighteen months ago, having cleaned up for the season, we started north. We were in the South Polar Seas, to the east of Cape Horn and considerably south. That is a close enough description of our position for the present. The nearest coastline of the Antarctic continent lay about a hundred and twenty miles southeast of us. The season, though well advanced, was extraordinarily mild and open. For eight days we had sighted no ice.

"One night shortly before eleven I was awakened by a peculiar jarring of the whole ship. It lasted fully forty seconds. The mate and the man at the wheel also felt it. Like me they could make nothing of it till daylight. Then we guessed. For the water was a peculiar milky green as if muddied by finely powdered chalk. There had evidently been a submarine earthquake and a volcanic eruption on the ocean floor during the night. All that morning the water grew milkier and milkier. By noon it was the color of a dirty river and as sluggish as molasses.

"Suddenly, about two o'clock in the afternoon, the whole surface of the water began to boil up in huge bubbles like a cauldron of hot porridge. The ship rattled and clattered as if it were being shaken to bits. The men, of course, acted like a pack of panic-stricken idiots. Discipline went to the devil. That fool of a mate's account of what probably was happening a mile or two beneath us drove them clean crazy. Then I took a fist in things and knocked some sense into their silly heads.

"But for the infernal boiling there was a dead calm. It was shortly after three o'clock that the first great bubble of black oil burst with a gurgling plop half over the decks. Inside of ten minutes the sea was a heaving blanket of heavy black oil three feet thick. If only we had been a fleet of tankers with pumping gear we could have made our fortunes within a radius of half a mile. Sheer to the horizon the whole sea was a dance of sleek black bubbles as big as whales.

"About five o'clock the oily mess began to boil more furiously. Our decks were one black slop from stem to stern. Then without warning a great gusher of sticky brown tar burst right under our bows and shot roaring straight up a hundred and fifty feet above our masts in a tumbling spout.

"We had banked our fires at the beginning of the row. Otherwise we should have been ablaze in a sea of fire hours before. Now the filthy brown tar began streaming down our funnels to the boilers. There was only one thing to do, stuck there as we were, and we did it, half smothered in the sticky brown mess. Somehow or another we got the funnels capped with tarpaulins. There we rocked and rattled in that boiling filth till dark, unable to get up steam and dodge the worst of it, stuck fast under that slapping deluge of brown muck.

"Night came down slowly. Except for the eruption of oil and tar, and the queer deadness of the air, the last hours of that rotten day were like those of any other open weather twilight in the South Polar Seas. Just as it began to get too dusky to see clearly that beastly tar spout gave a mumbling gulp and dropped down into the pitch as dead as a stone. That was the end of it.

"We thought our troubles were over. And so they were in a way. I sent the mate below to kick the men up to swab the decks. The sea was still boiling violently when he left. I was alone on deck when the next nightmare, and the jumpiest of all, leapt from the sea."

Captain Anderson paused for a moment in his narrative, seeking the right words to convince his curious audience of his veracity.

"The mate had just disappeared," he resumed, "when a terrific jar, as if the ship were being hit with a hundred battering rams, warned me that the devil was about to break loose. And he did. A huge chunk of black rock—the size of the Baptist Church down the street—shot from the heaving oil about a hundred yards east of the ship, whizzed clear over us in a crazy curve, and sent up a whooping splash of black muck as it dived that nearly swamped us. If that chunk had been aimed a trifle lower I shouldn't be here now.

"Well, that was only the first of them. At intervals of half a mile to a mile apart the whole sputtering mess of black oil began to spit up the floor of the sea in hunks of black rock as big as city hotels. None of them broke loose or hit closer to the ship than half a mile. The first was our one close call.

"That fool of a mate got the men on deck just when the show was at its best. They let out one yell and ducked back to their holes in the forecastle. The idiots missed a sight they'll never get another chance of seeing, for in five minutes that particular row was over. Either there was nothing left on the bottom of the sea to be thrown up, or sufficient vents had been torn in the floor for what was to come next. It came with a gurgling, oily rush.

"Before it happened, however, the black oil suddenly stopped heaving. No more bubbles rose. Evidently the intermittent supply of oil from below had given place to slow, even gushers. The surface of the oil became almost flat with the whirling ends of streamlines spinning up and twisting out everywhere. It looked just like a gigantic black millrace, gnarled over like the water of a river half a mile below a high fall.

"The mate and I are the only witnesses of what seethed up through the crawling oil. The only human witnesses, I mean. For if our pickled friend in the salt there could speak he might spin us a good yarn. He came up in that slow, churning motion of the pitch, one of thousands like him, and one small fry in a stew of huge beasts whose horny ugliness made him and his bigger sisters look like rosy June brides.

"All the three hundred foot nightmares of our dragon-ridden fairy-tale days boiled lazily up in that infernal black stew. Lizards as big as small trains with grinning mouths jammed full of six-inch teeth rolled over and over in the swashing oil as dead as Trojans, and huge armor plated, four-legged brutes the size of locomotives twirled round and round belly up in the twilight. Some of them had been split wide open, and their insides, black with oil, steamed and smoked like slaughter houses. Smaller beasts in thousands, and a thick scum of broken insects, littered the crawling oil between the slowly plunging carcasses of the big fellows.

"The mate is a fussy man given to footling hobbies. Photography is his messiest. He now dived below to fetch up his camera. Any fool could have told the idiot there was no use trying to get a snapshot in that light. But he kept at it like a mule and wasted five dollars' worth of films. He found out what an extravagant fool he had been about three weeks later when he got time to develop his rubbish.

"His idiocy gave me an idea. Nobody would believe our unsupported story. So I took a line and fished up this freak." He indicated the bird-reptile in its box. "I should have liked one of the big lizard brutes, but that we had no room to stow it on deck. And anyway the light was about gone."

"You said, Captain," Dr. Lane began, "that your catch was evidently just dead when you hauled it in. How do you know?"

"Because I stuck my knife into its neck to make sure. Thick warm blood oozed out. Here, I'll show you the place."

Once more he exhibited his scaly, feathered monster. It was as he had said. There was plainly visible on the left side of the neck a deep gash.

"It's a queer fish and a queerer story," Edith remarked, with a glance of distaste at the poor pickled monster.

Dr. Lane agreed with his daughter's estimate.

"For all its strangeness," he said, "I am inclined to take a chance. Captain Anderson, I will back your oil stock to the extent of ten thousand dollars, on one condition. You must take me to the exact spot where you picked up this wonderful creature. Mind, I am not swallowing your yarn whole. It is just possible that in your excitement you saw things that weren't there. The light, according to your own statement, was about gone.

"But the mate?" Captain Anderson protested. "Was he crazy too?"

"Possibly. Any psychologist will tell you that such things do happen frequently. Collective hallucination is the scientific name for such a state of affairs. Both you and he, I suppose, have seen pictures, or restorations, of extinct animals like the ones you thought you saw boiling up through the oil—dinosaurs, huge lizards three hundred feet long, the ceratops, and the like? You, Captain, must have seen such things when you were studying mining engineering."

"I know I have," the Captain admitted. "And the mate is such a hobby-ridden fool, always messing about libraries and reading rooms when he is ashore, that doubtless he's in the same fix. For all that you can't convince me that the whole thing was a nightmare. I saw it."

"Did any of the men see it too?" Edith asked. "Next morning, I mean."

"Not the main part of the show. All the heavy brutes had sunk. Nothing but the scum of broken insects floated through the night."

"It sounds queer," was Edith's frank comment.

"Indeed it does, Captain," her father agreed. "Now this is my guess. You found this bird-reptile right enough, for here it is. I don't think," he said with a smile, "that even I can explain it away to your satisfaction. What you took for thick warm blood oozing from the slash in its neck was nothing but brown tar."

"Well, suppose it was," the Captain retorted. "What does that prove?"

"Everything. And in a perfectly reasonable way. I accept the eruption of oil from beneath the sea floor as real. Your crew saw that?"

The Captain nodded.

"Very well, then, it's all clear. First let me tell you about a somewhat similar.state of affairs less than two hundred miles from here in Southern California. It is at the famous asphalt and oil hole on the Rancho La Brea. Some years ago the geologists from the University of California began digging out of the oily ooze all manner of bones and other remains of extinct animals—skulls of sabre tooth tigers that haven't lived in this part of the world for the past hundred thousand years, and many others equally interesting.

"The explanation of these remains is quite simple. Ages ago drinking pools of rainwater collected on the sticky surface of the oily ooze. The prehistoric beasts, not knowing the danger, picked their way out to drink. On trying to return to solid ground they quickly mired themselves like flies on tanglefoot. Now is it likely that in an entire continent of tar holes this one at La Brea should be unique as an animal trap?"

"So you believe my reptile or whatever he is was thrown up from some prehistoric asphalt hole buried under the floor of the Antarctic Ocean?"

"Undoubtedly, Captain."

The Captain grinned behind his gray beard. "A thoroughly scientific theory no doubt, Doctor. As such it does you credit. According to you my reptile should be full of brown tar, not dried blood and other stuff. Suppose you cut him open and see."

"That's a practical test," the Doctor assented, rising to get his implements. "If he has anything inside him besides pitch, like a badly cured mummy, I'll double my offer."

"Then you might as well hand me your check for twenty thousand now. I'll equal your offer. If you find nothing but mummy pudding inside I'll let you have my yarn for the stuffing."

The Doctor did not reply immediately. He was too busy making his incision where it would do the least damage to the appearance of the specimen. Presently he drew up with a gasp of astonishment.

"Why," he exclaimed, "it's as fresh as a newly pickled salmon."

"Of course it is. I packed it in salt the minute the mate had finished washing it off with rum and turpentine."

"Great Scott what a find! Edith, bring me the largest of those jars about a third full of alcohol. This beats me. The thing must have been miraculously preserved for ages. My offer stands, Captain. Take me to the place where you found this and the twenty thousand is yours the day we start."

"You will raise that to fifty thousand when I tell you the rest," the Captain prophesied confidently. "I asked you not to call me a liar until I had finished. As a matter of fact I am only half-way through."

"Have you more specimens?"

"No, but I have a round gross of first-class photographs."

"But you said the mate's pictures were a failure."

"So they were, that time. He had better luck the next, when I could boss him properly."

"Prehistoric animals?"

"Something much better, unless I'm badly off."

"Do go on," Edith begged, "and tell us what else you found."

"In a moment. Shall I telephone the mate to bring up his pictures?"

"Yes, do!" they exclaimed together, and Edith handed him the desk telephone.

Having got his number Anderson asked if Ole Hansen was still about. The answer apparently was satisfactory, for Ole was asked to step to the telephone.

"It's all right, Ole," the Captain shouted, as if his faithful mate were still in the vicinity of the South Pole. "The Doctor has swallowed it all so far, bait, hook and sinker. Bring the rest of the junk up here to his house. Get Christensen to show you the way. Jump on a street car and shake a leg."

3 A PUZZLE FOR DRAKE

"While we are waiting for Hansen," the Captain resumed, "I may as well tell you how he collected his photographs. As the blundering idiot will probably manage to lose himself between the gate and the back door, I have plenty of time."

"Is your mate Hansen so stupid as you make out?" Edith asked with genuine interest. "If so, he must be worth studying."

"Stupider, Miss Lane. You never met his equal for cracked theorizing. Well, let us leave him to find his way here and get on with our business. I'll tell you what I want from you, Doctor, when I reach the end of my story."

"Although you may not be aware of the fact," Dr. Lane replied shrewdly, "you have already told me. You want me to foot the bill for an expedition to tack down those new oil fields in your name. Well, it's all right with me. I'll take the fossils and anything else in that line and you can have the oil. Convince me that I should go in heavily and you need have no worry about finances."

"Hansen's pictures will put the finishing touches to what I begin. Well, except for one thing, the morning after the shakeup was just like any other perfectly clear South Polar calm. The sea was still covered with heavy black oil to a depth of several feet. Only a long, even swell heaved it gently up and down in billows a mile long.

"During the night I had ordered the fires drawn. We dared take no chances with the oil-soaked decks and rigging. With the first light the mate and I got the men out to clean up the mess. We drove them like niggers to keep their minds off the oil. It wouldn't do when we reached port to have them blabbing to the first shark they met. Later we decided to take the whole crew in on the scheme. They are to get a third share of all profits if they keep their mouths shut. That seems to be the only safe way. They're as mum as clams.

"All that day we sweated to get the worst of the oil off or covered up so it wouldn't be noticed when we reached civilization. By nightfall we had done a pretty thorough job. I decided to explain the oil-soaked hull by saying it was an idea of Hansen's to use crude oil instead of paint as a weather defier. It sounds just like one of his theories.

"The next question was how to swim out of the soup. With steam up of course it would have been easy. But the mate and I agreed—for once—that it would be a fool's trick to start any kind of a fire. The air reeked of natural gas and oil fumes. A spark, and the whole sea would be hell. There was nothing for it but to trust to the sails. By dark we were fully rigged and whistling for the breeze.

"It came like a thunderclap from seven directions at once. All in all that was the worst blow I have weathered through in twenty years of dirty squalls from the equator to Cape Horn. The mate of course had a theory to account for the suddenness of the hurricane. Like most of his efforts it came five minutes late. I'll tell you of it presently.

"For the moment I didn't give a damn for theories, being more interested in trying to save our masts. Except for a few whistling ribbons like rags on a clothesline the sails were gone. The filthy black oil broke over the decks in buckets and hogsheads, smothering us whenever we attempted to make a line fast. All our deck tackle went by the board, knocked clean off the plates by the sledgehammer kicks of the heavy pitch.

"After the first mad wrench the hurricane settled down to a steady, snoring gale from the north. The ship drove dead ahead for the ice barrier a hundred and twenty miles south of us. Nothing was to be done. We could only sit tight for the smash. Unless the wind fell we should ram the ice cliffs full tilt some time between midnight and dawn. The wind held.

"Tired of holding his breath, Hansen suggested that all hands join in prayer. He is always at it, before meals, at meals and after meals. I told him to go to hell and took the wheel out of his lily white hands. In the howling uproar he misunderstood the order. Evidently he thought I wished him to hold chapel in the forecastle. Anyway there is where I found him at daybreak with half the crew bellowing Norwegian hymns to beat the devil.

"Toward midnight I first noticed a cherry colored glow coming and going in the sky ahead of the ship. If I thought at all in the mad rush to the final smash I put the flickering down to an aurora, and tried to steer a course that would graze the ice when we struck. By my reckoning we should have been smashed about three o'clock in the morning. Four o'clock passed and still the ship staggered on through the oil under the terrific gale. I began to think I must have misjudged our speed. Five o'clock came, and with the first light the wind began to drop. In half an hour it was broad daylight over a sea with only a film of oil coating the waves, and not a sign of the ice barrier ahead. I left the wheel to hammer some sense into those hymn singing idiots of Hansen's.

"When they shot up on deck the wind was no longer a gale and the ship was manageable. Hansen said we had been saved by his bawling in the forecastle. About an hour later he sighted the volcano. Then he gave it the honor and glory for everything, including the wind.

"For a stretch of at least twenty miles the great ice barrier had been wiped out. Whether it had sunk, or whether it had been lifted up bodily by the eruption and tossed back on the continent I don't know. Hansen says the rock and ice just cracked apart that far in the earthquake. Anyhow the twenty miles of solid ice and rock was gone. In its place stretched a long broad inlet as straight as a street running clear out of sight into the continent.

"The wind dropped abruptly to a mere breeze, and the last of the oil film fell away in our wake. All about us the water was as white as milk, thick and soupy.

"When we came fully to our senses we noticed the unusual warmth. The air was as balmy as a spring day in California. It occurred to me to test the temperature of the water. One of the men drew up a bucketful of the milky soup. It was lukewarm.

"A yell from that excitable idiot Hansen made me drop the bucket. He was pointing up the inlet to a huge pillar of ink billowing up like the smoke from a burning oil well. I judged it must have been at least fifty miles from where we were. But I had no means then of making more than a crude guess.

"As we stood gaping at it the whole mass of ink was suddenly sucked down out of the sky. Only a dirty brown mist marked the place where it had been.

"'It's an eruption,' Hansen was good enough to explain. He meant well, but who ever saw an eruption acting down instead of up? There was no time to argue it out with him, for while we were looking, the show began in earnest.

"First an enormous black smoke ring teetered crazily up and mushroomed out over the sky line like an umbrella. Then a solid pillar of red flames gushed up after the smoke. My common sense was working in spite of me, for I found myself counting off the seconds. When I got to fifty-eight, the fist of the explosion struck us with all its force. Being ready for it I was braced against the funnel with my hands over my ears. Hansen, theorizing as usual, wasn't prepared. Nor were the men. For an hour after they had picked themselves up they went about staring like owls.

"If my count was right the volcano must be two hundred fifty to three hundred miles inland. At that distance I had no fears for the ship.

"The next thing to do was to get out before something started under our keel. Before doing so I could not resist the temptation of lowering a boat to see what had happened ashore—if anything was to be seen without dangerous delay. I decided to take Hansen and two men to pull the oars. When he understood what was doing—he was still deaf, like the rest of the theorizers—he made a dive below to bring up his everlasting camera and a bale of films.

"The pull through that beastly warm milk to the shore was both pleasant and disgusting. How these society women can bathe in hot milk—as I understand from the Sunday newspapers they do—beats me! That by the way, however. I see Miss Lane is blushing. Our landing was as easy as a picnic on a river. We at once tramped inland over the level snowfields to see what was to be seen.

"Hansen saw it first. About a mile ahead of us he made out a black dot on the snow. We made for it as fast as the loosely crystallized surface would let us. Coming up to it we found a chunk of black rock the size of a cow. At least that was all of it above the ice and snow. The rest lay buried in the star-shaped pit which its fall had dented through to the ice and underlying rock.

"One side of the rock was smooth. The rest was just a jagged nothing. Hansen took a photograph of the smooth side.

"I don't blame him for wanting to find another of the black chunks. Nor do I criticize him for stopping to take its picture. If the camera had been mine I should have been just as unreasonable. He dragged us over that forsaken wilderness of snow and ice for ten mortal hours hunting black rocks. There was no returning to the ship until he had shot his last roll of films. In all he got twelve dozen first-class negatives.

"Once I got him aboard our normal relations were resumed. He recovered his mind and obeyed orders. We steamed out of that photographer's heaven without another picture."

"Are you sure, Captain Anderson," Edith smiled, "that your mate's craze for photography isn't by your orders too?"

"Oh, quite. Still, I admit that Hansen is the keeper of my artistic temperament. Otherwise I should be mincing about Rio de Janeiro in pale lavender kid gloves instead of boiling blubber on Kerguelen like a Christian."

"What was Hansen's explanation of the storm?" Dr. Lane asked.

"The common-sense one, for a wonder. The sudden rise in temperature over the land caused the cold air from the sea to rush in toward the volcano and take us with it."

"In Hansen I recognize a brother," the Doctor laughed.

"You won't when you see him," the Captain prophesied grimly. "He looks like a fat barrel that has been well hammered down. Hullo, here's one of your mandarins."

The diplomatic Wong announced in faultless English that a gentleman by the name of Ole Hansen awaited the Doctor's pleasure.

"Show him up, Wong."

Hansen entered, as red as a lobster and shaped like a brandy keg.

"I've brought the photographs," he announced after the introductions.

"Dump them on the table and let the Doctor see for himself. They need no explanation—"

"But," Hansen expostulated, unburdening himself of his twelve dozen masterpieces, "I have a theory. If you will let me—"

"I won't, so don't try."

Giving his Captain a red explosive look, Hansen sat on the safety valve and obeyed orders. Heaven only knows what clouds of theories he generated under the suppression of all that superheated steam. A man of less robust build must have burst into a thousand hypotheses. The barrel-shaped Hansen merely swelled and held his peace.

Meanwhile Dr. Lane was devouring the photographs of the black rocks with feverish interest. Occasionally he passed one to Edith with a terse suggestion to "take a look at that." Each picture was that of a smooth black surface, in many cases badly fissured by the violence of the explosion which had disrupted the mass from its matrix, densely incised with pictograms.

"Call up Drake," the Doctor ordered before he had worked half through the pile, "and tell him we have a puzzle here that makes the Bolivian inscriptions look like A.B.C."

Edith reported that Drake would join them as fast as his legs would let him.

"Captain Anderson," the Doctor said, rising, "I'm in with you on this to the limit of my means. You can have the oil, I'll take the rest. It's worth more."

4 THE RIDDLE OF THE ROCKS

Lean, lanky, hatless, Drake arrived at the conference breathless and disheveled. Edith greeted him with applause and peals of laughter.

Drake shot one agonized glance at his long legs. Reassured that the worst had not happened, he drew himself up with the dignity of a stork and replied in frigid tones,

"I am perfectly dressed."

"Where did you leave your tie and socks, John?"

Drake groaned. The telephone message had interrupted the stream of his Mexican musings and here he was, just as he had flung himself together. Striking negligées in public were his specialty. Given ten years more of bachelor freedom, he would evolve into the ideal absent-minded professor who moons through the movies and the comic supplements, but scarcely at all through the business-like atmosphere of a living university. Drake was one of the extremely rare exceptions. Like many other mortals afflicted with the same failing, Drake always indignantly repudiated the insinuation that he was not as other men. Only repeated ocular proof, which he promptly forgot after each application, convinced him when he was a walking comic. Edith's attitude toward this embryo delight was a little philistine. She should have encouraged him for the sake of art. It surely would be a great pity to thwart his almost unique proclivities to play the idiotic part demanded of him by the practical man. And what would be the net gain of her motherly efforts? Drake at thirty-five would be outwardly like any ordinary scholar—except of course the professional quacks—and quite indistinguishable from any floor walker or bank cashier.

"Never mind, Drake," the Doctor consoled him, "I'll lend you things before dinner. In the meantime, here is something more important."

He handed the ruffled young archæologist a pocket lens and one of Hansen's photographs. With a nod of acknowledgment to Captain Anderson and the mate whom the Doctor introduced, Drake seated himself near the open window and peered through the lens at the photograph.

The fifteen minute silence lengthened to twenty and the atmosphere of the study grew unpleasantly tense. Half an hour passed without a sound. At last Drake rose and handed back the picture to Dr. Lane.

"Well, what do you make of it?" the Doctor demanded.

"Do you want the truth?"

"Of course."

"Very well. I do not wish to insult either of your guests," Drake began with anxious diffidence. "Especially as I have just been introduced," he added with an apprehensive glance at the compressed, husky Hansen. "However, you asked for the truth. I may as well let you have it before I know what parts precisely Mr. Hansen and Captain Anderson play in this affair. That photograph, in my opinion, is a clever fake."

"What!" the Captain exploded, bounding out of his chair. "You're crazy. Tell him about it, Ole."

But the outraged Hansen was beyond coherent speech. One of his round gross of masterpieces, and therefore the whole twelve dozen, had been pronounced fraudulent by this herring-gutted young dude without a shirt to his back or a collar to his neck.

"You'll eat those words," he spluttered in a turkey-cock fury.

Drake, with roseate visions of an early martyrdom in the cause of Truth, stood his ground before the advancing barrel of high explosives.

"Gentlemen!" the Doctor intervened sharply. "This isn't the forecastle. Be seated, Mr. Hansen. Drake, remember where you are. I won't have you making a prize ring out of my study. Sit down and explain yourself."

The bewildered Drake, by nature a pacifist to the marrow of his bones, subsided into a chair. Hansen, with a few choice compliments in Norwegian, also sat. Captain Anderson opened the attack.

"You're dead wrong, Mr. Drake. As a man of common-sense, would you suppose it likely that any fakir has money enough to manufacture a hundred and forty-four frauds weighing fifty to five hundred tons apiece? You wouldn't, eh? Well, neither would I. You've only seen the picture of one. Show him the rest, Dr. Lane."

Retiring once more with his glass to the window, Drake made a rapid inspection of the entire series of photographs. After the first few his frankly skeptical expression changed rapidly to bewilderment and finally to intense interest. Beginning again with the first he ran more slowly through the series, selecting fourteen of the pictures for further consideration.

"Well," said the Captain, "what do you make of them now?"

Like most specialists Drake saw his beloved hobby in everything.

"Pictograms," he announced incisively.

"Real or fake?" Hansen demanded with a red scowl.

"Real, I should say."

"What significance, if any, have they?" the Doctor inquired.

"That I don't know. In fact this is a problem that may well take fifty years or a century to solve."

"I have a theory—" Hansen began, but the rude Captain nipped it cruelly in the bud.

"Bother your theory!" he snapped. "Let us hear what Mr. Drake has to say."

"Perhaps," Drake hesitated, "if you told me where these pictures were taken I might be able to form a more intelligent opinion."

"No," the Doctor objected, "we want an expert's unbiased estimate. Mr. Drake," he continued, "is probably the best man in the world for our purpose. Whatever he decides will be worth learning and absolutely without prejudice. Go ahead, Drake. Take your time."

Drake picked up the fourteen pictures which he had selected from the pile.

"These," he said, "seem to go together. They are parts, I judge, of some much larger inscription. The rest of the pictures seem to be dislocated, but a close examination would be necessary before reaching a definite conclusion. I feel certain, however, of one very curious fact. Two widely separated ages of art are represented in this entire series. This feature is extremely puzzling for one peculiarity. Any archæologist will tell you that two such periods of art are never of equal brilliance. Yet these pictograms, in respect of artistic excellence, are all on a par—and a very high one at that. Now these," he continued, exhibiting the fourteen, "are not by any means nearly the whole of their story. They are nothing more than disjointed fragments. Yet they are the one evidence of some sort of continuity in the whole lot. On them, if at all, we must base our attempt at decipherment."

"I told you we should have spent a week looking for the rest," Captain Anderson bellowed at the indignant Hansen. "Why did you drag me back to the ship?"

"It was you who got as fussy as an old woman and dragged me back," Ole retorted, swelling ominously. "I knew we hadn't enough—"

"Oh, well. Go on, Mr. Drake."

"As I was saying," Drake resumed, "these fourteen hang together. But they are evidently not by any means the whole story. However they are enough to show that there must be some consistent scheme running through the lot. Whether I shall be able to unravel the tangle is another question. At present I doubt whether the inscriptions are more than mere picture writing. If so, what meaning are we to give all these excellent representations, literally by the thousands, of impossible monsters?"

"Not so impossible as you think," Lane objected. "Had your education been less lopsided you would recognize many of these monsters as first-class and highly probable restorations of extinct animals. They are life-like to an amazing degree."

Such was Dr. Lane's first opinion, reached after only a cursory examination of those remarkable inscriptions. He has since modified his estimate profoundly. Attentive study under suggestions from Drake in fact wrought a radical change in the Doctor's view within the year. For the present, however, it made a fair enough working guess.

"I must disagree with you," Drake replied. "In a way I can appreciate the obvious fact that these pictured monsters are vividly life-like, although I never saw anything resembling them. But in a more significant sense they are strikingly artificial and, if I may make a rough hypothesis, intentionally so. The people who cut these rows upon rows of pictures into the rocks must have been in a highly advanced state of civilization. The very perfection of the art was the chief thing that made me suspicious at first. Our own stone-cutters with all their modern appliances could do no better today. Now is it not at least curious, I ask you, that artists capable of such excellent work should deliberately go out of their way to cast an air of unlife-like unreality over certain aspects of their art? I shall not attempt at present to support my contention that the art is intentionally fantastic. The evidence is here; examine it for yourselves. Again, another circumstance roused my suspicions at once. There is a complete absence of any attempt to represent the human figure.

How are we to explain this? I confess I don't know. Such a lack is unheard of in the art of any known race."

"Would you expect to find portraits of human beings in a treatise, say, on crabs?"

"Yes," Hansen promptly and unexpectedly replied, with a hard stare at the Captain.

"I'll crab you when we get aboard," the Captain promised sweetly. "Your style is improving, Ole. But you must not interrupt the speaker. This is not a labor temple."

"I see your point, Doctor," Drake admitted. "Yet what race of human beings would go to all this trouble to cut into hard stone a work on prehistoric animals—as you say these are—when paper and printers' ink are so cheap?"

"Suppose printing hadn't been invented when these inscriptions were cut into the rocks?"

"Your hypothesis is fantastic. What—"

"I have a theory—" Hansen interrupted with desperate eagerness, but the Captain squashed it.

"Ole!"

"Since Drake is all at sea," the Doctor smiled, "perhaps it would be as well to hear what Mr. Hansen has to say."

"All right, Ole. Get it off your chest and don't take till next Sunday."

"It's like this," Ole began, rising to give his utterance all the impressiveness of his rotund authority. "I agree with Dr. Lane and therefore disagree with Mr. Drake. Those pictures are life-like. They are life itself! And now I tell you why.

"Two years ago in the Sailors' Free Reading Room at Rio de Janeiro I saw a book with pictures of extinct animals from some French and Spanish caves. Now who made those pictures? The damn fool who found them?"

"Ole!"

"All right, Captain. I forgot the lady. No, the d . . . , the fool I mean, who found those pictures did not make them. He had not brains enough, not what you call the artistic genius, to draw like that. Nobody any longer has so much genius. Those pictures were made by men who had never seen what you call modern art. They were too good, too much like nature, only better—if you know what I mean. Did the great Michael Angelo ever paint a herd of wild buffaloes? No. Michael Angelo only painted flocks of big she angels out of his head. Then came Rubenstein. Did he—"

"It's getting late, Ole. Cut out the wild asses and the encyclopædia and come to your theory."

"I am arriving, Captain. Therefore, I say, those long extinct buffaloes were drawn by men who had seen buffaloes, who had lived with them *en famille* as the French say. And therefore it follows in the same way," he concluded with a geometrical flower of rhetoric culled from his gourmand reading, "the men who cut the pictures of those monstrous animals into the rocks lived with them. They drew their likenesses from nature. For these animals are life-like, they are almost alive! Did those forgotten geniuses delay their masterpieces for Gutenberg? No. They needed no printing presses in their business. Which was to be proved, was it not?"

"Preposterous," Drake remarked as Ole, with a self-conscious bow, resumed his creaking chair.

"Is it?" the Doctor asked quizzically. "Precisely why is Mr. Hansen's theory absurd?"

"Because it would put the art of a million years before the Stone Age on a higher level than that of the Twentieth Century."

"Perhaps it was. It seems impossible that it could have been any lower. Edith, can you find the last number of 'Vanity Fair' with the latest masterpieces of potato peeling embroidery or whatever it is that the connoisseurs are raving over? Never mind, if you don't know where to look. After dinner will do."

"The point is, Drake," he continued, "that you know as little of what art was in prehistoric times as do I. Why, it is less than thirty years since you archæological chaps were telling us that all real art began with the Greeks. Then they found those Stone Age cave paintings that Mr. Hansen has mentioned. Since then we haven't heard so much of 'Greece, wonder-child of the Ages.' You are open-minded enough about your own stuff. Why can't you examine Hansen's photographs in the same spirit?"

"Never. At least not until I have deciphered them."

"Then go to it. That's just what we want you to do."

"How can I make anything out of a bald catalogue of dead beasts? Why, I don't even know their blessed names."

"Drake, you are deliberately playing the fool for some reason of your own. I believe you have guessed more than you admit."

"It is always best," Drake generalized, "to know nothing at the beginning of an investigation. For then one is certain not to know less at the end."

"Do you see any sort of regularities running through those fourteen you put aside?" the Doctor persisted.

"Dozens of them."

"That sounds encouraging. What, for instance?"

"First, about five-eighths of the monsters have four legs each. Second, approximately fifty-five per cent of them have no tails and the rest one apiece. Third, each of several has one eye by actual count, or two by inference, the second being on the invisible side of the profile. Fourth—"

"You're an ass," the Doctor interrupted irritably.

"Hear, hear sir," Ole agreed.

Drake grinned. "Did you ever try opening a live oyster with a toothpick? When I have something definite I'll let you know. Until then Mr. Hansen no doubt will be glad to hatch out poetic theories for you."

"All right," Lane assented good-naturedly. "Only don't spend ten years in finding out that all these inscriptions are nothing more exciting than a fossilized multiplication table."

"Or a treatise on the integral calculus," Ole gravely added.

"Oh Lord," said Drake, "do you know the name of that too? When do you find time to navigate your raft?"

"He doesn't know half of what he gabs about," Anderson explained. There was a distinct note of jealousy in the Captain's voice. "He owns the A, Q, X volumes of the *Encyclopedia Britannica*, the *Song of Solomon* in Norwegian, Balzac's *Droll Stories* in French—which I can't read, confound it, a third-rate pocket dictionary, Herbert Spencer's *Through Nature to God*, about three-quarters of

Maeterlinck's *Bluebird* in Swedish and half of it in English, and a seven figure table of logarithms. That's his whole damned library. Now if you think he's a blazing genius it's your own lookout."

"When I was in Boston two and a half years ago," Ole volunteered à propos of nothing, "I took an intelligence test. The psychologist said I was in the upper one per cent of the entire population of the United States."

"He lied," said the Captain.

"My library is not the only source of my erudition," Ole continued, ignoring the Captain's remark. "I also read much in public libraries while ashore," he concluded with smug modesty.

"Well, gentlemen," the Doctor remarked, "I am sure Mr. Hansen makes good use of his library, small though it may be. It isn't the gross tonnage that counts so much; it is the choice of one's reading matter. Mr. Hansen seems to have selected his 'five foot shelf' with a taste and care that has not been exceeded by Dr. Eliot himself. Would you like a copy of William Jennings Bryan's memoirs on evolution as a companion piece to your Herbert Spencer, Mr. Hansen?"

Ole blushed his thanks. The Doctor turned to Anderson.

"Now Captain, what about oil?"

"Are you coming in?"

"Yes, even if our friend Drake doesn't succeed before he's seventy in deciphering Mr. Hansen's photographs. We shall need a ship, I suppose."

"The old whaler will do."

"Not much ice, then, where we are going?"

"No more than she can buck. Our troubles will begin on land."

"So I have guessed. Would an airplane be of any use? Amundsen is taking one with him on his North Polar expedition."

"Who would fly the beastly thing if we did take one along?"

"Why not Drake? He's young and therefore teachable."

"Oh, let me learn too," Edith begged. "You know how useless Drake is when anything goes wrong with his typewriter."

"Indeed?" said Drake, deeply mortified. He truly was as helpless as a baby before any machine more complicated than a monkey wrench. Rather pathetically he imagined himself a first-class amateur mechanic, for Edith always tactfully let him do the bossing while she did the tinkering when his typewriter collapsed.

The Doctor turned to Edith. "Who said you were coming with us, young lady?"

"Nobody yet. But you were just going to invite me. Weren't you, dear?"

"What about it, Captain?"

"It's up to you. She's not my daughter. If she can stand forty below zero she may enjoy the trip."

"I'm afraid not," the Doctor said doubtfully. "You do so hate the cold, Edith."

"Fiddlesticks! Captain Anderson said the water was warm. Anyway I'm younger than you are. If I'm unfit to go it will be suicide for you."

"Well, we'll consider your case when the time comes."

Knowing that she had won, Edith sensibly said no more.

"How long will it take us to get ready?" the Doctor asked.

"About six months. You, Drake, and your daughter if she comes, must get thoroughly hardened before we start. Hansen and I can see to overhauling the ship and laying in the necessary stores. We're both old hands at the game."

"Where is your ship now?"

"Drydock. Rio de Janeiro."

"What!" the Doctor exclaimed. "Do you mean to say you came clear to San Francisco just to show me that reptile bird?"

"Why not?" the Captain asked complacently. "I knew you would join us."

"Am I as easy as they told you I was?"

"No, Doctor. You wouldn't swallow a mermaid."

"Such is the bubble reputation. Edith, this comes of your collection of freaks. I wish you would adopt some less humiliating form of charity in future."

"You haven't believed my story of all those big beasts in the oil yet," the Captain reminded him soothingly.

"No, and I'll be hanged if I do until I see them with my own eyes. Well, I'm game. That thing in the box is real, anyway. You can telegraph the Rio de Janeiro dry-dock to give your ship a thorough overhauling. Fit up quarters somewhere for a passenger or two."

"Ole and I saw to all that before we left."

"Easier and easier. Well, well. You *are* a surprising person." This bit of information seemed almost to surprise him more than the captain's strange tale. "It's too late for lunch and too early for dinner. Will you have tea with us?"

"We shall be only too glad to enjoy your hospitality," Ole sententiously replied.

"Ah, Hansen, I see you have a treatise on Dutch etiquette among your literary treasures as well as a table of logarithms. All right, boys. Edith, tell Wong to do his best in the true old Spanish style."

5 "BATTLES LONG AGO"

Seven strenuous months of physical toughening lay behind Drake, Edith, and her father. They had lost no time in setting about their preparations for the hardships ahead.

The day after the tea with Captain Anderson and the mate they were on their way to the Canadian Rockies. Before leaving, Dr. Lane gave the efficient Wong a sheaf of checks dated the first of each month for the next three years. With these Wong was to pay his own salary and keep the house in order.

To his rage and stupefaction Drake was dragged kicking from his puzzles to become a hardened mountaineer. The Doctor was determined that the obstinate archæologist should accompany them to see with his own eyes the originals of Hansen's photographs. Anderson and the mate left San Francisco the same afternoon to return to Rio via Boston.

The party of three had gone straight north to a fashionable resort in the heart of the Canadian Rockies. They planned to begin their training gradually. Arrived at the luxurious hotel, they hired guides and mapped out their program. Four hours' mountain hiking a day for the first week, six the second, and so on up to fifteen, when they would be sufficiently seasoned to dispense with the guides.

Drake, who had brought with him the fourteen most promising of Hansen's puzzles for study, proved a most refractory companion. As the daily marches lengthened he seemed to demand more and more sleep. It was a ten minute job to get him out of bed in the mornings. The Doctor became alarmed, thinking the rarefied air and violent exercise might have affected the young man's heart. A searching physical examination showed him to be in perfect health. Drake himself said nothing, enduring the interminable climbs up precipices and the endless crawls over glaciers with glum stoicism.

When the party left their quarters at the hotel to live in the bleak open with only their sleeping bags for shelter, Drake became positively morose. Edith declared in confidence to her father that the cranky young antiquarian was developing such a devil of a temper that the only comfortable course would be to send him home. She had stood all she could of the snapping turtle. The thought of a possible two years with him in a frozen wilderness appeared singularly uninviting.

"I should like to beat him up," she confided, "for I am sure there is nothing the matter with him but a vile disposition."

An unusually cold and foggy night on the snowfields gave her the key to Drake's ailment. Unable to sleep for the wretched discomfort, she lay on her side staring wide-eyed at the soupy mist. Presently she became aware of a tiny, faint glow in the direction of Drake's quarters. Slipping from her bag she crawled on all fours over the soft snow toward the source of the light. Unobserved, she got close enough to see Drake lying flat on his stomach in his sleeping bag, his head propped up on his hands, intent on one of Hansen's photographs. The dim illumination came from an improvised reading lamp consisting of two inches of candle in a small tomato can on its side. She stole back to her bag and crept in, to keep a lookout on the dim glow. After what seemed an eternity it vanished, only to reappear half a minute later. Drake had lighted another two-inch candle. And so it went until about an hour before dawn when the glow finally disappeared and Drake presumably slept the sleep of the unjust.

Edith said nothing of her discovery to her father. The next night was clearer. Between cat naps she watched again. Once more the light vanished an hour before dawn, and the criminal slept. Edith decided not to peach. Instead she contrived an ingenious plan for the salvaging of whatever survived the general wreck of Drake's temper.

She had not long to wait before putting her plan into action. The two men shared the labor of splitting wood and keeping the campfire going while she cooked. They planned at least two hot meals a week, descending from the snowfields to the timberline to find fuel, for with their heavy packs it was impossible to carry oil. On these occasions the men peeled off their coats and went after wood with a will. The prospect of a well-cooked steaming hot meal put enthusiasm even into the dissipated, cantankerous Drake.

Edith bided her time. When next the perspiring Drake, having collected twice as much wood as he could carry, was swearing under his breath like a bobcat, she quietly abstracted the fourteen photographic puzzles from the inner pocket of his discarded coat.

"It's a dirty trick," she murmured, stowing them safely away inside her shirt, "but it is for his own good."

That night Drake was like a forlorn cow that has just lost its beloved calf. Edith heard him rooting about in the dark, scraping his shins and swearing at anything and everything. That night, she said later, was just one long, whispered curse.

She let him suffer for his calf three days. Then, with a six-foot crevasse between them, she confessed. Drake looked murder at her. But by the time he scrambled the mile and a half which she, with rare foresight, had placed between them by going rapidly ahead of the party, the out-raged Drake was too exhausted to fight. He regained his fourteen tormentors only on the solemn promise that he would blow out the candle every morning at two o'clock sharp. Thus, unless the enthusiastic Doctor insisted upon routing them from their bags ahead of schedule, Drake would get a full four hours' sleep every night.

"If that isn't enough to sweeten your disposition," Edith stipulated, "I'll add half an hour at a time until we hit the right dose."

Under the new ordering of his disreputable habits Drake became as suave as melted butter. Not that he talked much more than he had, for he still emulated the oyster. What little he did say, however, was all that Edith desired in affability. The Doctor, noticing the change, ascribed it to a sudden, bone-freezing drop in the temperature.

"Drake will do famously when we get to the real thing," he told Edith. "Just see how this cold snap bucks him up."

"Oh, he will be all right," Edith agreed. "When he gets something to do he will lose his grouch for good."

After twelve weeks of roughing it on the snowfields and glaciers of the Rockies the three went to Alaska for a more drastic course of the same training. Little by little they accustomed themselves to scantier and scantier clothing, until by the end of their hardening they were clambering over ice and snow in howling blizzards with no clothing but a single loose overall garment of wool. The Doctor in his joyous enthusiasm was inclined to go farther, pointing out that if stark nakedness in the snow is the proper thing for consumptive children, surely a breech clout in a blizzard should be sufficient for tough campaigners like themselves. But Edith wouldn't hear of it, although Drake seemed to entertain the suggestion favorably.

And now all this, the hardship and the fun, lay behind them. That night they were sailing from Montreal for Rio de Janeiro, there to meet the rest of the expedition and undergo their last training. They must learn to fly. Dr. Lane still believed that an airplane might prove the decisive factor in the success of their venture, although Captain Anderson, with all an old sailor's conservatism, belittled the idea and grudged the two months' delay which it would cost.

Ole, on the contrary, by letter and cablegram, fairly gloated over the prospect. A mastery of flying would bring him many steps nearer the omniscience which was his ideal in this imperfect life. The Captain's letters reported him already past master of the art of flying—on paper. He had even invented an improved type of flying machine which, according to the envious Anderson, resembled a wheelbarrow with wings. This masterpiece of Ole's unsuspected mechanical genius was still in the chrysaloid stage of development, being as yet only one-third drawings and two-thirds pure theory. Still, all in all it justified Ole's high rating in the Boston intelligence tests. Anderson could never have done anything like it.

Except for Drake's alleged seasickness the voyage down to Rio de Janeiro was uneventful. Drake had telegraphed from Vancouver to one of his antiquarian cronies to meet him in Montreal with half a ton of carefully selected books, for the most part profusely illustrated works on biology, geology and evolution. With these he shut himself up in his cabin, admitting only the stewards who reported him in the last stages of seasickness. Smelling a prosperous rat, Dr. Lane left the sufferer to his agonies and hopefully promenaded the decks or played quoits with Edith.

On the morning of the last day of the voyage the doctor's patience was rewarded. The invalid emerged from his cabin looking, as Edith informed him, as fresh as a young string bean.

"I'm better," Drake announced.

"That's good," said the Doctor. "How are Hansen's photographs?"

Drake tried not to look pleased. He failed. His face broke into a grin.

"Doing as well as could be expected, thank you," he replied.

"Have you deciphered them?"

"If I say 'yes' you will pester me to death with questions; if I say 'no' you will set me down as a blockhead. So I shall evade the question by answering both yes and no. And that, as a matter of fact, is the exact state of affairs."

"The Lord should have made you a woman," the Doctor remarked.

"A beautiful blonde," Drake sighed. "A perfect thirty-six," he added with an admiring glance at Edith's lithe figure.

"I'll give you a swift kick unless you come through with what you have found," the Doctor snapped. "Come on; out with it."

"Before violence I am powerless. I am too proud to run away." He became more serious. "You were right when you said my education was lopsided. A thorough knowledge of biology, geology, evolution and half a dozen tougher sciences is just what I lack now to read those fragments fully. I have been doing my weak best to make up the deficiency and learn something worth knowing. At present I can guess at the meaning of those fragments, but only through thick blankets of wooly ignorance. Unless I am clean off there is vastly more than can be read at a glance in those rows upon rows of prehistoric monsters. I don't believe those inscriptions will ever be fully deciphered by any man who like me is an ignoramus on all the sciences connected with living things."

"You evidently have found more than you admit. Tell us what you know. If you need more science to go ahead I'll give you all I have."

After a brief tussle with his antiquarian conscience Drake yielded.

"First," he began, "this sort of work is very deceptive. Take the case of the Etruscan writing for instance, or the Hittite inscriptions if you prefer. Either one has been 'read' in half a dozen different ways. One man making perfect sense of a particular inscription says it is an extremely modest account of a marriage ceremony. His opponent and critic reads precisely the same signs as a detailed description of the slaughter of forty bulls. Both can't be right, unless of course the forty bulls are a poetic metaphor for the bridegroom. And so it goes; what one theorist reads as a beautiful prayer to the goddess of love another deciphers as a simple recipe for lentil soup. Unless there are dates, numerals, or other mathematical signs that can be definitely checked against facts in such work it is all likely to be a mere reflection of the decipherer's personality. So when a man says 'forty bulls' I know what to think of him."

"And you are afraid now," Edith smiled, "of giving yourself away? Never mind, I'll forget all the compromising parts."

"I have nothing to be ashamed of in my private life," he retorted, drawing himself up like a stork.

"That is what they all say when they begin to tell their dreams," the Doctor laughed. "Then they are as mad as tarantulas when they find they have given away the whole show. But go ahead; those beasts of yours are not all purely subjective."

"That is where you are wrong. It is the ideal, the subjective part that matters in these particular inscriptions. And that is precisely what I can't decipher. The rest is easy enough. Superficially those fourteen inscriptions are fragments of the history of a terrible war. It is the symbolism behind the bald account of battles and sieges that I can't get at. It is like one of those sentences that can be read in a dozen different ways to give good sense. The surface meaning seems perfectly clear. Then when the sentence is read a second time another meaning begins to appear, and so on, until the whole shows up as a most ingeniously constructed cipher.

"Consider, for example, the simple statement 'It rained yesterday.' Ordinarily we should think nothing of it. But suppose you were an intelligence officer in the army and you found one of your men sneaking over to the enemy with 'It rained yesterday' sewn into his left sock. You would ask for the code, wouldn't you, before shooting him?

"Well, so it is in my case. At first sight those inscriptions record only fragments of a hideous war. But only at first sight. The account of the war is consistent and thorough, even if it is appalling in its stark insanity. Intelligence, if I may say so without becoming oratorical, is dethroned. There never was another war like it, and there never will be again. For the fighting material has gone out of existence."

"Beast against beast?" the Doctor hazarded.

"No. Beast against intellect and intellect against beast. Only I can't make out whose intellect it was or what, exactly, the beasts were.

"That, however, is not my main difficulty. The whole story, I am convinced, is merely the symbol of the real conflict which those inscriptions record. I have no definite knowledge that this is the case. Yet I feel it to be the absolute truth. Some terrific struggle has been disguised under the fairly straightforward account of a war unique in the history of the world. It is my guess that the real conflict was of so terrible a character that the survivors deliberately wrapped it up in a symbolism that may never be explained."

"What could have been their motive for recording this struggle at all if they took such pains to obscure its history?"

"Can't you see? Perhaps they guessed that some day a similar devil might break loose, and they left this hint of their own chaining of the fiend. They suppressed a plain history lest some idiot be tempted to try again what had wrecked them. Such things do happen. If it were not for the lofty patriotism of certain old men we younger fellows might never have to face gas and other horrors never intended for the destruction of life. The makers of those inscriptions decided to disguise the truth so that only beings as intelligent as they themselves could decipher its meaning. This is only my theory, as our friend Hansen would say."

"Still," the Doctor objected, "I fail to see in your theory why a record of the horror should have been left at all, even in the most obscure form. If they wished oblivion for it, surely the safest way would have been to leave no record, symbolic or otherwise."

"If that was their only anxiety, yes. But what if they wished to leave a warning to anyone intelligent enough to read and take it? Suppose, for the sake of argument, they had discovered some secret of nature. And suppose that this very discovery undid them. Would they not wish to leave a caution to the next race of investigators who might blunder through to the forbidden door?"

"Your imagination is running away with your brains, to say nothing of your tongue. What about the actual war that is recorded?"

"I'm feeling seasick again," Drake prevaricated, diving for his cabin. "Some other time."

And that was all they got out of him, for he locked his stateroom door.

6 A WITNESS TO THE TRUTH

Their two busy months in Rio de Janeiro passed pleasantly enough. With the help of a young lieutenant from the Brazilian navy one at least of the adventure seekers became an expert aviator. Possibly it was Edith's striking beauty that caused the young officer to lavish his skill and patience upon perfecting her in those finer points of aviation which she probably would never use unless she became a stuntist at a county fair. It is at any rate certain that he took far less pains with the industrious Ole who, after one shocking misalliance with a gilded virgin—on top of a church,—developed into a safe and sane air navigator, largely self-taught.

Captain Anderson gave it up immediately after his first stomach raising flight with the daredevil lieutenant. He refused flatly to learn the knack of being seasick all over again.

Dr. Lane, learning easily, showed a bad tendency to loop the loop without due provocation. Edith begged the Captain to set her father to work on the ship's stores—taking inventory, anything to keep him out of the dazzling sapphire sky. The Captain consenting, Edith was left a clean heaven which she shared with the lieutenant. Ole, an indiscriminating admirer of Maeterlinck, remarked to Drake that Edith's airy antics were precisely those of the queen bee on her prenuptial flight. What Drake replied is unrepeatable.

Poor Drake had proven himself a hopeless duffer at the game. After a truly conscientious attempt to teach him the rudiments of flight, the lieutenant announced with considerable relief that Mr. Drake would make excellent ballast in an emergency, but was otherwise useless. So Drake, discomfited and humiliated, returned to his inscriptions. Such at least was the outward appearance of things. But Ole evolved a deeper theory which he generously confided to Edith.

"No man, Miss Lane, can be such a fool as Drake made of himself. Drake does not want to fly. He goes back to my photographs. That young man has brains. Some day he will have a theory." Ole spoke in the hushed tones of a fat old woman contemplating her buxom daughter-in-law.

And Edith, reflecting that she had begged Drake to let her give him private lessons, felt like boxing Ole's red ears. In her heart of hearts she knew that the mate's theory was the truth; Drake was infatuated with a lovely abstraction. And sighing her exasperation she resumed her bee-like flirtation with the lieutenant. He at any rate was aware of her charms. But she would have liked to set her even white teeth in the one apple just beyond her reach.

By the end of the first month in Rio Drake's habits were ruined. He now had the whole of Hansen's masterpieces in his room for study, one hundred and forty-four dumb tormentors of the reason. Although the heat was terrific, the long, lean Drake seemed not to suffer. But his food did, intensely. Meals brought to his door remained outside until the porter devoured them with ghoulish glee or took them away for burial. At last, however, the sympathetic landlord concocted a villainous ration which was both meat and drink, and which could be downed at one gulp with a minimum of attention to details. Oysters and cream formed the basis of this ghastly diet to which rum and a dash of absinthe gave the finishing flavor. The intervening strata were a horrible mystery. A suspicious granulated blackness about the middle suggested caviare. This perhaps was confirmed at the curdled surface by the unmistakable odor of finely chopped garlic. The necessary balance of carbohydrates was supplied by a liberal admixture of brown sugar. A quart of this ambrosial hooch placed four times daily in his hand, with unlimited coffee "as black as the devil, as sweet as love and as hot as hell" in the Spanish phrase, kept the wolf from Drake's vitals.

Lane spent his nights aboard ship, while Edith danced till three in the morning with the amorous lieutenant under the perfunctory chaperonage of his aged mother. So Drake had a free hand to do what he liked with the twenty-four hours between dawn and dawn. He slept when sleep stole upon him from behind and overpowered him in his chair. If when exhausted he instinctively sought his bed he lay down without bothering to undress. Within four hours he was at his problem again. Refuting all theories of the hygienists he took no exercise whatever and remained in perfect health, as hard as a rock. After all, a busy mind is perhaps the perfect tonic and the best exerciser.

Ole, gleaning daily bulletins from the landlord, developed an awed respect for this unprecedented young hatcher of theories. That something huge and universal must at last leap forth from such an aeonial gestation he had not the slightest doubt. On the morning of departure he led Drake aboard to his quarters on the old whaler—now cleansed and rechristened the *Edith*—with all the solicitude he would have shown an expectant mother.

The *Edith* slunk under her own steam from the grand harbor, rounded the point, and headed due south in the sparkling air, cleaving a sea of chrysoprase. Officially they were on a whaling expedition. The airplane was sophisticated to the Brazilian officers as a freak hobby of the rich and eccentric Dr. Lane who wished before he died to harpoon a whale from the air.

The great adventure had begun, but what was to be its outcome not one soul aboard the silent ship had the slightest idea. They were headed due south for the undiscovered oilfields and for a stranger thing which, could they have foreseen it, they would not have wished to discover. It is in this unreasoning way that human beings are forever blundering into the mysteries of life.

By Lane's orders Drake was left to himself. Hansen's reports had impressed him, and he knew from experience the powerful drive of unbroken thought.

As the days flew over them like azure birds the breeze freshened and a knife-edged cold cut the unhardened members of the crew to the bones. The old-timers and the well-seasoned beginners merely quickened their movements and went about their work with a new energy. The greenhorns would soon get used to it. In the meantime they must stamp and swear and get on with it as best they could.

The lightly ballasted *Edith* beginning to pitch and roll like a porpoise, the oysters, caviare and brown sugar of Drake's orgy had their revenge. His abused stomach, protesting at the sound ship fare, rejected honest salt horse with ineffable scorn. Edith forgot his inconstancy, pardoning him all his theories, and ministered to him like a white robed angel of forgiveness. His recovery was as sudden as his collapse. And with the return of his vigor and his temper—he had been as sweet as a consumptive curate during his prostration—he once more jilted Edith for his houri.

"Let us go to the Captain's cabin and talk over what we are to do," he suggested. "You bring your father and I'll rout out Ole. This is the second mate's watch. They will all be off duty."

Seated comfortably round the red baize of the Captain's table the five discussed their plans. Anderson and Lane had decided to head directly for the inlet which the Captain had discovered the morning after the submarine eruption. They were then to steam up the inlet as far as possible. Then they were to leave the ship in charge of Bronson, the second mate and a capable seaman, and travel inland by dogteam and sledges to the volcano whose smoke and flames Anderson and the mate had seen from the inlet. If practicable to use the airplane two of the party could return for it.

The men under Bronson's charge were to wait at the ship three months for the party to return. If at the end of that time they had heard nothing from the explorers they were to despatch a relief party to go in search. The organization of the relief had been planned to its last detail. Should circumstances so dictate Bronson would have only to carry out his written instructions to the letter.

Anderson had made only a rough guess as to the probable location of the oil which he expected to find. Although this first conjecture was founded on a theory of Ole's the Captain refused to give him any credit. With a rare flash of common sense Ole had observed that since the heavy black smoke and ruddy pillar of flame which they had seen from the inlet looked like burning oil, probably it was burning oil.

The one stumbling block which this sensible hypothesis had to surmount was, as Lane pointed out, the Captain's estimate of two hundred fifty to three hundred miles inland as the distance of the explosion which they had heard. It hardly seemed probable that an outburst of burning oil could make itself heard and seen at such a distance. A volcanic eruption, on the other hand, easily might carry that far. Krakatoa, Katmai, Pelée and many others among the more famous eruptions had carried even farther.

The Captain, however, would have none of Lane's objections. To him the mere vastness of an oilfield was no slur on its probability. The bigger the likelier was his theory. And staring up at the swinging kerosene lamp he beheld a beatific vision of stocks and shares floating like all the leaves of Vallombrosa on an ocean of unlimited liability.

Lane was curiously reticent about what he expected to get out of the expedition. Since that afternoon, now ten months ago, in his San Francisco study, he had not once alluded to the Captain's tale of dead prehistoric monsters boiling up as fresh as life through a sea of pitch. If questioned he would have said that his judgment was suspended, as undoubtedly it was. The indubitable bird-reptile obstinately continued to exist as an awkward reality not yet satisfactorily explained away.

On mature reflection he had abandoned his first theory that the reptilian bird had been preserved for ages like a sardine in oil. But he refrained from acquainting the Captain with his changed state of mind lest that imaginative ex-mining engineer and inventive whaler should be moved to show what he really could do in the way of a yarn when put on his mettle. In the true scientific spirit the Doctor was resolved to await further facts before abandoning himself like Ole to seductive theories.

One sore spot in his memories hardened him in this decision. He had not yet forgiven the Captain for assuming that he was a gullible enthusiast eager to swallow the first mermaid with a cocoanut head dangled before his mouth. Above all, still holding the opinion that Drake was the greatest decipherer of his time, he wished to hear what the young archaeologist had to report as to the outcome of his intense concentration on Hansen's photographs. Edith, with Drake's permission, had revealed the secret of his vile temper in the Canadian Rockies.

"Well, oyster," said the Doctor, turning to Drake, "are you ready to open up yet?"

"Have you a theory?" Ole blurted out.

"Two," Drake replied.

"Two theories!" Ole rhapsodized. "Young man, you are a scientist. What are your theories?"

"The first, and the one which I favor, is that I'm crazy."

"So impossible as all that?" the Doctor asked, raising his brows.

"I told you in San Francisco it was impossible," the Captain asserted. "Now Drake is going to prove what I said. Wait till you see it with your own eyes."

"It is not that part of it which is impossible," Drake replied. "After what I have guessed as the true meaning of the symbolism of the inscriptions your stew of monsters sounds a little tame. I am willing to accept your account as true to the facts, even if Dr. Lane is still too cautious to commit himself. But the other thing, the real meaning of that fragmentary history recorded in the inscriptions, is a subject which I must decline to discuss until events have proved me either crazy or right."

"I appreciate your stand, Drake," said the Doctor. "Under like circumstances I should feel the same way. Still, you can tell us this much without prejudicing your case. From what you have made out so far do you believe that we shall find any tangible evidence of the true struggle? I mean of course the one which the makers of the inscriptions took such pains to disguise."

Drake gave him a shrewd look. "You have guessed the nature of that conflict?"

"Perhaps, reasoning from other data, I have. In that case you can understand why I prefer to wait before venturing my guesses. Shall we find any traces of the real fight?"

"I don't know. To me it is incredible that we should."

"Some things are eternal," the Doctor remarked quietly. "For all we know life may be indestructible."

"Have you ever whiffed a dead whale?" the Captain interposed. He was a practical man.

"That isn't what the Doctor means," Ole expostulated, beginning to redden.

"I know, Ole. I know what the Doctor means. He's talking of the soul. Now, Doctor, did you ever see a whale with a soul?"

"Not after it was dead," the Doctor admitted with a smile. "However, that was not what I had in mind. My idea was something much more prosaic—a question of energy and cells, and all that commonplace sort of stuff."

"Cells?" the Captain snorted. "Rotten fish is rotten fish, cells or no cells."

"That isn't—"

"Shut up, Ole. No, Doctor Lane, I'm not fool enough to argue with you on your own deck. But when you show me a whale that I can't set stinking ripe in three weeks I'll begin to believe in the indestructibility of life."

"That—"

"Shut up, Ole. Well, Doctor, where's your immortal whale?"

"In Heaven," the Doctor replied without the flicker of an eyelash.

"Father," Edith protested, "you are irreverent."

"Not necessarily, Chick. Remember the prophet of Nineveh. Now Drake, what is your second theory?"

"That the whole thing is literally true."

"And that is mine," said the Doctor.

"Mine too," Ole echoed before the Captain could squelch him.

"It can't be, Ole," the Doctor replied. "For, prolific as you may be, you are constitutionally incapable of hatching such a nightmare."

Ole looked crestfallen. He was rebuked. Edith felt for him as she was suffering acutely from repressed curiosity.

"I wish you two wouldn't talk as if I were a baby in long dresses. If I'm old enough to be here I'm certainly old enough to be let in on things."

"You might take the plane and fly back to Rio in the night," her father laughed, "if we frightened you with all our half-baked theories. Better wait and see—"

He was cut short by a jarring tremor that shook the stout ship from stem to stern.

"My God!" the Captain shouted, bolting for the door, "we've struck! All hands on deck!"

They reached the deck a second behind him. Instantly an overpowering stench enveloped them body and soul, searching out the secret convolutions of their brains with a sense-destroying, paralyzing nausea. Hardened old whale pirates were leaning over the rail in a paroxysm of the extremest misery.

On the less calloused members of the expedition the effect was instantaneous and drastic. It was complete. No chemist in the distorted ambition of his wildest night-mare ever dreamed of a smell such as that which defiled the very soul of this night, otherwise so beautiful and serene.

A full moon silvered the calm meadows of the sea. Nature, dead and living, lay peacefully asleep. Athwart the silver road through the ripples floated majestically the vast corpse through whose middle rottenness the sturdy ship had churned her filthy way. Four pillars, two at either end, towered up in the mystic light like the ruins of a shattered temple on a hill in Greece. These were the creature's legs. What else of it the moonlight revealed had better be veiled.

"There's your immortal whale, Captain," the Doctor sobbed when from very emptiness he ceased his calisthenics.

"Whale be blowed. That carcass is the size of four whales. It's one of them."

"I believe," said the penitent Doctor, "smelling is a severer test of truth than seeing. Lead us below and give us asafetida from your medicine chest to take the taste of truth out of our mouths."

Returning to the Captain's cabin they sought forgetfulness in rum tinctured with Jamaica ginger.

"How shall I ever get it out of my hair?" Edith wailed.

"Shave your hair, dear," the Doctor prescribed, "and then boil it in lye."

7 BEACHED

Shortly after midnight Captain Anderson called the sleepers.

"This is the spot, Doctor," he said. "You wanted to see it with your own eyes."

"What spot?" the Doctor sleepily inquired.

"Where all those big beasts boiled up from the bottom of the sea."

They stood gazing over the rail at the cold, glittering Antarctic waste of black water. Far to the south the dim shapes of five huge bergs towered up like vast frozen ghosts in the moonlight.

"The water looks clean enough," the Doctor remarked suspiciously. The smell having dissipated, his skepticism was returning. "Where's your oil?"

"Blest if I know. Washed ashore months ago, I expect."

"In what direction is the nearest land?"

"Southeast. Directly in line with the southernmost of those bergs."

"When shall we reach it?"

"Within twelve hours if the wind doesn't rise."

The Doctor glanced at the cloudless sky. "Everything looks serene. Well, we should see your inlet sometime tomorrow afternoon. By the way, has the lookout sighted any more dead—whales?"

"Whales? That was no whale we cut through, I tell you. It had four times the bulk of the biggest whale afloat. Think what you like, that was one of those brutes that boiled up when I was here before. And the lookout saw three others."

"How close?"

"About two miles. Of course he couldn't make out exactly what they were at that distance. But I'll bet they were not floating islands, or ice, or dead whales. If we sight another I'll steam up close to give you a whiff if you like."

"For mercy's sake don't," Edith begged. "My cabin is full of the last one still."

"A mere smell proves nothing," the Doctor remarked dryly.

"Mere smell?" Drake exploded. "Great Scott! What is your idea of a full-blown reek?"

"I mean," the Doctor explained, "the smell may have come from putrefying whale blubber. The odor is notorious and far reaching I'm told."

"You bet it is," the Captain asserted. "Twenty years of it have made me an expert. And I tell you straight that a ripe whale smells like a bunch of violets beside that beauty we cut through."

Disdaining further argument the Doctor retired to his cabin, and the others after a last look at the austere grandeur of the icy night turned in to their warm bunks.

About nine o'clock the next morning the breeze veered and blew from the icebound land far to the southeast. It was still a mere sigh. The Captain and Ole anticipated a safe and early arrival at their goal. That after-noon would bring them to the mouth of the volcanic inlet.

No spot on the oceans of the earth could have been more coldly serene, more vastly mysterious. The water, almost black in the mass, curled over in hard glassy waves intensely green as they broke, and far to the south the airy peaks and pinnacles of huge bergs swam like dreams athwart the taut horizon. Then the offshore breeze freshening brought with it the first faint hint of an indescribable pollution.

"Dead whales," the Captain laconically remarked to Lane.

"Undoubtedly," replied the Doctor through his handkerchief.

Edith gazed longingly at the high-powered airplane under its tarpaulins.

"We must have run over another of them," she sighed.

Anderson laughed. "Did you feel a jar, Edith? No? Well, neither did I, and my sea legs are more sensitive than yours. We're not running over the rotten brutes; we're running into them."

And with that comforting assurance he swung below to see if the engineer could crowd on more steam. He was tremendously eager.

Lunch time passed unobserved. Those of the crew who were off duty followed the example of the passengers and sought seclusion below decks. But the ever increasing stench found them out like a forgotten sin. Every mile less between them and the land multiplied their misery tenfold. To the inexperienced passengers this penetrating torment which prostrated hardened whalers became unendurable. At last Lane, reaching his limit, went in search of medical relief.

He had no definite idea of what he wanted, trusting blindly to the stores for inspiration. And he found it. Presently he returned with three improvised gas masks of surgical gauze soaked in spirits of camphor.

"Who ever would have guessed that we should need gas masks in the Antarctic," he laughed ruefully as he adjusted Drake's. "Edith, get out your needles and thread and make nosebags for all hands."

Under her father's supervision Edith labored diligently at a new style of mask designed to filter the tainted air through finely sifted ashes. If the temperature kept up the ashes might be soaked in deodorizer. Otherwise the sufferers would have to put up with the lesser efficiency of the dry material.

Ole, coming in to see how the greenhorns were bearing up, found Edith at her task. The poor fellow was the sickly hue of cheesy white phosphorus. Some of the men, he reported, were on the point of mutiny.

"Order them to make masks for themselves," Edith advised. "They can all sew. Here, take this one as a pattern."

His rotundity drooping from his shoulders in soggy folds, Ole departed. Although his faith in the vanity of nosebags was slight, yet in the true scientific spirit he would test any theory before condemning it as useless. The men, therefore, were soon in the throes of a sewing bee. And it may be said here that the masks later made endurable a labor which without them might well have proved impossible.

Land was sighted at two thirty-five. Due south along the horizon stretched the great barrier cliff of black rock and sheer ice, shadowy in the distance and unsubstantial as a vision. Anderson joined the three at the rail and passed Lane his binoculars.

"Look about two points east of south and you will see the opening of the inlet."

"Ah, I get it. Not very wide, is it?"

"No. Just a twenty mile crack in the Antarctic continent that wasn't there two years ago. I imagine it narrows down fast after it gets farther inland."

He turned and left them to go about his business. They stood watching the distant shadow assume definite outline. Presently Lane hailed the Captain on the bridge.

"We're getting off our course, aren't we?"

"No. Dead on it."

"But we are going thirty degrees east of the inlet."

"Thirty-three, Doctor. There's an eight mile stony beach over there that I want to have a look at first. It might give the men fresh seal meat if there's any way of landing. We have plenty of time to make the inlet before dark if we decide to go on."

"Oh, all right. You're the captain."

Although their changed course drifted them across the breeze instead of directly into it, the stench became more terrific. Without their masks they could not have faced it. Presently the Captain called Lane up on the bridge and handed him his glasses.

"There's the beach, Doctor. Now if smelling isn't believing perhaps seeing is. Take a close look at your whales."

Lane almost dropped the Captain's best glasses.

"Good Lord," he gasped, "hundreds and hundreds of them! Full steam ahead, Captain!"

He ran down the steps to tell the others to keep their eyes open. As the *Edith* rapidly neared the long beach they saw at first only a coal black slope littered with what looked like huge rounded lumps of black rock. Then a blast from the whistle raised a cloud of scavengers from the black masses and the truth leapt out before their eyes. The eight mile beach was a refuse heap of huge oil-soaked carcasses festering in the sun.

Piled five and six deep where the winter hurricanes had hurled them the monsters of a forgotten age rotted in the delayed death which should have been theirs nine million years ago. On that beach there must have been hundreds of thousands of the gigantic brutes. The smaller monstrosities wedged and packed between the mountainous carcasses were without number. The Antarctic cold, their long immersion in the salt water and their thick coating of oil had but postponed the colossal corruption which now, at the height of a mild open season, preyed upon their mountains of rich flesh.

A boat was already being lowered. They sprang in with Ole and the Captain and were rapidly pulled ashore. The landing on that shelving beach was easy. They stood up in the oozing slop of oil to gaze as in a nightmare at the horror of the shambles surrounding them.

"Well," said the Captain, pointing to the sheer black cliffs barring the beach from the frozen continent, "there's what is left of my oil. The wind swabbed those rocks with some of it and blew the rest inland or wasted it all over the ocean from here to Cape Horn. Is there any money to be made out of these carcasses, Doctor? What about blubber? That big brute over there,' he indicated a twisted dragon mailed in triangular two-foot plates of horn, "looks pretty good to me. He's not so ripe as some of the others."

"Money be damned!" snapped the Doctor. "This is a bigger thing than the Standard Oil and Dutch Shell combined. It would be nothing short of an infamous sacrilege to hack these beautiful things to pieces for the sake of a few dirty dollars. No sir! I am financing this expedition, and so long as you are on land you will obey my orders. Aboard ship you are the master, but only for so long as I choose to employ you. I am the owner. Now, is that clear?"

"All right, Doctor. Keep your shirt on."

The soft answer mollified the indignant lover of beauty.

"Do as I tell you," he said, "and I'll see that you find your precious oil. You can go prospecting while the rest of us are discovering our treasure. And although it isn't in our contract I'll give you gratis all the very best expert mining and geological advice I can. To begin now, there is not the ghost of a possibility of striking oil on a beach like this. For your encouragement, however, I may tell you that I have already formed a pretty rational theory where to look for the main reservoir. Your earthquake tapped only a top bubble of it."

"So have I a theory," Ole announced with modest pride.

"Shut up, Ole. I want to hear what the Doctor thinks."

"I was only going to say," Lane continued, "that if my guess is right all the oil you saw is only a bucketful of the big tank. Unless I'm all wrong you will stumble into a reservoir of the highest grade oil as big as the State of California. To settle this thing once for all, I promise to finance another expedition for oil prospecting if you return from this a cent poorer than you wish to be. If we don't get your oil this time we certainly will next. There is no argument about it; I am positive. Now let us get to something more important and inspect some of these gorgeous jewels while the light lasts."

They followed him into the thick of the shambles.

"Ole," he continued, "I see you have brought your camera. Get busy. Begin with the big fellows and be sure you take enough pictures of each to show clearly the head, neck, position of the legs, pattern of the scales, and tail— if there is one. Take in the small fry too. They're just as important as the big fellows."

While Ole industriously clicked away at the mountains before him, the rest of the party clambered over monsters whose horny armor still afforded a sure footing, carefully avoiding the inviting slopes of the colossal three hundred foot lizards. A step on those smooth, bloated bodies meant a plunge up to the neck in corruption.

From many of the hideous skulls most of the flesh had already disappeared, leaving only irregular patches of blackened skin above the arsenals of sabre teeth and around the huge glasslike masses of lustreless jelly in the eye sockets.

As they passed from monster to monster along that shambles of a beach, Lane's expression changed gradually from reverent wonder to puzzled incredulity. His theory was taking shape before his eyes. Yet so strange was it that he doubted the evidence of tangible proofs. The thing he had imagined was unbelievable when seen. What, he wondered, lay behind this veil which his own speculations and those of Drake had lifted ever so little? Had they guessed the whole truth, or did an unimagined catastrophe wait for them at the end of their untrodden path into the unknown? At this first partial confirmation of their theory his belief in himself faltered. For once he hoped that he had been misled by reason.

Going up to one huge head he peered into the gaping cavity of the mouth and began to count the teeth. Their number would either confirm or destroy Drake's theory and his. Hoping that he had made a mistake he counted the teeth a second time. He had made no error.

"As I thought," he said, wiping the sweat from his forehead. "These things are all wrong."

"Is an ugly brute like that ever right?" Anderson asked.

"Always, in nature. At least according to their fossil remains they are invariably true to type. What would you think of a man with forty-eight teeth instead of the normal thirty-two?"

"As a practical seaman," said the Captain, "I should advise him to go to a dentist and have sixteen pulled. It would save him a lot of toothache on the high seas."

"That wouldn't work on this fellow. It would take a steam shovel to dig out his eight superfluous molars."

"Perhaps," Drake suggested hopefully, "this one is a freak. Try another. There are plenty lying about."

"Yes, but I don't see one of the same species. That's another curious thing about all this. There are not more than a dozen specimens of any one kind, I should judge, in the whole stew."

"Isn't that one over there the same sort as this?" Edith asked, pointing to a huger brute that resembled the monster of too many teeth.

The Doctor surveyed its frozen death agony. "I believe you are right," he said. "Let's count his teeth."

The count checked. Again the monster had eight molars in excess of what nature should have given him.

"That settles it," the Doctor muttered, sitting down on the treacherous tail of a defunct reptile.

"Oh see what a mess you are in!" Edith cried. "Stand up. You can't come back to the ship till you've burned your clothes."

"Clothes don't matter in a crisis like this. Science is rotting to its foundations."

"That's no reason why you should sit down in the basement," Edith retorted. Her mask had slipped, and naturally she was inclined to be severe.

"If this is science," Drake remarked, "I agree. It's putrid from cellar to attic."

"Don't play the fool. If you have guessed as much as I think you have, you should be able to appreciate what this may mean. This is serious. Not one of these creatures, I'll wager, is all that it should be. Each at first glance is like its supposed type. When you look at them closely and begin to apply scientific tests you find they are all either deformities or new species. Offhand one would say that nature had been practising and had forgotten her art."

"That," said Drake, "isn't your theory, however. Is it?"

"No," the Doctor admitted. "But the facts, all theories aside, can be ascertained either to establish or to refute my contention that these things are not as nature should have made them. Now here is a crucial test. See that blue brute like a potbellied crocodile over there? No, not the one with the saw ridge of three-foot spines down its back, but the one with the red bags hanging down from its jowls. All right. According to all we know from fossil anatomy that beast was comparatively harmless. Its only weapons were its teeth and its claws. I don't know what those obscene looking pouches mean—they don't show in any fossil remains yet found. Nor do I know whether red is their natural color, or whether it is due to faster decay owing to all the oil having dripped down off them. So much for its supposed identity.

"Now I suspect," he continued, "from the shape of that beast's head and snout that it was venomous when alive. The true animal, the one in the fossil beds, was as innocuous as a tame worm. I'm going over to see. If that brute has poison glands above its evil fangs the question is settled. It is some reptile utterly unknown to science."

Accompanying him to the grinning head they watched while he inspected the rows of yellowish knives bared by the upward snarl of the dry, scaled lips. The great cavern of the mouth gaped open, revealing a single five-foot row of teeth on each side of the gums. Having carefully selected the fang for his test, Lane picked up the largest stone he could heft and hurled it with all his strength at the point. The stone rebounded like a pebble from a brick wall.

"Here, Ole!" the Captain shouted. "Come and play handball."

Ole with his knotted strength was more successful. Behind his thirty-pound pebble he put the full barrel of his strength. The fang was jarred. The deep musical boom which it emitted died gradually away and Ole took another shot. At the fifth impact the fang was loose. The sixth, aimed at the base, sent it crashing out of the monster's head. Lane peered up in the gaping cavity.

"There's a sac of something up there," he said, "but it may only be a cushion of fat. Ole, will you fetch an oar from the boat?"

When the car arrived Lane thrust the blade far up the cavity and prodded hard. The sac broke, and a heavy oily green liquid oozed down like cold pitch on the decaying remnants of the reptile's tongue.

"I want some of that," the Doctor exclaimed, hastily emptying the brandy from his pocket flask. "Ole, scoop up a ladleful on the end of the oar. I'll hold the flask; you let the stuff pour in like molasses."

"What is the decision?" Drake asked curiously, as the Doctor carefully tucked away his pint of supposed venom.

"We can't tell until this stuff is tried on some living creature. Nevertheless I am willing to stake my reputation on the outcome. That brute, when alive, was as venomous as a regiment of rattlesnakes."

"Then it is like no prehistoric monster known to science?"

"As different as a hen is from a hippopotamus. And so, I am willing to wager, is every other creature that we have seen on this nightmare of a beach. They are all new. For one thing the majority of them are enormously bigger and bulkier than they should be. That in itself, however, is not conclusive. It would be possible for such a state of affairs to exist in, say, a herd of cattle. If all suffered from the same disease of certain glands—those regulating growth—they might all be enormous giants and yet not unnatural. These are abnormal in a far more radical way."

"But," Edith protested, "several of them look very much like the restorations in some of your books on fossils."

"That is the strangest part of all this unearthly dream. They are like bad copies, botched imitations if you like, of those huge brutes whose bones we chisel out of the rocks from Wyoming to Patagonia. Nature must have been drunk, drugged or asleep when she allowed these aborted beasts to mature. Every last one of them is a freak. It is just like looking at a shambles of all the deformities of a nation."

"The whole thing is inexpressibly hideous and depressing," Edith shivered. "And these masks are becoming useless."

"Hideous? Depressing? Why this is Heaven!"

"Then I wish I were in hell," the mate remarked.

"Hadn't we better be getting back to the ship, Doctor? We shan't want to plough our way through this in the dark."

"Perhaps we had," the Doctor reluctantly admitted, feeling like Adam when the angel showed him the back door of paradise. "How many pictures did you get, Ole?"

"Twenty dozen."

"You look it," said Drake with a glance at Ole's bulging sweater. "Are you always half loaded or is part of it natural?"

"Pinhead," said Ole under his breath, beginning to pull on his oar.

Drake, who had been unusually taciturn on the beach expressed himself before reaching the ship.

"Doctor," he said, "your conclusion that all those rotten brutes are only half natural confirms my theory of the inscriptions."

"Mine too," said the Doctor, "And you still want to go on with this?"

"Of course."

"Well, I don't. I'm beginning to turn back and go home right now."

"When it is just beginning to get interesting?"

"I don't believe you know what you are up against."

"Neither do you. But we both seem to have made a pretty good guess. I'm going to see it through and find out what is at the other end of the chain."

"Then I shall have to stick it out too. For I'm hanged if I'll let an old man like you get the better of me."

"Old man?" Edith exclaimed indignantly. "He's only eleven years older than you are, baby. And he's not half so frightened of the dark."

8 A SIGNIFICANT HINT

The Doctor and Ole would have been deliriously happy to spend the rest of their days among the monsters on the beach. The weather however cut short their ecstasies in the middle of the fifth week.

It had been growing gradually colder, although the sky still retained its crystal clarity. The wind steadily freshened. Twice the party had been caught by a "woolly" which knocked them sprawling in the evil-smelling brown slush. Young ice beginning to tinkle and chafe against the ship, Anderson became anxious lest they be frozen fast for the season over three hundred miles from their goal. He counselled an immediate withdrawal to the inlet. Ole and the Doctor reluctantly gave him best.

They were not ten hours too soon in their decision. All about the ship the water curdled rapidly into a churning waste of young ice which in another twelve hours would render the propeller useless. As it was, the propeller several times on their short run to the inlet jammed, and the Captain's heart descended to his boots to rise again as the desperate expedient of full steam ahead sent the screw kicking.

If the worst came to the worst, Lane reflected, and if they were caught, they could leave the ship in charge of Bronson and make their way over the pack to the mainland with dogs and sledges. But to be forced to this expedient would disrupt the plan of their whole campaign.

Anderson, still obstinately trusting to his volcanic theory, expected to find open water in the inlet. And indeed as they bucked their slow course toward the mouth the severe cold moderated several degrees and the pack became less dense. Lane and Ole began to regret their precipitous flight from the heaven of their dreams.

The sudden departure from the slaughter beach had cut short the Doctor's most ambitious project. Another day might have seen it accomplished. With the help of Bronson and Ole he had rigged up a tackle by which he planned to transport one of the larger horn-plated monstrosities intact to the ship. The crew had already cleared a place for it on deck. Over the protests of Edith, Drake and the crew, all was ready for the reception of the huge evil-smelling brute when the sudden necessity for getting out or being frozen in caused Lane to abandon the beast and tackle at the water's edge.

"Never mind," Anderson consoled him, "we can hoist your lily aboard when we come back this way. It will be no sweeter then than it is now."

With a sigh of regret Lane resigned himself to the loss of his loved one. It was the prize of the whole filthy brood. Whatever may have been the state of its interior, the heavy armor of its enormous scales had preserved it, outwardly at least, from the more distressing features of dissolution. Edith rejoiced openly at her father's misfortune, and the crew wore smiles that even a knife-edged blast from the south was powerless to chill.

Despite his heartbreaking loss Lane did not quit the beach in absolute poverty. Every available nook of the *Edith* was packed with his well-salted and pitch-soaked mummies. His collection as it stood would be the scientific sensation of a century.

More valuable still were Ole's photographs. An able-bodied Norwegian seaman with the most expensive cameras and an unlimited supply of films can take an overpowering abundance of excellent photographs in five and a half weeks. Under Lane's expert direction he had photographed practically everything visible on that eight mile beach.

This indeed was but the minor part of Ole's Herculean labor. His greater masterpieces had been achieved by the freehanded expenditure of Anderson's dynamite and blasting powder. This the sagacious Captain had stowed aboard the *Edith* in ton lots, confident that he should have heavy blasting to do in his oil prospecting. He expected to find his oceans of wealth under rocks buried beneath the accumulated ice of ages. An incautious remark to the Doctor, who was bewailing his stupidity in not having brought crosscut saws, steam shovels and other modern implements of surgery in the large, had betrayed the Captain's hoard to the rapacious zoölogist. The three weeks' orgy of judicious blasting which followed gave Ole his unique collection of interior views.

In this filthy business Lane and the mate toiled alone. The others refused point blank to be present at the opening ceremonies. A day's practice with its attendant disasters, which may be imagined but not described, made the adaptable Ole expert in the planting of the charge. By the evening of the second day he was splitting open swollen monsters with the expert neatness of a specialist on pre-historic appendicitis. A second charge skilfully inserted when the Doctor so desired brought forth the creature's stomach for detailed examination.

Lane was anxious to learn all that he could of the dead monsters' life habits. Anatomy alone, as revealed by Ole's beautiful interior photographs, was not enough. He must find out on what the creatures had lived. As a rich byproduct of this work he obtained, from the undigested contents of the stomachs of the carnivorous reptiles and mammals in the shambles, many of his most curious specimens. Seclusion from the air in the stomachs of the huge lizards and enormous salamanders had preserved many of these beautiful objects practically fresh.

One remarkable incident of all that surgical saturnalia deserves to be recorded here. At the time it gained only a passing notice from Ole and the Doctor, absorbed as they were in the larger beauties of their obscene orgy. But had Lane given it the attention which it merited, and which he as a scientifically-trained man should have accorded it, the party might later have avoided a disastrous mistake. Through ignorance of its inevitable consequences they were all but destroyed.

Late one afternoon Ole had placed an unusually heavy charge against the belly of an enormous brute whose car-cass, from its well-preserved condition, promised a rich mine of vegetable treasures. An inspection of the teeth showed Lane that the dead monster had been an eater of herbs, leaves and grass. The charge exploding prematurely only half did its work. The downward force of the dynamite tore a deep pit in the loose, oil-soaked shale of the beach and shattered the underlying bed of perpetual ice. The broken surface of the deepest ice lay clean of oil. Immediately after the explosion some undigested green fronds of a mossy plant dropped from the creature's torn stomach upon the clean, freshly broken ice.

The half accidental explosion having ruined the specimen for further investigation, Lane and his assistant shed no tears over the mess but hurried on to the next. They had but three-quarters of an hour's daylight left, and their time was too precious for regrets.

Having finished their next operation successfully they prepared to return to the ship while the light still served.

Their shortest way back led past the botched job. Glancing down at the ice pit, Lane called Ole's attention to the rich bright green mass of hairlike vegetation which, presumably, had fallen from the rip in the creature's stomach. Already overburdened with their implements and specimens, they abandoned their intention of immediately collecting some of the curious plant. Reluctantly deciding to leave it till tomorrow they hurried on through the dusk to the boat.

During the night the temperature rose several degrees. This otherwise fortunate incident robbed them of their expected prize. For when they visited the hole in the ice they found that the oily slush oozing down through the shale had made of the vegetation a dirty brown soup.

Nothing was to be gained by crying over rotten vegetables. They proceeded at once to their surgery elsewhere, confident that the next herb eater would furnish them with a ton of the green stuff.

In this they were deceived. It was not until some weeks later, however, that Lane discovered their serious error. They found an abundance of green vegetation in the stomachs of such monsters as were plant feeders, including tons of a particular variety whose green fronds and masses of long tendrils resembled closely those which they had missed.

Mere resemblance is far from identity, as the Doctor realized when it was too late. When knowledge finally came the party was fighting for its life with a foe which gave no quarter. But for this unpardonable negligence on Lane's part the explorers need not have brought upon themselves a hideous warfare for which they, as twentieth century human beings, were totally unprepared. The dropped fragments of Ole's and Lane's green loot littered the clean shore, the fresh young ice from the beach to the ship, and the decks. Had Lane used his scientific eyes he would have noticed immediately the sinister difference between the habits of the plants he had collected and that which, through force of circumstances, he had abandoned.

This oversight and its subsequent consequences gave Lane the scientific chastisement of his life. Since that ghastly fight on the ice he has not scorned the humblest detail in his battles with the unknown.

The *Edith* reached the mouth of the inlet not an hour too soon. Snow began to fall as the gap of the inlet swung into view. Within ten minutes the opening disappeared behind a thick grey confusion of whirling feathers. The ship crushed her way through a thickening ice pack, cautiously feeling for the door in the iron wall ahead. To take the pack at a rush was impossible. Every yard of the way must be felt out or a smash against the barrier would send the ship like a brick to the bottom. Along this barren coast the ice cliffs plunged sheer down to deep water.

The slow going all but blocked the propeller with floating ice. At each succeeding jar the Captain's face became whiter. He had no physical fear; his anguish was purely mental. It was the prospect of losing his hypothetical oil that froze his nerves.

Suddenly the nerve-racking grinding lessened. In fifteen minutes it has ceased completely.

"We're in," Anderson announced with undisguised relief. He would die rich after all. "No ice, as I expected."

A sounding gave no bottom. The volcanic crack in the earth's crust, if such indeed was its nature, was deeper than the Captain had anticipated. Although before them loomed the impenetrable gray wall of tumbling snow it seemed safe to proceed at half speed.

"For twenty miles at least this thing is as straight as a street," the Captain explained, "and we want to get on."

Occasional blasts from the whistle reverberating from the high cliffs nearest them gave a check on the course and kept the ship off the rocks. By daylight they had made only thirty miles, having slackened speed for greater safety during the darkest hours of the morning. The snow had thinned and now showed signs of clearing. Shortly after nine o'clock only a dazzling glitter of finely divided crystals scintillated in the sunlight. For the first time the party saw its surroundings.

Ahead, and due south, stretched the inlet, at this point about a quarter of a mile wide, to disappear finally as a jagged black line on the white waste.

Not a particle of ice floated on the water. Anderson ordered one of the men to draw up a bucketful and take the temperature. The reading gave forty degrees Fahrenheit—eight degrees above freezing, while all about them the bleak wilderness beneath its shroud of dry snow crystals lay locked in perpetual ice.

"What do you make of it, Doctor?" the Captain asked.

"Nothing, yet. I just accept it as a fact. What current is there?"

"About two miles an hour against us. Shall we go ahead, or land here and have a look at things?"

"Go ahead, full steam. For all we know this may freeze over with the first blizzard. Besides I am anxious to see what is at the end of this long street."

"So am I. Full steam ahead it is."

Their progress was finally blocked in a most peculiar manner. Sixty odd miles of the roughly straight water-course lay behind them when they began to notice a decided rise in temperature. Simultaneously a heavy fog met them, rolling up from the south toward which they were headed. The dazzling sunshine and the stark blue sky became memories. Anderson now proceeded as slowly as it was possible to do and still make headway against the current. The street showing unmistakable signs of degenerating into a crooked alleyway, he kept the whistle tooting almost continuously. The engineer kept the screw just turning, ready to reverse at the first blackening of the mist ahead. But it was water, not rock that stopped them.

A sudden gush sweeping down the channel in a three-foot wave sent the *Edith* spinning. Full steam ahead kept her barely abreast of her former position. A second torrent brought with it clouds of steam. Instantly the ship was racing to keep her place in a scalding deluge. The waves breaking over the stem drenched and blistered the deckhands with boiling water.

There was but one thing to do. Taking a desperate chance in the blinding steam, Anderson slewed the ship about in the narrow channel and went down with the torrent, trusting to sound signals to keep him off the cliffs. By midnight the immediate danger was past. Once more the *Edith* lay where she had started ahead at full steam.

"No lobsters boiled yet," said the Captain with a sigh. "Even Ole is still raw." The stars glittered in the hard black sky like crystals of icy fire. "I shall drop anchor for the night here. The lookout can see far enough ahead to give warning if anything breaks loose."

"We should be safe enough here," the Doctor agreed. "The last of the steam fog is all of forty miles away."

And so it proved. However, the night was not to pass without a flurry. At three in the morning the lookout called Captain Anderson to view a spectacle which had been troubling him at intervals for the past two hours. Having seen it, Anderson at once routed out Ole and all the passengers. They found the watchman staring straight ahead at a heavy pall of low black clouds suspended above the southern horizon.

"Keep your eyes on those clouds," Anderson directed. He had barely spoken when the underside of the pall burst into vivid crimson. For perhaps three minutes the cloud pall pulsated from crimson to cherry red like the intermittent reflection from a forge fanned by old-fashioned bellows. Then suddenly the light went black.

"How long before it lights up again?" Anderson asked the watchman.

"Thirteen and a half minutes, sir. Regular as a clock."

The interval passed and again the clouds burst into fire. And so it went till dawn when the rising winds of the upper atmosphere, tattering the pall, flung it far to the frozen south. During all that time the party had watched in fascination, not heeding the stiffening of their joints in the cold. The unearthly beauty of that distant inferno, and the mysterious regularity with which its manifestations recurred, made conversation trivial. Little was said until daylight, when the upper winds and the rising sun obliterated the awful grandeur of the night.

"Is that your volcano?" the Doctor asked.

"Ole's burning oil well, you mean. No, I'm sure it isn't. Those clouds were not more than fifty miles away at the most. My estimate of the other thing, you remember, was between two hundred and fifty and three hundred miles inland. That would make it over two hundred miles from here."

"Then what do you make of it?" Edith asked.

The Captain grinned. "Like the Doctor, I'll wait and see what's ahead before I jump."

"I have a theory," Ole began.

"Bottle it. When it's ripe enough to blow the cork let it fizz."

Ole rolled off rumbling to vent his emotions on purely masculine ears.

"What is it to be, Lane?" the Captain asked. "Do we try it again upstream or shall we take to the land?"

"How long will it take to get ready for the land journey?"

"Four hours. I saw to rationing the sledges while you and Ole were enjoying yourselves."

"Are the dogs in fit shape?"

"They will do. The four weeks' exercise on that rotten beach wasn't all it should have been, but it will have to do."

"Why not compromise?" Drake suggested. "Let us go by ship as far as we can before taking to the sledges. I don't relish dragging the beastly things over the ice. For that is what it will come to when the fool dogs give in. Sooner or later they are bound to go. We can't pack four months' grub for them and ourselves."

"What about it, Captain?" the Doctor asked. "Are you willing to risk the boiling water?"

"Now that we know what to expect I see no great danger. Unless," he added, "boiling mud comes down with the water and mires us a hundred miles from the sea."

"We'll chance it," the Doctor decided. "If there has been no more of an eruption than boiling water so far it

seems improbable that there will be one now just to welcome us."

"There is always the airplane as a last resort," Edith
pointed out.

"Yes," said the Captain, "and who would be the happy
pair to escape while the rest stayed behind and starved?"

"Don't you see? The pilot could take off the men one
at a time. In a pinch five or six could crowd on somehow.
The plane can lift the weight of ten men easily."

"And get the last of them off the night after Judgment
Day. No, Edith, if we do get caught your plan won't work.
However, I'm as game as your father. And what I say the
men will do—and be damned quick about it, too. Now,
Doctor, since we are going back I should like to ask a
favor."

"Go ahead. If it's anything reasonable, consider it
granted."

"It is this. I want to find out what caused that glow on
the clouds. Suppose we take a side trip to find out before
going on to the main show?"

"That sounds all right to me. And it will give the dogs
some real exercise."

"To say nothing of ourselves," Drake prophesied gloomily. "I know the brutes will be unmanageable. One tried
yesterday to take a piece out of my leg—and I have no
meat to spare."

Without further discussion the ship was put about.
They proceeded upstream at full speed. By noon they
reached the point where they judged it would be wise to
leave the ship and take to the sledges.

Within two hours Anderson, Ole, Drake, Lane and Edith, who refused to be separated from her father, were on their way over the ice with a week's provisions. Bronson was left in charge of the ship with orders to head her downstream and keep a sharp lookout for trouble. At the first hint he was to steam for the mouth of the inlet. Should the party send no word to the contrary before the seventh night out, he was to organize a relief and go in search.

9   INTO IT

The party had two sledges. Anderson and Ole, being the only members experienced with dogs, taking charge of the sledges, instructed the others. One who has never had the pleasure cannot appreciate how much sport goes with the skilful manipulation of a dog team. The greenhorns soon learned. A temperature several degrees above zero, dead calm, a blinding glare from the undulating snow-fields, and their own panting exertions quickly brought out the perspiration. Edith bore it with compressed lips, the Doctor grinned like a cat in pain, and Drake, wishing he might lie down and die, contented himself with a continuous profane commentary on the dogs, the desolate landscape and the idiot who had dragged him into this brainless mess.

Drake's misery reached its climax when he was just on the point of abandoning the expedition after three gruelling hours of elaborate awkwardness. His sledge at the moment was careering sideways like a crab down a gentle ice slope which the winds had swept clean of ice crystals. Reaching the bottom without mishap he stubbed his toe on some hard obstruction cunningly concealed beneath the loose drift. At the same instant one runner of the sledge found another stumbling block. Before Drake knew what it was all about he was sprawling on his back like a lanky frog in the snow, his sledge was upside down, and the dear dogs had tied themselves into a true lovers' knot.

Scrambling to his feet he forgot Edith, his surroundings, everything in fact but his fluent vocabulary. His rhythmic denunciation of the universe brought a blush to the ears of the sensitive Ole, who at that moment was acting as Edith's instructor. Quitting Edith's side with alacrity Ole hastened over to extinguish Drake. Anderson and the Doctor, taking things easy, were some distance ahead. In that clear, cold air every syllable carried like a bullet. They spun round as if shot by a machine gun.

"Great Scott!" said the Doctor, "I didn't know he had that much in him. Let us go back and see what brought it out."

Ole discovered the cause of offense before the others reached the spot. Drake's eruption had ceased abruptly in an ominous calm. With a glare of suppressed rage he stood regarding Ole's dangerously inviting pose. The mate was on his knees scratching like a terrier to scoop away the loose snow from a black object, of which the pointed cap had already been exposed by his frantic enthusiasm.

"Ah," he puffed, "you are a born researcher, Mr. Drake. Invisible though this was to the naked eye you found it. You have the scientific penetration, the genius that sees through deceptive appearances to the underlying truth."

Drake, speechless, considered. Should he give Ole a thundering kick, or was his toe too sore? By habit he kicked only with his right foot, the one which had 'researched' Ole's treasure. He decided for peace.

"What is it, idiot?"

Ole ignored the compliment. "See for yourself. Inscriptions!"

Drake was now on his knees, rooting with Ole. An exclamation from the Captain proclaimed the discovery of the second black stone which, buried in the snow, had wrecked the sledge. All hands now began digging. In a few minutes two small, jagged fragments, evidently pieces of a larger rock which had been shattered by its impact on the ground ice, lay clean for inspection.

At first the result was deeply disappointing. One of the fragments had been so badly scarred by its rough treatment that not a single pictogram remained on its surface, while the other exhibited only the broken remains of half a dozen. Neither was worth photographing. Anderson, having set Drake's disaster to rights, suggested that they move on.

But Drake appeared to be deaf. The more badly damaged of the two fragments seemed to hold him hypnotized. Presently he rose to his feet and kicked the black mass savagely with his heel.

"Fetch a sledge hammer," he ordered Ole.

"Where in hell am I to get one?"

Edith had already located the handaxe which she now offered to Drake. With one sharp blow he split the black fragment into two along a plane of cleavage. The sight which met their eyes brought a cry of astonishment from all but Anderson and Ole. One surface of the divided rock was covered with the deeply incised pictograms of prehistoric monsters, while the other, like a relief map, bore the raised replica of the same inscription. Yet the whole fragment before Drake split it into two had seemed to be an ordinary chunk of black, cement-like rock. Drake's brain was at work.

"If you found twelve dozen of one kind, Hansen," he said, "it is against all probability that you saw none of the other. Why didn't you photograph some of them too?"

"I did," Ole replied like a stolid keg. "In all I took over one hundred pictures of the raised kind of inscriptions. They are in my chest aboard the ship."

"Then why on earth didn't you show them to me?"

"Because," Anderson informed him, "we knew what sort of men you scientific chaps are. We didn't want to give you too much to swallow all at once—just enough in fact to make you hungry for more."

"You win," said Lane. "I want everything you have."

"That's the lot, Doctor, honest. From now on we are as green as you are."

"And that's saying a good deal. Does this throw any light on your difficulties with Ole's photographs, Drake?"

"Enough to show me why the whole series doesn't hang together. No wonder the drawings of those animals are in two different styles belonging to two totally distinct epochs of art. It also explains a thing you would have noticed if you had taken the trouble to examine the pictures carefully. Even I, with my vast ignorance of natural science, can see that the monsters represented belong to different ages of the earth's history. Roughly they seem to be alike. But the resemblance, although real, is no deeper than the similarity between men and apes. They belong to the same races of creatures, but are separated by millions of years of evolution."

"You're wrong there, Drake. I prefer to think that the differences are merely the varying expression of a fixed idea. The minds of the artists have evolved, not the creations of their art. I'll argue it out with you later. For the present, does this find affect your guess as to what's ahead of us?"

"Not materially. The struggle that I deduced from the symbolism of the inscriptions must have been longer than I thought. That's all."

"Where did you find your inscriptions, Ole?"

"A good seventy miles north of here."

"Then there should be more in this neighborhood, because it probably is nearer the source of the explosion. If so, we shall find enough to write a prehistoric encyclopedia from A to Z."

And so it proved. At intervals of half a mile to a mile they found the vast undulating snowfields littered with colossal fragments of black rock, many of which on their level faces were covered with the deeply cut figures of prehistoric monsters. As many more smaller chunks doubtless lay buried beneath the snow and ice of two winters. Not stopping to photograph these now, they hurried on to their goal, the source of the eerie light which they had seen from the ship.

That night, without much wind, was cloudless. Although the temperature dropped below zero none of the party experienced any serious discomfort in their dry sleeping bags. The months of hardening in the Canadian Rockies and Alaska had well prepared the newcomers to the Antarctic for hardships which otherwise might have proved unendurable. The absence of high winds on the bleak plateau was an unexpected piece of good luck. By rare fortune they had penetrated one of those mysterious, almost windless regions of the Antarctic Continent which have puzzled explorers.

The first day they covered only twenty miles. With the experience of a march behind them they made a little over forty miles through the dead calm of the second day, to creep into their bags at night exhausted. The men took watch by turns in two-hour spells. Not a flicker of the strange fire they were seeking stained the cloudless night sky. Beginning to doubt the correctness of their route they were wholly unprepared for the inferno into which they blundered at five o'clock of the third day.

The start at five o'clock on that memorable morning was made under a sky blazing with the icy jewels of innumerable stars. At sunrise they found themselves ascending a sharp declivity of blue ice. Up that long ascent the going was necessarily slow. By slogging ahead they had risen two thousand feet shortly before ten o'clock. As nearly as they could judge they were now climbing over a huge fold of rock running almost due north and south. The view from the crest of the rise confirmed their guess. Below them they saw a broad trough running north and south as far as vision carried, filled almost to the brim with tumbling white mist. Some thirty miles distant the farther side of the trough towered high above the rolling mists in an unbroken barrier of jagged black peaks.

Although it looked hopeless they decided after a brief consultation to continue on their course. Should the black barrier prove as forbidding as it looked from thirty miles away they must turn back. They were not going to be balked, however, by the mere aspect of difficulties. Without further debate they descended the long ice slope into the heaving pall of white fog.

The descent was made without accident. Arrived on the floor of the trough Anderson produced his compass and led off through the swirling mist. Lane assumed command of one sledge with Drake as helper. A few yards behind the leader Ole and Edith managed the second. So thick was the fog that Anderson's figure only some forty feet ahead was invisible to the tenders of the second sledge. Nevertheless the Captain set a stiff pace over the blue ice and hard packed snow crystals.

They had now but four and a half days left in which to make their objective and return to the ship. The Captain was determined to find out the nature of that black barrier before Bronson could overtake him with an unwelcome relief party. The stiff pace, almost a run, suited the others, for the clutching cold of the fog sought out and gripped the marrows of their bones.

For perhaps three-quarters of an hour all went well. Then a horrified shout from Anderson brought the party to a palpitating halt.

"Don't come here," the Captain called back. "Wait till I fetch you."

One by one he led the others to the brink of the death which he had escaped by half a second. There it gaped, a sheer well in the blue ice thirty feet across and of depth unknown. The lip of the circular hole lay flush with the surrounding ice. Its sides dropped straight down as if carved out with a huge knife. It was a perfect circular well, over a hundred feet in circumference and of a depth which they could only guess, for it was full to the brim with white fog.

Edith had an inspiration. She returned to the first sledge.

"Here," she said, handing the Captain a pound tin of soup, "throw that down and listen for the echo. Then we can figure out how deep it is."

Anderson tossed the can into the centre of the hole. Only the breathing of the dogs broke the intense stillness. Not the ghost of an echo rose from the well.

"Probably there is soft snow at the bottom," the Captain remarked. "Well, I'm glad I'm above instead of below."

Not suspecting what lay before them, the party proceeded through the fog at a brisk trot. An astonished shout again brought them instantly to a halt.

"Here's another of the damned things," the Captain announced. "Ole, fetch a rope. There's one on the second sledge."

"You're not going down it, are you?" Drake asked nervously.

"Not if I can help it, nor the next one either." He tied one end of the rope securely about his middle and passed the other end to Lane. "Make that fast to both sledges. When they begin to shoot ahead, pull back hard. All right, come on. These may be oil wells for all we know."

He marched rapidly forward through the blinding mist. "Follow me exactly," he called back. "I've just gone two yards south of another."

From that time on they passed at least two of the wells every five minutes, occasionally cutting across the narrow strip which separated three or four in a cluster. Prudence urged them to return, but the determination to see the thing through held them to their course.

They had neither time nor inclination to speculate on the significance of those sheer pits in the ice and rock. All their will was concentrated on their feet. One slip and they might learn more of the mystery than they cared to know.

Anderson forged steadily ahead without speaking. He was bent on reaching the barrier before turning back, holes or no holes.

At five o'clock they had been marching almost continuously for twelve hours. The constant strain on their nerves no less than the pull on their muscles was beginning to tell. Anderson suggested a brief halt and a warm drink. It would take half an hour to prepare the chocolate. That would leave them about an hour of such daylight as there was in the cheesy fog.

They were just about to enjoy the steaming drink when, with a rapid up and down vibration, the ice beneath them began to shake violently. The dogs howled dismally and tried to bolt. Suddenly a terrific jar directly under them sent the party rolling. Staggering to their feet they succeeded in cowing the dogs. The jarring ceased. In dead silence the last tremor died.

White and still, they stood staring at each other's scared eyes in the ghostly mist. Few things so terrify even the most courageous human being as a violent earthquake. There is about the terrific jarring an impression of uncontrollable and insane force that temporarily upsets the balance of the reason, and the helpless victim, powerless to escape, can only wonder when the torment will cease. Lane had experienced earthquakes in central China. This, however, was of a different order. To the other members of the party it was a new test of courage. Drake's knees turned to water. He almost went down when Edith, suffering from the same malady, clung to him for support. Ole said nothing. He was too scared to pray. Anderson stood it best.

"That's nothing," he said. "It will save my blasting powder."

The words were hardly off his tongue before it began again, worse than ever. In ten seconds it was over.

"That's the queerest shake I ever felt," said the Doctor, wiping the perspiration from his face. "The motion was entirely vertical. It felt exactly as if someone miles below us was hitting the roof over him with a heavy iron bar. Listen!"

Miles under their feet they heard a muffled crashing like the slamming of thousands of doors along a hundred mile corridor. With a last crescendo of slams the noise ceased, to be followed immediately by a hollow rumble as of water bursting underground from the sea through labyrinths of rock. Rising to a sudden, deafening thunder directly beneath them the shattering noise passed, to mutter itself out in the bowels of the earth leagues to the south. Then the mist all about them took sudden life. A great wind, eddying like a maelstrom, spun them helplessly on the ice.

By instinct rather than reason Anderson got his clasp-knife open and cut the rope which bound him to the sledges. At the same instant Drake and Ole each clutched one of Edith's arms, Lane seized Anderson by his collar and with the other hand grasped Ole's coat, and all five huddled together, flattened themselves on the ice. Not one of them afterward recalled any thought in all of this. It had been purely the instinct of self-preservation acting automatically.

Spinning like straws in a whirlwind, now this way, now that, they were too dazed to comprehend what was happening. Only a dim consciousness that the air was being swept clean of fog penetrated their numbed consciousness.

The vortex motion of the atmosphere ceased as abruptly as it had begun. Staggering to their feet in an air as clear and hard as glass they found themselves less than two feet from the brink of a well fifty yards across. The last vestige of the fog had been sucked down the innumerable blowholes. These they now saw thickly pitted over the desolate ice in all directions to the range of vision.

It was some seconds before they realized the full horror of their plight. Drake was the first to come out of the stupor.

"The sledges?" he muttered, staring about him in a daze.

They were gone. Anderson took in the situation at a glance. He kept his nerve.

"Out of this as fast as we can," he said quietly.

He still clutched his compass. They followed him at a run. There was no time to speculate down which of the wells the sledges had been sucked. Every nerve strained to get out of that ghastly maze of death traps.

"It's beginning again," Lane said presently. "I felt a slight jar. Down on your stomachs and all hang together. Hansen, you're heaviest. Get in the middle."

They cowered on the ice, their hands joined round Ole's stout figure, waiting for they knew not what.

Chapter 9

10 UNDAUNTED

Huddled on the trembling ice they set their teeth and prayed inwardly, expecting to be hurled skyward. A rushing roar, like the tumbling of flames in a furnace when the door is suddenly opened, rose with incredible speed to a high, singing pitch of shattering intensity. Just when the shrill whistling grew unendurable there shot from the innumerable wells dotted over the ice hard white pillars of compressed mist. With explosive violence the fog which the wind had sucked down into the bowels of the rocks was being expelled.

Straight up shot the thousands upon thousands of dense white columns to fray themselves out in a whirling tracery on the roof of the sky like the groining of a vast cathedral.

Then the bottoms of the rushing fog pillars soared free of the wells. The shortening columns, sucked up into the newly formed clouds flattened themselves upon the misty roof in thousands of rings that vibrated, clashed into one another, rebounded, clashed again, and finally rolled along the underside of the cloudy dome in a mazy tangle of spinning filaments.

The pitch of the singing note from the blowholes heightened. Air or gas was being forced up under tremendous pressure from the interior of the earth. Speechless with awe, the huddled watchers beheld the tops of the invisible columns burst into pale blue conical flames. Almost immediately after they heard the thudding of the ignition.

For perhaps ten seconds the whole cloud roof over the vast ice trough was hung with the thousands of these pendant cones of blue flame. As the sustaining pressure now rapidly dropped the shrillness of the whistling diminished, and by great trembling bounds the blue cones descended toward the wells, reddening as they fell.

Half-way between the blood-red ice and the crimsoned cloud roof the downward-rushing cones of red flame halted, suspended in mid-air, roaring like ten thousand blast furnaces. Then with a tumbling reverberation the innumerable tongues of crimson lengthened, swooped upon the wells, and with a last earth-shaking thunder disappeared.

Although daylight still lingered beneath the high gray pall of fog, the party, blinded by that last downward rush of fire, saw nothing. Dazed and trembling, they got to their feet. Gradually vision returned. Without a word Anderson peered at his compass and led off. They were too stunned by the mere magnitude of what they had seen to attempt as yet to comprehend it. Only the instinct of self-preservation urged them to immediate flight.

They had made a little less than a mile when again the subterranean thunder shook the ice under their feet. Then they remembered for the first time their night vigil on the deck of the *Edith*. That periodic glow on the distant clouds had recurred every thirteen and a half minutes.

For safety they again huddled together on the ice. Again the surface air was sucked down the wells, but with considerably less violence. Apparently the initial disturbance had stored up fuel for the succeeding flames. Once more the shrill whistle from innumerable vents announced the coming of the fires, and again the blue cones hung from the massive cloud roof, to hover down presently in crimson fire before the final swift plunge to the darkness of the wells.

Long before they escaped from the trap, night overtook them. Their march had been a succession of panting runs while the tumbling flames and the crimson glow lit up the icy desolation like a frozen hell. When the flames vanished, and the air all about them became a black well, they halted breathless with fear while the rapid jarring of the ice rocked their brains, and the fierce whirlwinds clutched at their bodies to hurl them down the bottomless pits of fire.

The terror of the fiftieth grim watch was no less than that of the first. At any instant the gyrating wind might get a surer hold of their shrinking bodies and dash them all to a horrible death. Ordinary courage, steeled by lifelong habit to brave the commonplace dangers of human existence, availed them nothing. Their minds being unprepared for this torture they could only cower under its fiendish recurrence.

Dawn found them still crouched in the trap or stumbling blindly forward under the lash of instinct. They had no idea how many miles they had reeled through during the night. For all they knew they might be two miles or twenty from the comparative heaven of the icy desolation between them and the ship.

With the coming of full daylight the temperature rose and the heavy pall above them began slowly to descend. A new terror gripped them when the icy mists swirled down, enveloping the party in impenetrable gray. They must now grope their way forward a step at a time. Haste meant death in the wells, which still with maddening regularity shot up their pillars of descending flame. Numb with cold and stupefied by fatigue as they were, they yet had feelings of awe for the mysterious beauty of the infernal dream when the crimson flames, smoky as milky-red opals through the shrouding mists, paused for a fraction of a second above the wells for their final plunge.

Three hours after dawn the last rumble jarred the ice, and the blowholes droned wearily, but no flame issued. It was as if some titan chained beneath the rock had expired his last flaming breath. For that day at least the strange terror was ended.

Through the searching cold of the dead mist they groped their way in stunned misery for another four hours. Only the necessary words of caution as the leader avoided the pitfalls at his feet broke their dazed silence.

At last they felt themselves climbing uphill. They were out of the inferno. Urging their jaded bodies to the limit of endurance, they panted up the long slope. Two hours later they flung themselves on the ice, face up in the glorious sunlight.

For half an hour they lay there in silence, soaking in the light of heaven. The heat of their bodies melting the ice, presently their clothes were sagging with freezing water. In spite of themselves they slept.

"We can't stay here," Anderson said, getting to his feet. "Wake up, everybody. We must go on as far as we can and trust that Bronson will find us."

The Captain was right. Sleep with no covering but their clothes, even in the afternoon sunshine, was almost certain suicide. Like automatons they followed Anderson over the dazzling snowfields, tramping monotonously till dark. Among the weary five of them there was not a particle of food. And having no fuel they could not thaw out the hard frozen snow or ice to drink. The bits of ice which they sucked in the stinging cold to allay the raging thirst cracked their lips and seared their tongues, causing them exquisite torture.

Never slackening his gait, Anderson crunched steadily ahead. Fatigue to him might have been an alien mystery. The three men followed him doggedly. Hansen appeared to notice nothing more than the ordinary day's work. He bobbed along like a jogging barrel directly behind Anderson, treading down a firm foothold for Edith, who trudged after him. Lane came next, some yards behind, and Drake, cursing softly to himself to keep up his spirits, brought up the rear.

The deepest darkness of the early morning made no difference to Anderson. He kept on. It is a perennial miracle what the human body can stand when it is driven by a relentless mind. All that night, half-mad with thirst, the party slogged on through the black cold.

Dawn found them still marching.

"Anybody for a rest?" Anderson croaked through his cracked lips.

Edith nodded, and sank down in her tracks. Instantly she was asleep. Taking off his outer coat, Ole rolled her in it and slapped his sides to keep from freezing. To the protests of Drake and Lane, who peeled their coats, Ole replied that he, having more blubber than both of them together, could better stand a freeze.

None of the men attempted to sleep. They sat on the ice or stamped about when they began to stiffen.

"Hereafter I carry my sleeping bag on my back," the Captain croaked. "Damn the dogs."

"Captain Anderson!" Ole reproved him.

"She's asleep, idiot. Shut up."

Stirring uneasily, Edith rolled over on her cramped side. Suddenly she sat up with a start.

"Oh, I'm dreadfully ashamed," she cried, scrambling painfully to her feet.

"How long have I slept?"

"Five minutes," Anderson lied nobly, and Drake nodded.

"It felt like five seconds," Edith sighed. Then she noticed Ole's coat. "Oh Ole, how generous of you," she exclaimed, helping him into it. "But you shouldn't have done it; I'm not a baby."

"That's nothing," Ole protested.

"It's a great deal," she replied. "My, but it's cold."

"All right," Anderson croaked, "we'll go on. You will soon warm up."

From that hour Edith became a firm adherent of the theory that five minute naps at the proper time are as refreshing as a night's sleep. None of the men had the heart to explode her theory. They never told her that she had slept three hours and twelve minutes.

Another rest of two hours in mid-afternoon refreshed them all. By huddling together three of the men generated warmth enough in the clear sunshine to enjoy a profound sleep. The fourth kept watch, rousing the next man when his turn came. Edith slept straight through the two hours.

That night they marched briskly from dusk to dawn without a halt. Another two hour rest restored them for the final effort. The men had found their second wind. Edith's sufficient sleep and youth made her a good match for the men. She would go through with it to the end and come out smiling. Curiously enough, hunger did not greatly distress them. After the first sharp pangs they forgot food in the intense longing for copious draughts of water. Putting their wills to it they forged ahead almost at a run over the hard, packed snow.

Seventeen hours later they saw the rubies and emeralds of the ship's lights gleaming through the crystal night air. In fifteen minutes they were wallowing alternately in cold water and steaming hot chocolate.

"Never again," said the Captain, limping off to his cabin. "I'll leave that sort of thing to professional explorers who enjoy talking about it afterwards from a platform."

This, however, was the rash statement of a pessimistic and leg-weary man. By twelve o'clock the next day he was up to his neck in plans for another assault on the black barrier which he was determined to cross. He persisted in his belief that oceans of oil lapped the farther side of the jagged range which they had failed to reach.

Lane regarded this as a delusion. Finally as a geological expert he convinced the Captain that sweet pickles were a likelier prospect than oil in a rock formation such as they had seen. Later he modified this verdict.

"Have patience," he said, "and you will get your oil. Don't expect it to rain down on your head like blessings from above."

"Listen to me," Ole broke in. For some time he had been suffering agonies from the high pressure of his super-heated theories. "Those blowholes," he said impressively, "spouted natural gas. Therefore there is oil at the bottom of them. There are our wells, Captain."

"Idiot," said the Captain, "how are we to get at the oil if it is at the bottom of those hell holes?"

"Pumps."

"Pump yourself and dry up." The Captain turned to Lane. "What is it to be?"

"Full steam ahead as far as we can go. Then deposit a cache of dynamite and provisions, send the ship down-stream a safe distance, and make it inland by sledges to your volcano."

"Burning oil well," Ole corrected under his breath.

"We shall see when we get there," said the Doctor. "Suppose we can approach to within fifty or even a hundred miles of the volcano—pardon me, Ole, burning oil well. We could establish a base there—bury our supplies in the ice, if necessary—and deposit caches of food and fuel every ten miles to the place itself. There are plenty of able-bodied men aboard to chop holes in the ice and pack in the stuff. Then we won't be bothered with those beastly dogs."

"There are only two teams left, anyway," said the Captain. "Your plan sounds reasonable."

"And I know John will go wild over it," Edith added. "He would rather fall down one of those wells than coo to a dogteam again."

Drake was absent from the council, having locked himself in with Ole's photographs.

"Oh," the Doctor replied, "I was planning on Drake managing one sledge and you the other. We shall need all the transport we can scrape together, for there is no telling how long we may be away from our base. Ole, Anderson and I will be busy looking for oil wells."

Edith ignored the suggestion.

"May a mere woman participate in the councils of the gods?" she asked with mock humility.

"Yea," her father answered, "even a mere child may prattle about our feet. 'Out of the mouths of babes—' you know. Proceed, infant."

"I shall do so," the child replied. "And presently you won't be able to see me for my smoke. For I intend to take Ole with me on a tour of inspection while you and the others are breaking pickaxes and your backs over cast iron ice."

"How so, child?"

"I have wings, have I not?"

"Even so, angel child. You were born with feathers on your back."

"Then I shall fly. In three hours I shall find out more about this country than you and the blessed dogs will learn in ten years. If Ole's cameras are good for anything we shall supply you with a map of this continent from here to the South Pole. Then you will be able to find your way to the Captain's oil field without your toes over every brick on the road stubbing as poor John did. Ole, consider yourself engaged as official photographer of the air reconnaissance. In the meantime, Captain Anderson, full steam ahead while our luck lasts."

The last order being confirmed by Lane, the Captain obeyed. Returning to the cabin, he found Lane with his back to the wall fighting his last battle against Ole and Edith.

"Help me to talk these lunatics out of their insanity," he begged, "before they break their silly necks."

But the Captain, having reflected, was less inclined than the Doctor to the lunacy theory.

"Let me take a squint at the barometer, first," he said.

"Set fair," he announced. "This seems to be an almost windless region. Those tornadoes round the blowholes don't count. The devil alone is responsible for them. Having his hands full there he won't bother us here—at least not for twelve hours unless the barometer is a worse liar than he is.

"Now here is my vote," he continued. "If the weather stays set until we reach our anchorage, I say Edith and Ole should go. She is right. In three hours they can find out what it would take us years to bungle through. At the first sign of wind or dirty weather she can scoot back to the ship. She is the best air pilot of us all. And I'll say this of Ole: he is second best."

Ole blushed appreciatively. "You bet your boots I am."

"Also you are as dumb as a barrel," the Captain resumed, "so you won't put Miss Lane up to any foolishness. She will do the thinking for both of you."

"Ole can take the pictures and theorize," Edith promised consolingly.

"And mend the motor when you bust it," Ole added with a touch of vindictiveness. It is one thing to call a man a master builder of theories and quite another to say he theorizes. Ole sensed the distinction.

The Doctor was finally routed. And so it happened that Edith and Ole took not one reconnoitering flight, while the men and dogs toiled fifteen hours a day at the caches, but several.

That afternoon they proceeded upstream to within fifty miles of their projected goal. For twelve days of perfect calm they anchored in the narrow channel, ready at a second's notice to race from the deluge of hot mud which they half expected but which never came. The stout ship was to leave her timbers in that desolate spot to the end of time, but it was not mud or lava which held her fast.

The powerful airplane had been unshipped without difficulty. A level stretch of hard packed snow made an ideal landing ground. When tanked to capacity the plane carried enough petrol for a thousand mile flight. Taking no chances, the explorers carried the full complement on each trip.

"Au revoir," Edith said as she climbed in for her first flight. "We'll be back before midnight. I promise."

"How far are you going?" Drake asked.

"To Hades."

Edith's answer had been given merely to shock Ole. Yet it contained an unsuspected element of truth. That was precisely where she landed before the end of her explorations.

11 HOT WATER

Edith's intention was to fly due south. She wished if possible to discover the source of the eruption which Anderson had observed on his first trip. The account of the gigantic smoke ring, visible at over two hundred and fifty miles, "teetering crazily up the sky" had taken her imagination by storm. She wished to see for herself what sort of a monster blew such delightful rings. Ole's burning oil well theory did not seem entirely satisfactory. Edith rather expected to find a crater pursed up through the ice like a smoker's lips, lazily generating smoke for the next puff.

So far the party had seen no sign of the distant disturbance from the ship. The cordial gush of hot water which had first welcomed them, however, they regarded as highly significant.

If there was hot water in the vicinity Edith longed to be in it. Her rather inactive part in the expedition so far had made her feel young and unimportant. She now wished, as she said to herself, to return from her trip distinguished or busted. Giving the engine more gas she let it out to seventy miles an hour, humming through the zero air in a bee-line for her hive. If Anderson's estimate had been correct she should reach it in less than an hour.

Ole set himself with stolid perseverance to photograph the Antarctic continent as seen from above. With the results of his labors it would be possible, he hoped, for subsequent explorers to find their way blindfolded to the South Pole.

Forty freezing minutes flew behind them before they noticed any feature of interest on the desolate, icebound landscape rolling up from the south to meet them. The jagged black crests of what appeared as an almost perpendicular rock barrier pricked the horizon.

Nearing this barrier at the rate of a mile a minute they saw it rise by leaps above the white wilderness. Ole had charge of the navigating instruments. By a rough calculation, half guess and half arithmetic, he estimated the barren cliffs to be not over three hundred feet high. A glance vertically down showed an undulating ice plain thickly dotted with huge fragments of black rock. Occasionally one of these jagged fragments, having fallen with the flat side uppermost, presented a thatch of last winter's snow to the observers, but for the most part their stark pinnacles were bare and black.

Presently Ole gave a shout that was audible above the droning of the propeller.

"Blowholes," he bellowed, handing Edith his binoculars.

Peering over the side Edith beheld a pockmarked expanse of blue ice, pitted with bottomless wells and littered with huge fragments of rock. Putting her trust in Providence not to "blow" the wells until she had flown over them, she gave the engine more gas and spun toward the low barrier at a hundred mile clip.

Coming directly over the barrier they saw that the apparent wall was a tumbled desolation of huge rock masses at least five miles broad. It would be impossible to traverse that jumble with dog teams. If the goal of the expedition lay beyond that chaos they must traverse it painfully on foot with packs on their backs.

Edith flew on. The speedometer showed eighty miles an hour. Some minutes later they saw the black mass beneath them curving precipitously down like the slope of a steep mountain.

Determined to ascertain the extent of the vast crater—for such they judged it to be—Edith continued to fly due south with one eye on the speedometer. The walls of the huge depression below them were soon no longer visible. Only a sheer void with slowly heaving sooty black clouds at the bottom, apparently several miles below them, met their awed gaze.

That deep expanse of inky billows seemed never ending. On they flew at eighty miles an hour until seventy minutes lay between them and their starting point at the lip of the gigantic crater, and the precipitous slopes of the farther side soared suddenly up out of the black smoke to meet them. The crater, they inferred, must be ninety miles across. Vast as this estimate made it, they could not be sure that it was adequate, as they had no means of judging whether they had flown above a diameter.

When they finally cleared the last of the shattered buttress and level ice stretched unbroken for miles beneath them, Ole signified his urgent wish to descend. They landed without mishap.

"Where are you going?" Edith demanded as Ole started on a run back to the lip of the crater.

"I have just had a theory," he bellowed, forgetting in his enthusiasm that he was no longer competing with the propeller. "Now I test it."

When he rejoined her forty minutes later his face bore the smug expression of one who has looked on Truth and found her all that he hoped.

"Just as I thought," he said. "The south sides of those rocks on the edge of the crater are covered with lichens."

"Well," said Edith, testy from the cold, "did you expect to find barnacles?"

"No," he replied with the bland complacency of a sunfish, "I knew I should find lichens."

"Then it was stupid of you to waste nearly an hour looking for them," she retorted. "Get in. I'm going on."

"But," he expostulated, "I have proved my theory. That is no new crater. It must be very old. Therefore Captain Anderson did not see it erupting."

"Then what did he see?"

"An eruption within an eruption. Just the old floor of this volcano has blown up in our times."

"And the floor was covered with inscriptions? Yours is a likely theory, I must say. Who ever heard of people carving inscriptions on the floor of a volcano?"

"Who ever didn't hear of it?" Ole retorted, not quite sure of his logic. "Why shouldn't they? Perhaps those inscriptions were only tombstones. Haven't you seen the flat ones in the churchyards? Those ancient makers of inscriptions wished to bury something."

"So they dug a hole in the red hot lava and put a lid over it?"

"Not of course. I mean," he corrected himself, "of course not. No, that isn't what I mean. I want to say it doesn't follow. The main eruption may have been millions and millions of years ago." Ole grew poetical. "When the earth was but an infant in swaddling clothes that ancient eruption moved, and lived, and had its being."

"Colic?" Edith asked innocently. "Is that from the *Song of Solomon*? It sounds familiar."

"No," said Ole, as stolid as a keg of soused herrings, "Solomon sang of other things. All those rocks I photographed," he continued, "are parts of that old cracked floor. Satan has recently been unchained again down there"—Ole's polite way of saying that hell had broken loose again in modern times—"and those far hurled tons of inscriptions testify to his inordinate vehemence. We are witnessing a recrudescence of that prehistoric calamity which rocked the Pole to its roots."

"I too have a theory," Edith announced.

"Yes?" said Ole eagerly.

"My theory is that you will be left here talking through your hat forever if you don't climb in at once. I'm going on."

The unappreciated Ole took the hint. They were off again.

Edith decided to fly home in a wide circle, following the southern rim of the crater until it began to turn sharply to the north. Then, leaving it behind she hummed on due west for about a hundred miles. She was on the point of turning north again, and home to the ship, when a peculiar dim blue line across the western horizon caught her attention. To investigate would take only half an hour. She investigated.

So did Ole. He again discovered innumerable blow-holes in the ice over which they whizzed, and called Edith's attention to the significant detail.

"This looks promising," she said to herself, for Ole could hear nothing. "Now if Nature knows anything at all about logic she should have planted another big hole in the ice over behind that blue line."

Nature proved herself logical. The blue line became the sheer edge of a tremendous ice precipice sweeping in a gradual curve round the horizon. Fifty miles was a conservative guess at the diameter of this vast depression. Unlike the other no jumble of black rock cluttered its edge or the surrounding plain.

Half a mile from the edge Edith landed. In silence she and Ole hurried over to the edge of the precipice. Reaching it they stood a few yards back and gazed into the immense void before them. No smoke obscured the sunlit floor of this vast amphitheater. So far below them it lay that it appeared only as a dim blue shadow.

"Come," said Edith, "that's too good to spoil today. We shall return tomorrow and see it properly. Don't say anything to the others about this. One thing at a time is enough for those doubting Thomas cats."

"I won't," Ole promised. "My theory is," he jabbered before Edith could choke him off, "my theory is that Satan is still chained down there."

"There will be the devil to pay," she said simply, "if he breaks loose tomorrow while you and I are exploring. I hope you are on good terms with him."

Ole was shocked. Never before had he heard a young lady use such language outside of a church. He registered his disapproval by climbing into the machine without another theory.

Edith's report brought tears to the Captain's eyes.

"That fool Ole was right," he admitted generously, "What he and I saw from the ship was a burning oil well. Now you have found it."

"Full of black smoke," Ole added gloomily. "Probably all the oil is burning away."

"No, idiot," the Captain replied, "or you would have seen flames."

"I suppose it was just smouldering?" Ole suggested with a nasty touch of irony.

"Oh, undoubtedly," the Captain sneered. "The obvious, practical solution always escapes your colossal mind. Can't you see it? That smoke is simply what has settled down after the fire went out."

"And burned up all the oil," the pessimist supplemented.

"Oh, shut up. If what he says is true, Doctor, isn't there likely to be more oil under the floor of that hole in the rock?"

"I'll tell you when I see the floor."

"Well, whatever theory you and he may hatch between you I'm going to tear up an acre or two of what's left of that floor with dynamite. Tomorrow we begin packing my part of the show to the circus tent."

Before sunrise the next morning Edith and Ole were stirring in preparation for their trip. They were off with the first ray. The Captain having assured Lane that the cold, windless spell was certain to continue, Edith coaxed her father into giving his consent at the last minute. She departed with the Captain's heartfelt blessing and his best thermos bottle full of hot chocolate. What souvenir the blessed girl might bring back to him today he could only speculate, but he hoped it would be another oil well of even vaster dimensions than her first.

What Edith and Ole expected to find on their private expedition they kept to themselves. Neither had the least suspicion of the handsome surprise which Nature had generously prepared for their welcome.

Turning sharply to the west as soon as the airplane lost sight of the ship, Edith steered a straight line toward her find. Ole as navigator gave her the signals keeping her on the course. She made the propeller hum. Not being interested in the dreary Antarctic landscape she shot over it at a hundred and twenty miles an hour, the limit of the machine's capacity.

The dim blue line on the horizon raced forward to meet them. Slackening her speed to eighty miles an hour Edith spiralled down like a seagull. Reaching the level of the lip she circled for a turn near the precipitous wall and then, to Ole's horror, made a nose dive for the bottom of that vast well. Cutting out the engine presently she tilted to forty-five degrees, and glided down, down to the sunlight of the blue plain below.

"Where are we going?" Ole gibbered in his fright.

"Down there, of course. It looks nice and sunny. I'm half frozen."

"What if we can't land?"

"Then we must fly out again."

"But suppose something goes wrong with the engine?"

"Then we shall be a pair of scrambled eggs with no toast, but only the hard ground, beneath us."

The sunlight swam up to meet them, and to their astonished eyes was revealed an azure river winding through a green plain. Dropping lower they saw the huge trees rush out, and then, farther away, the innumerable silvery plumes of the pampas grass undulating to the warm breeze. Entranced they saw the long billows of light rising and falling like the swell of a silver tide. Here, sunk deep in the icy heart of the Antarctic Continent lay paradise of flowing water and a luxuriant vegetation.

Accepting it for what it was they flew on in silence, looking for a spot to land. For once Ole was without a theory. Later he hatched several. The probable solution of the mystery was not, however, his work alone. Drake supplied the egg; Ole merely brooded on it and gave it wings wherewith to soar.

The dense vegetation by the river thinned here and there into rolling meadows of lush grass. They flew over these, seeking more level ground for a landing. At last they spied what they sought, a long sandy spit cleaving a still blue bay in the river.

They made a perfect landing. Then, when they stood with their numbed feet on the warm sand they realized the wonder of the place and its beauty. They were almost in the centre of the vast well. Twenty-five miles distant in whatever direction they looked towered up the sheer blue cliffs fifteen thousand feet above the floor of the valley.

Age-old ice bound the brows of those precipices, and over the circular opening to the sky howled the winter blizzards of the Antarctic, powerless to freeze the water in this blue river or blight the tenderest flowers of the valley's perpetual spring. By what miracle had time preserved this deep garden against the advancing cold? Dying ages had piled on the once tropical regions above a crushing desolation of ice a thousand feet thick. While overhead the yelling gales of winter warred against themselves with whirlwinds of frozen sleet and splintered shafts of clanging ice, only rain fell through this mild atmosphere above the valley. How had this spot, this very heart of a forgotten paradise retained its life-giving warmth, while all about lay the stark body of life frozen cold in the death of ages? Or had it always been as they now saw it? These were questions which they could only ask themselves but not answer.

"This is more beautiful than a California valley," Edith sighed, "and on a far grander scale than any of them. No other valley in the world is an almost perfect circle like this one, nor is there another with cliffs like those to shelter it. Those walls are three miles high."

"Less about a fifth of a mile," the precise Ole corrected her. "I watched the barometer as we dropped down. Say two and four-fifths miles high."

"Ole, you are impossible."

They strolled off the sandy spit to ascend a little knoll whence they might obtain a view of the whole valley. Not until they had been walking about five minutes did they notice the oppressive discomfort of locomotion. Thinking that it must be due to their own thawing out in this mild air after the long flight through zero temperature, they took off their heavy sealskin coats. Twenty steps farther they shed their sheepskin tunics. Another ten yards and they stripped their jaegers.

"At this rate," Edith laughed, "we shall be shedding our skins before we reach the top of the hill."

Ole, puffing like an overfed porpoise, tried hard not to look shocked. He took a mental oath not to shed another rag. Respecting his modesty Edith forbore her next impulse and toiled up the slope lugging only her outer garments. She wished she were Eve and he Adam.

"I know what it is," Ole exclaimed, not stopping to do his theorizing. "We are two and four-fifths miles below the surface of the earth, aren't we?"

"Three," said Edith. "But it's too stuffy to argue. Go on."

"Then we are at the bottom of a mine. I mean," he explained laboriously, "it is just as if we were at the bottom of a mine. All that air is crushing us."

"You do seem to bulge more than usual," Edith admitted.

Ole ignored this verification of his theory.

"And," he continued, expounding the article on *abyss* from the *A* volume of his sample of the encyclopedia, "the internal heat of the earth can be felt at this depth. It gets so hot in the deep mines that the miners have to stop going down, and just burrow out sideways like moles."

"Thank Heaven," Edith sighed, "you don't own the entire Encyclopedia Britannica. I simply couldn't stand it all in this infernal heat."

"Miss Lane!"

"Oh, I shall swear in a minute. Don't mind me; it's my nerves."

At the crest of the hill they flung themselves panting on the thick, mossy grass.

"I shall never growl at the cold again," Edith declared. "This place must be like a steam bath when the sky is clouded up over the opening."

"And the clouds blanket in the radiation," Ole added appreciatively. This evidently was a gem from the one masterpiece of Herbert Spencer's which he possessed. It certainly seems unlikely that he found anything so sensible in either the tattered "*Bluebird*" or his sevenfigure table of logarithms. "On such occasions the humidity must be very high."

"As muggy as lukewarm pea-soup for breakfast. I'm fed up. Let's get out of here. Put on your clothes. It's less bother to wear than to carry them."

As she stood up to shake on her sealskin a darker blue stain on the azure of the distant wall caught her eye. Looking intently at the deeper blue she imagined that she could see clear through the vast cliffs into a dim azure world beyond. Then dismissing the illusion with a laugh at her own fancifulness she started slightly at a new aspect of the shadow. It was in the form of a perfect arch at least three thousand feet high. Ole's remark about the miners burrowing out sideways when the heat grew unendurable stuck in her mind with an odd persistence. What if this were an old mine, disused since a million years before the dawn of history?

"What do you see?" Ole demanded nervously. He was struggling with his heavy tunic.

"Nothing. But you have a look. What is that shadow on the cliffs over there?"

Ole stared long and hard. His seaman's eyes made out no more than had Edith's. Not wishing to commit himself to an untenable theory he wheeled slowly round, searching the whole hundred and sixty mile precipice.

"There is another," he began cautiously, "three points east of south."

"Yes," said Edith, "and I have counted four more. That makes six in all. Let's investigate."

"Right, Miss Lane. I'm with you."

Their lassitude vanished at the prospect of adventure. Joining hands they raced down the little hill by shortcut which would take them through a clump of high bushes directly to the airplane. Laughing like a pair of children off for a picnic they romped into the shade.

Suddenly a huge gray boulder blocking their path came to life with an earth-shaking screech. Edith screamed and clung to Ole. He stood frozen in his tracks, paralyzed with terror.

How they ever reached the plane they were unable afterwards to recall. Edith remembers being thrown in bodily by Ole. He only has a blurred memory of cranking the propeller, climbing and kicking madly at the evil red eyes in a hideous serpent head that shot up after him on a massive thirty foot neck. He swears that he struck one glaring red eye just before the motor lifted and the heavy bodied brute flopped on its belly in the sand, fanning the air with the vast spread of its ineffectual, bat-like membranes.

12 TRAPPED

To the Captain's anxious inquiries the fliers replied that they had returned early on account of the cold. Although sorely disappointed that Edith had not discovered another oil-hole for him, Anderson said nothing. He contented himself with putting Ole to the dirtiest job in sight. Lane was far inland, superintending the caching of stores. Drake had gone off somewhere to exercise his beloved dogs.

Edith and Ole conspired to keep their find to themselves until they should have explored it thoroughly. They began to regret their panicky flight straight back to the ship. Tomorrow, however, they would keep their nerve and spend a heavenly day investigating the abode of the dragon. A landing in the open should be sufficient protection from surprise. By avoiding clumps of brush, rock piles and the pampas they might see much before being chased.

That evening they gathered in the Captain's cabin. The Doctor, having unpacked his scientific paraphernalia, was absorbed in an attempt to analyze the green venom which he had collected from the giant reptile on the beach. The scanty equipment proving insufficient he put away his test tubes with a sigh of disappointment.

"I shall have to wait for a living victim."

"Let me see your flask, Doctor," Ole begged.

"Have you a theory?" the Doctor laughed, handing over the pint of thick, evil, green fluid.

"Not this time. But I have a knife."

To the astonishment of the party Ole proceeded to anoint the eight-inch blade of his murderous knife with the sticky green venom.

"There," he said complacently, brandishing the knife to dry it, "nobody gets fresh with me any more."

"It may be harmless," Edith remarked with a meaning look. "You had better not put too much faith in that messy stuff."

"I'll chance it."

As he spoke he unconsciously fixed his eyes on Anderson. The Captain stirred uneasily.

"Look here, Ole, I set you at that job this afternoon because all the men were away with Lane."

"That's all right, Captain." Ole was not going to let his accidental advantage slip. "It gave me a touch of lumbago. Can Bronson take my watch tonight?"

"I'll take it myself if he can't. With lumbago like that you're not fit to be on deck. Will you be able to fly tomorrow?"

"Flying rests my back. I'll be better in a week or two."

Edith rose to retire. As she went out she shot Ole a significant glance. Mumbling an excuse he followed her.

"Why not take a revolver tomorrow?" she whispered.

"No use. I couldn't hit the side of the ship at ten yards."

"But suppose we do get caught again? That stuff may take hours to act. I doubt whether it is a poison at all. Father really knows nothing about it."

"What can we do? A guess is better than nothing. Besides, I don't mean to get caught."

"Neither do I. Oh, that awful brute. I shall have a ghastly nightmare. Good-night, Ole."

They were off at sunrise in the stinging cold. Drake for a spell at breakfast had grown quite peevish, not to say profanely rude, when Ole harmlessly asked him to pass the butter. The memory of what Drake had said was food and warmth to Edith on the freezing spin south. Having nothing to cheer him but the shadowy prospect of sticking an overdeveloped lizard with wings in the gullet, Ole froze. It was with reckless relief that he shed his sealskin when at last they landed.

Today they had come down in the centre of a five mile meadow. Unless the enemy flew they were safe.

Ole had brought the Captain's strongest binoculars. With these he now slowly swept every mile of the vast precipices, blue in the hazy distance. On each of the Six sapphire shadows he lingered a full five minutes. The dim shadows, he decided, might be weather stains on the cliffs. If nothing more, a three thousand foot stain should be worth investigating.

"You take a look, Miss Lane."

"Those are caves full of mist," she said decisively, handing back the glasses. "Which one shall we try first?"

"The nearest. That one to the southeast. If we don't like what we find, this is a good place to fall back on."

"You think we may wish to turn tail in a hurry?"

"We can't tell," he said uneasily. "I am no coward."

"Of course you are not. Neither am I. Shall we go?"

"My eyes are better than yours, Miss Lane. Remember, I have been half my life at sea."

"Well?"

"I thought I saw things moving at the base of those cliffs. They were only shadows."

"Afraid of a shadow, Ole?"

"Yes," he admitted frankly. "Show me something real and I'll fight it like the next man. Put me up against a nightmare the devil himself never dreamed of and my legs turn to water. Now you know how I feel."

Impressed by his outspokenness she held out her hand for the glasses. Long and curiously she searched the base of the cliff.

"I believe you are right. There is something over there at the foot of the precipice. How far away from it are we?"

"About twenty-three miles."

"Even if the shadow were an elephant's we couldn't make it out at that distance."

"Not with these glasses," he admitted.

"Has it struck you that those moving things can't possibly be shadows?"

"Why not?" he queried nervously.

"Because that whole sector of the cliffs is itself in deep shadow."

"I hadn't thought of that," the unpractical builder of theories admitted. "Are you going on?"

"Yes."

"No woman ever got the better of me yet, and I'm damned if a kid in short skirts is going to make a monkey of me now."

"Ole!"

"Oh, it's all right, Miss Lane. The Captain isn't here."

"You behave yourself or I'll leave you with the reptiles."

Flying as slowly as was possible they cautiously approached the mysterious stain on the southeastern wall. At that hour of the morning the shadow of the precipice lay in a great blue crescent on the valley before them. Soon entering the shadow they experienced a sudden drop in spirits. To the superstitious Ole the semi-twilight was a gloomy omen of disaster.

Edith began to wish she had been less daring. Hating to back out after her bold front to Ole she kept her forebodings to herself. Nevertheless she had a strong premonition of trouble. The thought that the motor might fail them at a critical moment almost made her sick. Swallowing hard she anxiously scanned the terrain for a safe landing place. To her joy she observed a gentle three mile grassy slope from the base of the precipice to the edge of the pampas.

They were now near enough to make out the nature of the stain. It was indeed what they had first guessed, a colossal archway over half a mile high in the face of the sheer cliff. Smoky with blue mist it might have been either a huge cave or the entrance to a tunnel under the continent. If the latter, Edith made a sudden resolution to explore it to the end—some day. At present she felt too shaky. Her nervousness soon received a shock that acted as a counter irritant.

Ole had been making efficient use of the binoculars.

"Let me have the wheel," he said presently, "while you take a look with the glasses."

They were now within five miles of the cliffs. Although it was not exactly a sane proceeding, they changed places in mid-air. Ole now became the pilot and Edith the observer.

Her first observation stopped her heart for two sickening seconds. The green slope at the base of the cliffs was a crawling den of gigantic monsters. The huge, torpid beasts blundered and crawled over one another's sluggish carcasses like blind salamanders. Evidently they were just awakening to greet the sunlight which in a few hours would stir them into activity. The vast cave or tunnel no doubt was their den and breeding place.

"Fly lower," Edith ordered, "and let us see what the brutes look like." Her stomach had resumed its normal position.

Without the flicker of an eyelash the stolid Ole obeyed. No snippy kid in short dresses could outdare him. He dropped sharply to the fifty-foot level, let out the motor to its limit and shot straight as a bullet toward the misty cavern. Edith shrieked. She had met her master.

The droning roar of the propeller roused the lethargic brutes to a trumpeting rage. A hideous forest of writhing necks shot up; flat, brainless heads swayed up to spit their hatred and their venom at the breaker of their bestial sloth, and the obscene red membranes of the huge brutes' aborted wings clattered impotently against their bloated bodies. The fetid stench of their breath mingling with the reek of their foul lair defiled the morning with an unforgettable sickness. A flashing vision of innumerable eyes red with brainless ferocity, a din of yellowed fangs clashing after their unattainable prey, the penetrating breath of a living decay, and the hideous flight was a memory.

Was Hansen insane? Again Edith shrieked as he shot full speed into the blue mists of the cavern. Shutting her eyes she instinctively braced herself for the obliterating crash.

It never came. Whether or not she fainted she doesn't know. Ole swears she did.

When she opened her eyes she thought for one wild moment that she was in hell. The blue mists had given way to a rapidly flickering crimson glow. The oppressive heat all but stifled her. Great gushers of flame thundering up from the floor of the vast tunnel flattened and curled in fronded fire over the arched rock half a mile above. Down the endless distance colonnades of pillared flames dwindled in vistas of alluring terror, enticing the damned to their torments.

Ole had been less rash than he seemed. While Edith was taking her fill of the den over which they shot he, like a born navigator, was minding his own business. As the blue entrance of the tunnel rushed forward to meet him he saw that its interior was approximately straight and sufficiently well lighted for safe flying. The chance he took was negligible. A mile from the entrance he sighted the first flaming well, and thereafter the tunnel became a well lighted corridor, broad and lofty, ideal for rapid flight. Danger of a collision with one of the roaring flame pillars was nil, the highway down the tunnel being over a mile broad and the avenue of flame wells at least half a mile wide at its narrowest point.

Those three thousand foot pillars of flame were absolutely without smoke. Ole's reasonable theory—inadequate, as later events proved—made them vast natural gas jets. He recalled that there are on record in Asia oil wells and escapes of natural gas which have been flaming continuously for over two thousand years. Therefore, he said, this probably was the same sort of thing on a much grander scale. The age-long action of water opening fissures in the rocks had first let vents into the subterranean oil and gas reservoirs. Then the heat of chemical reactions between the water and the minerals in the rocks had ignited the gas. This detail of his theory led him seriously astray. Had he chanced upon the true explanation of how those gas pillars took fire—which any competent physicist would have guessed at once from the peculiar behavior of the flames over the blowholes which Anderson had discovered—he would not have rushed like a fool into the trap which nature had prepared for him.

Granting the ignition of the gas the astute Ole reflected that the rest of the inferno explained itself. Intense heat and the constant high pressure of escaping gas had enlarged the first vents into huge circular wells, up which the solid flames shot until they impinged on the rock roof three thousand feet above. Doubtless, he reflected, the red hot rocks up there were constantly flaking. In time an avenue of blowholes would burst through the roof of rock and ice for some later explorer, far in the future, to find and wonder over. He inferred naturally that under Anderson's trough of blowholes there probably extended another vast tunnel through the solid rock. The six shadowy arches which he and Edith had observed on the wall of their circular valley no doubt were all of one kind. The continent must be, in this strange region, a vast rabbit warren with tunnels branching in all directions, some even to the sea.

At this point of his meditations Ole experienced his first qualm. Those other blowholes onto which the party had blundered differed in one significant respect from those which the future explorer of his musings was to discover. The escape of gas and flames through the first was intermittent and its period strangely regular. The periodicity of the first blowholes was the disturbing peculiarity. These gushing wells of fire in the tunnel seemed to be continuous. Did they ever go out like the others? Ole's imagination leapt ahead of the racing machine. What if those pillared flames should suddenly drop down their vents and disappear? In the dark he must smash himself against the tunnel wall like a ripe tomato.

This squeamish reflection passed from his mind to make way for another. One detail of his inadequate blowhole theory received a sudden and disconcerting confirmation. Half a ton of red hot rock shattered itself with a crash on the floor of the tunnel not a hundred yards to the right of his course. The whole roof must be cracking under the fierce bombardment of flames from those thousands of gigantic blast furnaces.

For the first time he now noticed the stifling heat of the tunnel. The rushing air positively scorched. What if his petrol tank should explode And what if a red hot fragment of stone set fire to the airplane? Ole began to sweat from a combination of too many clothes, too much heat and too little nerve. He was not having the best time in the world. Nevertheless he shot on like a courageous fool at a hundred and twenty miles an hour down that vast tunnel into the bowels of the earth. No snippy little kid in short dresses should make a monkey of him.

The kid had recovered her senses. She was having a heavenly time. Her one regret was that her father had not seen all those nice beasts. She must take him back an egg if the beasts were that sort.

The air in the tunnel began to grow faintly smoky. They were now over an hour from the entrance. Consequently at least a hundred and twenty miles lay between them and daylight.

The same thought occurred to the pair: they should now be nearing the vicinity of the smoke-filled crater which they had discovered first. Theorizing rapidly Ole concluded that the tunnel joined these two, the ruined crater and the vast depression still green as a paradise. Doubtless the explosion of a huge reservoir of oil beneath the first had sent its floor skyward to litter the surrounding desolation with chunks of black rock. Then, he speculated, had the first also been a den of prehistoric monsters—or, as Lane maintained, botched imitations of such—before its destruction? It had.

The verification of Ole's speculation was twofold and twice convincing. Like a dead memory from a forgotten existence a nauseating stench assailed their nostrils. They remembered that moonlit night on the Antarctic ocean and the soul destroying pollution of the winds from the beach of monsters.

Presently through the thickening smoke they saw the shambles. The tunnel was all but blocked by the rotting carcasses of huge brutes which had trampled one another to pulp in their panic to escape the fumes which finally suffocated their multitudes.

Cutting out the engine Ole glided toward the mountain of decay. Just as he turned the plane to escape from the immense corruption he spied the second confirmation of his theory.

Great, slow-moving brutes, each the bulk of three full grown hippopotami, mailed in horn and with a ridge of jagged armor sticking up along their spines from the flat, broad head to the tip of the thirty-foot tail, were crawling like huge newts over the rotting mountain, or splashing heavily through the foul brown ooze from its base.

These gigantic scavengers took no notice of the intruders, continuing with voracity their filthy feasts. The whole decaying pile crawled with them. Their number could only be guessed, for the end of the tunnel was invisible through the murky smoke. For all the explorers definitely knew, they might be one mile or twenty from the ruined crater.

They decided it was time to fly. Both felt faint from the awful stench. Ole let out the engine to its limit. The sudden roar startled a flapping horde of lesser scavengers which they had not seen. Being almost the color of their obscene food these had escaped notice in the murky light. They now arose in thousands, cloud upon cloud of long-necked reptilian "birds" with the wings of bats. From tip to tip the spread of their leathery membranes averaged a good eight feet, and on each six-foot neck a grinning head the size of a horse's stretched hungrily forward. Hard round eyes like those of gigantic serpents stared stonily at the intruders, estimating their value as food. The six-inch teeth clashing aimlessly at nothing filled the air with a hideous cacophony.

Either their own foul banquet was more to their taste or the reptilian birds were by nature peace loving scavengers averse to combat, for they contented themselves with flapping round and round this unknown bird of the twentieth century. Their lineage went back millions of years; this parvenu was an infant yesterday. With hard stares of contempt they circled back in wide spirals to their interrupted repast.

Thanking Heaven for this deliverance, Edith breathed again. But her thanks were premature. A strangely familiar rumbling was but the prelude to a remembered thunder of subterranean explosions. She knew what was coming.

So did Ole. Anticipating it he cut out the engine and dipped gradually. Taking the desperate chance that no considerable mass of shattered rock littered the floor immediately ahead he brought the plane down. Luck favored him. They came to rest whole on the rocky floor.

They climbed hastily out. The jarring under their feet all but threw them prostrate. They heard the sudden suction of the rushing whirlwinds rushing down to the subterranean chambers, and saw what they dreaded. As if struggling for their life with the demon winds the pillars of descending flame quivered for an instant in mid air. Then with a knelling roar they disappeared in absolute night down the wells.

13 HADES

An hour in the impenetrable darkness of that suffocating stench was a hundred years long. Unfortunately Ole had a liberal supply of matches. Under ordinary trials these would have been a godsend. Here they proved an exceedingly cunning gift from the devil.

The instant the terrific jarring ceased Ole lit his first match. It was just half past eleven in the morning. Five hours before he and Edith had been enjoying an extensive breakfast. For lunch they now had nothing but the air, such as it was. They had given up the attempt to eat their sandwiches after the first mouthful. The meat tasted like carrion, and the bread had made of itself a sponge to soak up all the noisomeness of that foul shambles.

They climbed back into the machine to await the next earthquake and the rekindling of the gas wells. To pass the time Ole theorized and struck matches every five minutes. The brief light showed him a set white face, the large brown eyes with their dilated pupils almost black, and the resolute, finely shaped mouth compressed in a firm bow. The kid, he admitted to himself, was sticking it like a hero. He had expected her to blubber.

"I have been wondering," she said about the fifth match, "how we are to get out of this beastly tunnel if the darkness continues for, say a week." She laughed ruefully. "'Beastly' is right in more ways than one. The smell is beastly, there is a hideous den of prehistoric beasts at the less obscene end of this filthy burrow, and a stinking mountain of dead beasts blocking the back door. Suppose we do have to walk out, which way shall we go? All those scavengers and hideous bird things are behind us too."

"Whatever happens," he replied with savage conviction, "I am not going to walk. To the living devils it is a hundred and twenty miles. What kind of a fool would walk that far to be torn to pieces? Especially on an empty stomach?"

"Not my kind," she admitted ruefully enough.

"And do you think I'm going to swim through those miles of muck behind us?"

She shuddered. "I couldn't go that way even if those vile bird creatures and the huge crawling brutes weren't there."

"No more could I. No, I shall not walk."

"Then if the wells have gone out for good we must stay here forever."

"We can fly," he asserted.

"And smash ourselves in the dark like a pair of goose eggs. I can think of nothing stupider than two unhatched geese unless it be three."

"Well, isn't a quick smash better than slow rotting? It wouldn't be suicide," he added to pacify his conscience, "because we should be doing it on the chance of saving our lives."

"Yes, a quick death is better. I wonder if I shall ever see my father again. And my garden, and the dear cats in San Francisco."

Ole was touched. The poor kid was going to cry. He struck a match. Her eyes had grown larger and darker, but there were no tears. After all she was a brick.

"Listen," he said confidently, "I have a theory."

"If it's as depressing as the rest of this nightmare please keep it to yourself."

"But it isn't. You remember how long it was between blowoffs at those holes the other day?"

"About thirteen minutes."

"And the flames only lasted a few minutes after they caught. Now those jets in here were going full blast for over an hour. Suppose they had been going for a full day when we flew in."

"I'll suppose it. What then?"

"They will light up again as the others did. But not for a much longer time."

"A week, perhaps? We shall suffocate long before we see."

"No. The same cause must be at the bottom of those flame holes and these."

"And that cause may operate only once a month, once a year, or once a century for all we know. The next flare may light our bones."

"For two reasons I say no. The first is practical, the second is theory. First, those bat birds have eyes. They can see. I know that is so from the way they glared at us. Now animals that can see don't stay long away from the light."

"The encyclopedia has fooled you, Ole. All that you say may be true. But there is probably a back door to this tunnel, and those filthy things just swoop in here to feed.

When they are gorged they flap out again to roost in their dens. They get all the fresh air and sunshine they need for perfect health in their rookeries."

"I hadn't thought of that. Still, having eyes they must be used to seeing their food."

"Eyes for such creatures in this stinking place are an ornament of luxury. They have nostrils. I saw them myself—two holes on the snout like a snake's."

"Well, listen now to my theory. You can't knock out that, anyway, because it is all pure reason."

He lit another match. Her eyes were fixed straight ahead on the impenetrable soot. The match died.

"Why do these blowholes come and go?" he continued. "Why don't they shoot off burning gas all the time?"

"Is it a riddle?"

"Not to me," Ole replied proudly, lavishing two matches on the invisible stench.

"I give it up. What's the answer?"

"The moon."

She wondered if she could climb out unnoticed by the theorizer. Poor Ole; his mind must suddenly have given way. She was sorry for him, but sorrier for herself. A lunatic on top of her other troubles would be too much.

"Where are you going?" Ole demanded.

The flaring match revealed a scared pair of eyes searching his. Edith had started to climb down.

"I thought you had gone crazy," she said, climbing back just as the match expired and burnt Ole's fingers. "But you seem no more insane than usual. Go on with your theory."

"The moon does it all. Really it is quite simple when you get the idea. As a practical seaman I know how the moon raises the tides—they follow it round the earth. The moon attracts the water. Then a big heap of water gathers in the middle of the sea, and the bulge follows the moon."

"I wish I could follow you."

"When the moon gets so far ahead that the bulge can't keep up the tide falls. When the bulge sweeps over a place it is high tide there. Anyhow that's something like it."

Ole proceeded to elaborate his account by an obscure reference to that bane of all amateur theorizers, centrifugal force. With the squaring of the circle and perpetual motion this mystical conception forms the unholy trinity of the born paradoxer. Not one of them knows what it means, yet by invoking its magic powers they explain everything from germs to God. Edith, trying not to listen, felt like a quart of milk in a cream separator. Centrifugal force was separating her mind from her body, but which was which she could not have told. Mercifully it did not last long, and Ole soon reached the practical application of his moonshine.

"Now my theory is," he said more rationally, "that there is a vast tank of oil—perhaps several—under the whole region."

"Won't Captain Anderson be pleased to hear that? I'm glad somebody will be happy in all this mess."

"Not all oil, perhaps. I think it may be floating on salt water."

"I wish it were carbolic acid."

"Now when the moon raises a tide on all that oil it rushes through the underground galleries of this continent and forces up all the collected gases of twenty-four hours through the blowholes."

"And somebody is waiting to set a match to it, I suppose?"

"You mean how does it catch fire?"

For a moment the inventive Ole was badly stumped. Then his chambered mind gave up its buried reminiscences: all gases when compressed get hot. Keep on compressing them far enough and they get red hot—if gases ever do behave in such a revolutionary way.

"Compression," he answered offhandedly, as if the effort had cost him no labor. "Compression heats up the gas. When the wave passes it presses the gas into a small volume next to the roof. That makes it red hot. Then it escapes through the blowholes. Friction on the sides makes it hotter still. Of course it catches fire-high up in the air, high enough so the rush of escaping gas can't blow out the flame. It couldn't light up, could it, before it reached the air? Then the tide falls, air has to rush in to fill up the place left by the falling oil and water, and the flames are sucked down."

"Tides don't rise and fall every thirteen minutes. Your theory is up the spout."

"My theory is irrefutable. Of course tides don't happen every thirteen minutes. But haven't you ever seen the way the water swings back and forth, up and down, when you set it going in a long bathtub?"

"I do bathe occasionally when I'm in civilization. And you may be sure I shall spend a month in the first real tub I see. Yes, I may even have time to try your experiment."

"When the tide rushes into some vast underground cavern, half filling it, big waves must be set up travelling back and forth, up and down along the trough. Suppose the wave comes in by a long tunnel into a vast hole, and has to squeeze out by another tunnel. In trying to squeeze out all at once the waves will be started at the wall above the tunnel. And all the time the hole is filling up, compressing the gas against the roof. Now suppose it takes a wave thirteen minutes to run the length of the underground tank. Then it will force up the gases at a particular place once every thirteen minutes.

"As it passes the place," he went on with enthusiasm that fed upon itself, "the air will be sucked down again. That explains our first blowholes. Now for these. The tank under them must be much longer. The waves therefore take a longer time to pass under. It follows that the flame jets will burn much longer. Which was to be proved."

"You have proved also," she pointed out, "that the flame pillars will be dead for half an eternity. We must wait at least until the next full moon raises the gas for our torches. And by then we shall be in Heaven—I hope."

"No, I think every tide must raise the gas enough to send up a flame. Of course at full moon the flame will be hotter and last much longer."

"And where does your blessed salt water come from to float the oil and gas and raise the tides?"

"Where all salt water comes from—the sea."

"These tunnels, or others like them—bigger and longer, of course—must stretch far out under the floor of the Antarctic ocean." He became encyclopaedic, explaining how, gradually weakening under the pressure and seeping of ages of water, the bottom of things aqueous had suddenly given way letting the ocean burst down to the subterranean fires, flooding them and the innumerable tunnels. This, he said, accounted for everything. The oily stew of prehistoric monsters which he and the Captain had witnessed was merely the backwash, the jetsam of the sudden deluge which had drowned out perhaps a dozen of the interconnected paradises such as the one Edith and he had discovered. Some day the floor of the unruined one would give way too and there would be another grand boiling up of monsters somewhere between South Georgia and Cape Horn. Or the accumulating gas under its rock bottom might suddenly hurl it skyward at some tide higher than the usual one.

The origin of these vast tunnels and semitropical paradises in the frozen continent he was as yet unable to explain. At them his theory balked, baffled. He doubted now whether the monsters of the stew had been so recently dead as he and Anderson imagined. Their freshness and the still uncoagulated blood of the baby devil they had fished up could be rationally explained on a twenty-four hour immersion in warm oil and water.

Theorizing thus freely Ole was happy despite the ever present, all enveloping, stinking darkness. Edith's respectful silence flattered him. He outdid himself. Never before had he lectured to an audience so sympathetically appreciative. During his interminable harangue he forgot even to strike a match. When finally he did, Edith's eyes were closed. She was fast asleep.

Although deeply chagrined Ole considerately let her sleep. Taking out his pipe he rammed it full of twist. The coarsely cut tobacco refusing to burn he reached into his pocket for his knife. Only when he was about to cut up the tobacco in his palm did he remember what he had done to the blade. In a cold sweat he closed the knife and returned it to his pocket. A scratch, for all he knew, might be deadlier than the fangs of a hundred cobras. Any way he would take no chance of a slip in the dark.

Refilling his pipe he tried again to smoke. Finally he compromised at the rate of a match to a puff. It became a continuous performance. The tobacco in that smoke-fouled atmosphere reeking with an unspeakable corruption lacked the rich, nutty flavor emphasized by the billboards, yet it was some consolation. The matches, especially their heads, tasted even better than the tobacco smoke.

The devil betrayed him just as he broached the fourth box of matches. He became aware of a wet, dragging noise. Instantly he had a theory that made him sick. Those filthy scavengers also had eyes. Not only the bat-birds were by nature lovers of the light. One of those huge foul brutes, dripping corruption at every move, was wallowing toward Ole's friendly little beacon in the universal darkness.

The noise stopped. Then a measured slopping announced that the filthy monster had paused to lick itself. Having swabbed off its lunch, or having performed its unseemly toilette, it sighed prodigiously and rattled the grating armor of its horny scales. Once more there was silence.

Presently a hideous rasping proclaimed that the obscenity was scratching its parasites. Again it sighed heavily, profoundly. The companionable candle of its quest was perhaps but the disordered illusion of an overloaded stomach. A long-winded, slobbering belch automatically begot and confirmed this hypothesis in Ole's paralyzed brain. He struck no more matches.

Should he wake Edith? If she made any sound the monster must find them. On the other hand if she woke suddenly when the beast had crawled closer, as it might, she would go mad from terror and be unmanageable. He decided to rouse her as gently as possible.

"What is it?" she said, and remembered. "Oh—"

He clapped his hand over her mouth. Again thinking him demented she struggled violently.

"Danger," he whispered in her ear. "Be quiet."

All her muscles tensed, she instantly became still. Then she heard the dragging shuffle of some ponderous body approaching the airplane. In a flash she realized what was upon them.

"Your knife," she whispered.

He opened the blade. Of what use was this toy against a mailed brute weighing over a hundred tons? Yet it was his one weapon, and instinct compelled him to be ready for his feeble best.

The creature heard their movements. Its lurching drag, bringing with it leprosy of smells, quickened. It was abreast of them, on Edith's side. Was it going past the machine? In the sooty darkness the brute blundered forward. Its horny side rasped and rocked the plane, all but upsetting it.

For some seconds the slow brain of the brute failed to interpret the unusual sensations. Then it registered, and the foul monster squatted. The plane tipped sideways. A foot higher and it must capsize.

The dull brain proving inadequate for its problem, the huge brute resumed its wallowing progress. Presently, to judge by the sounds, it turned at right angles to the line of the machine, slewed round on its belly, and squatted. Was its head or its tail toward them? And in which position could it hear the better? They soon learned.

One or other of the occupants of the machine moved slightly and something creaked. For some ten seconds the brute took no notice. Then, the significance of the noise penetrating its ganglia, the monster moved slightly forward, directly toward Edith's side of the plane.

"Quick!" she cried, "the knife! Light!"

A cold breath, unutterably foul, blasted her own and extinguished Ole's half handful of matches. But the flare had shown her where to aim. With her whole body she struck at the brute's eye. The keen eight-inch blade cut it like a jelly. Her hand plunged into the slit, burying the knife.

No injury to the slow-witted creature's eye alone could account for the terrible sound which tore the silence of the tunnel to tatters of screaming agony. The green paste on the blade was indeed a venom. It had shot along the blood vessels and the optic nerve directly to the monster's brain.

Its every nerve was in hell. In its excruciating agony it bounded furiously about the tunnel, missing the plane by bare yards, and thundering down from its convulsive leaps in a writhing mass of torment that shook the very rocks.

No human being could hear those terrible screams without pity. In the minute and a half that it lived the wretched thing suffered all the agonies of all the hells imagined by human beings since the beginning of the world.

With a last shivering yell of absolute pain it was dead.

"Oh my God," Edith gasped, "I did it. Hell, hell, hell!"

In a paroxysm of sobbing she beat her clenched fists against her ears.

14 THE DEVIL CHICK

Their brother's death agonies had roused the bewildered scavengers in a bellowing horde. Blundering into one another in the darkness, the monsters fought and screamed till the roof shook. And the multitude of reptilian birds, alarmed at the tumult, clattered down the black tunnel in flapping clouds, screeching their fright or pain where they dashed their brainless heads against the unseen walls. Their broken bodies, raining down on the rock floor, flapped convulsively till the maddened monsters trampled them to smears.

Twice when a bat-winged bird became entangled for a moment in the guy wires the plane jarred dizzily, and once a bellowing monster lumbering from its pursuer set the whole machine spinning like a top. Unless the pillars of fire burst forth soon it would be only a matter of minutes until the plane was splinters and the bodies of its occupants pulp.

Above the jarring din they sensed a deeper tremor and a heavier reverberation. The subterranean waves were buffeting their way through the labyrinthine corridors beneath the tunnel. In a moment the solid rock floor heaved like a swell of the sea, the blowholes roared, and ten thousand pillars of flame burst thundering to the roof.

Panic-stricken, the huge monsters scuttled for their burrows in the mountain of corruption. On a vast scale it was the scurrying of a multitude of beetles when a board is lifted, letting down the sun on their secret world.

Blinded by the sudden glare, clouds of the reptilian bat birds crashed against the walls of the tunnel, breaking heads and wings and necks. Most horrible of all, hundreds dashed directly into the pillared flames to be roasted alive and shot to the rock vault, where they exploded. Their steaming viscera rained upon the floor.

Before she realized what he was about, Ole had cranked the propeller and was back in the machine. The impact of the bewildered scavenger had reversed the plane.

"The shortest way," Ole shouted, and headed for the shambles.

Soaring over it, he plunged into the smoke and stench above. They saw now the cause of the dimmer light above the festering pile. The blowholes were choked with the huge carcasses which had rolled down from the vast heap undermined by the feeding of the scavengers. Until the rushing flames could incinerate these obstructions they must bell out in roses of fire. Heavy black smoke billowing up from these fierce crematories filled the narrow channel above the mountain of corruption with an indescribable foulness.

Mile after mile they flew down the shallow channel between the corruption and the rock roof, lighted only by the flickering crimson reflected from the vault. Would it never end? Twenty miles fell behind them, twenty-five, and still the obscene bat birds rose at their approach to circle down to their interrupted banquet when the droning parvenu had passed.

The smoke thickened, but became less foul. Like a breath of heaven they recognized the reek of burning petroleum. A cleaner wind cut their faces. Black with soot, the plane shot clear of the tunnel into the relatively clean night.

They were still enveloped in billowing smoke, but it was not unclean. An occasional banner of crimson flame unfurling for a moment at the bottom of the black sea revealed the source of the conflagration. A vast lake of oil was burning far down there on the floor of the ruined crater.

Rising sharply, they pierced the heaving smoke pall up to the wonder of sweet air and icy stars.

The moon had just set. They had emerged into the ruined crater of their first discovery far west of the line along which they had previously flown.

Edith, as a rational being, assumed that Ole would fly straight for the ship at top speed. He, however, had a nobler intention, and one which did him great credit. Taking the shortest air line to the jagged rim against the northern stars he let out the engine, soared over the wilderness of black rocks, black now as Tophet in the moonless night, and then, when the dim gray of the icy desolation swam into sight, cut out the motor.

"What in the name of sin are you going to do?" Edith demanded.

"I am going to land on the snowfield beyond these rocks."

"And what for? Are you crazy?"

"Not crazy," he replied solemnly, "although the scoffers would call me so. And why? Because I am thankful."

"You're raving."

"This is not the first time I have been scorned and mocked for my faith. If I can forgive Captain Anderson's blasphemous jeers I can put up with yours."

"I haven't jeered at you, and besides I'm not blasphemous. Just now I wish I were."

"Whosoever lusteth in his heart after an oath to say it hath committed the unmentionable sin."

The plane was running along the snowfield parallel to the outlying mass of jumbled rocks and about eight hundred yards from the nearest.

"On my knees," Ole announced as the plane came to rest, "I shall offer up thanks for our merciful deliverance to God."

"If you do any such thing in this absurd place I shall box your fat ears till they sing like all the hosts of Heaven. Don't be a fool. Get on home to the ship. I'm freezing."

"I pray that you may not some day long for a lump of ice to cool your tongue."

And with that hypocritical intercession he climbed down to the frozen snow.

"Look here, Ole," she flung after him, "if you think the Creator is as big a fool as you are, you are jolly well mistaken. It will serve you right if you fall down a blowhole. You might at least have the decency to crank the propeller before you commit suicide."

But Ole was absorbed in his search for the most uncomfortable square foot on the Antarctic continent. To offer thanks from a bed of downy ease would not be treating his audience with due respect.

Having found what he sought, he knelt down, uncovered his head, and opened fire. Edith suspected that his extreme humility, voiced in an unnecessarily loud tone, was aimed at her instead of at Heaven. His impersonal allusions to hardness of heart, a stiff neck, a disagreeable temper and an ungrateful disposition were put with remarkable skill. Although Edith's name, age, sex and color were meticulously omitted from his oration he yet contrived to give her a severe and exceedingly long-winded lecture on her numerous shortcomings. Bitterly did she regret that her aim was like that of any girl. Otherwise she would have heaved the heavy thermos bottle into his fat, smug face. It was such a lovely chance to miss; with his eyes closed like a sleeping lobster's he wouldn't see it coming.

But common sense and the Lord were on her side. Ole had overlooked more than the blowholes. In so astute a theorizer his oversight really was unpardonable. He should have observed that all the monsters of his acquaintance were confirmed lovers of a mild temperature. And he should have reflected that such of the poor brutes as had wandered back to their ruined home, would naturally gather round the cheerful hearths to drool over the good old times.

In short, Ole should have known that these heat-loving, carnivorous monsters would frequent the vicinity of the blowholes. To be snugly out of the draughts they would retire between eruptions to their spacious lairs in the jumble of rocks. When the home fires burned again they would emerge and gather round the blaze. The spells of cold between roasts would be excellent sharpeners of the appetite. Undoubtedly the home-loving beasts were communists, sharing all things. When a journey from the cheery blowholes to the gloomy banquet halls of the tunnel seemed long and unattractive, they stayed at home and ate one another.

To these simple-minded beasts the thankful Ole was literally a godsend. Their pious instincts perceived him as manna dropped from Heaven. It chanced that he had selected his uncomfortable spot opposite one of the poorer rookeries. For a week all the famished beasts had been of two sizes only: mere babies just born and therefore still dear to their ferocious mothers, and huge, agile brutes of approximately equal fighting abilities. All intermediate sizes had devoted their lives to the welfare of the community.

Being of extremely low intelligence, the strapping survivors had not yet mastered the theory and practice of cooperation. It never entered their brainless heads that any two of them were more than a match for an unlucky third. Consequently all starved, whereas two-thirds of them at any time until the Armageddon between the last gigantic pair might have wallowed in luxury. Lacking farsighted statesmen they lived in armed neutrality and hunger until such time as the babies of the community should develop militarism. But this sporadic sort of uprising furnished pretty lean pickings.

Unaware of his grateful audience, Ole prayed vigorously. He thanked Heaven that the blowholes in his immediate vicinity were not as other blowholes. These were orderly and quiet, the others roaring furnaces of the devil. He proceeded to inform headquarters that he had a theory.

"This chain of blowholes, O Lord, vents the gas of another tunnel. The oil tank under these is not connected with the tank under the others. Thus, O Lord, hast thou prepared a safe place in the wilderness that thy servant may give thanks unto Thee."

To say the least, Ole lacked neither brazen nerve nor conceit. To give Edith the full strength of his lecture he continued facing her. His back, therefore, was toward the rookery. Nevertheless his remarks carried in all directions unimpaired by distance in that intensely still air. Staccato echoes from the black rocks repeated his vainglorious theory. The echoes even improved on his remarks. To Edith, trying not to listen, it seemed that over there in the rocks there was a sound of sleepy revelry, a drowsy, incredulous chuckling as it were, reinforced by subdued squawks. The infernal brood was awake.

Curiously watching a shadow against the starry sky she saw it move, black out a dazzling planet, and grow larger. Evidently it was not a lump of rock. A long neck cautiously raised itself above the black mass like a periscope. Having sighted its prey, the hungry head was quickly lowered. The black mass effaced itself on the blacker slope of the rocks.

"Look out!" she cried. "It's coming."

Ignoring the unseemly interruption, Ole theorized louder.

"You idiot! Crank the propeller—run for it!"

"The Lord is mindful of his own," Ole responded unctuously, and proceeded to give thanks for the fact.

A piercing shriek from Edith brought him to his common sense. One glance over his shoulder and he was on his feet, running as he had never run in his fat life. After him like a gigantic ostrich raced the enormous lizard on its long hind legs, the tail curved up like a scimitar, and the twenty-foot neck stretched forward to the elastic limit. No turkey after a hapless grasshopper was ever more eager.

Ole's seven or eight hundred yard start saved him. He fell into Edith's lap just as a vicious swish of the monster's tail cut the air under the machine in two.

Looking back toward the rocks, they saw the whole black brood boiling out over the dim gray desolation. As aimlessly as brainless hens they darted hither and thither over the snowfields, seeking a prey which had escaped. Far over the black expanse they raced like great scuttling lizards, and behind some of the huger shadows trailed three or four tiny dots like pursuing vermin. These were the babies of the brood following their eager mothers.

Evidently these creatures were of a breed distinct from any that Edith and Ole had yet seen alive. On the slaughter beach Ole and Lane had operated on three roughly similar giants.

So entranced were the observers with the ludicrous steeplechase that they failed to note the familiar thunder preceding a "blow." Before Edith knew what was happening the plane was bounding and tumbling like a glass ball in a fountain.

She came to her senses just in time. As she shot the plane up for a sixty degree climb the air immediately below them burst with a dull roar into thousands of blue flame cones. It was a sharp rebuke to Ole's irreverent conceit. The theory which he had confided to Heaven evidently was faulty. After all, the oil tank under this region of blowholes probably was connected with that under the tunnel. The backwash of the tide under the tunnel was now forcing up the compressed gas through the secondary chain of vents.

Looking down, they saw the flame cones descending rapidly. In a moment they would disappear down the wells. Such, at least, was Ole's confident prediction. As if to teach him caution in theorizing, the flames did nothing of the kind. This eruption of gas was not of precisely the same sort as that first one into which Anderson had blundered with his party. It was more like the neighboring one under the tunnel. The flames did not disappear, but lengthening downward to the blowholes became short pillars of fire. These, however, were on a much smaller scale, mere conical candles a hundred feet high and from five to thirty feet thick.

The home fires were again burning merrily. It was impossible not to feel a twinge of sympathy for the exiled monsters scurrying over the icy plain to the friendly fires. Mothers abandoned their trailing young in the race after their more agile mates to the cheery hearths, and many a small monster was left squawking piteously in the cold. Around the invigorating warmth and light of the blowholes sociable groups of three or four huge lizards squatted in amiable content, their hunger and its consequent animosities for the moment forgotten. Edith was touched; Ole wasn't.

Mother instinct is said to be universal. Those brainless females hobnobbing with their ferocious mates around the comforting fires while their babies cried miserably in the cold, disproved the theory. Again Edith was deeply touched.

Wheeling back in the starlight, she dipped and circled low above the forlorn little monsters on the ice. All her dormant mother love awoke and strode rampant over one particularly shameful case of abandonment. The isolated little creature, no bigger than a Newfoundland dog, could not have been more than a few days old. Its ridiculous little tail was a mere stub, and its grotesquely disproportionate head all but overbalanced the emaciated body see-sawing on two feeble pins.

"Ole," she exclaimed, "we must take that darling little devil chick back to the ship. It is perishing for warmth and its mother."

"You're not its mother, and I'm blowed if I'll warm it."

"Oh yes you will. For you are going to catch it."

"Who is crazy now?"

"Not I. You will be perfectly safe with the parents away selfishly enjoying themselves. Besides, you will have a fair start of nearly three-quarters of a mile if the mother sees your kidnapping. If you can't outrun her at that distance you're no good. Here we are. Climb out and fetch the baby. Grab it well up by the neck so it can't bite."

"I'll be damned if I do."

"You will be if you don't. Now look here, Ole. Either you get that chick for me or I make your life miserable forever by telling the Captain how you ran away from your prayers. You will be famous from Liverpool to San Francisco and from there to Hong Kong as the grateful seaman whose able-bodied prayers raised the devil. Get that poor little beast for me and I swear never to tell a soul what kind of fool you looked racing that two-legged reptile."

It was rank blackmail, and as such succeeded in a continent where there is not a single lawyer.

With elaborate but unnecessary caution Ole sneaked up on the squawking foundling from behind. In its hunger and pathetic loneliness it would have welcomed him with open mouth. Grabbing its long thin neck with one hand, he clutched its stubby tail with the other. Then putting forth all his barrel of strength he started to lug the kicking little monster toward the airplane.

Who would have suspected that the puny wretch had such a fight in its emaciated body? And who would have dreamed from its plaintive squawk that the little devil had lungs of leather? It bawled for its daddy, screeched for its big brother, and yelled for its gadding mother. They came bounding in great hops.

All things considered, we must conclude with Edith that Ole, not the abandoned chick, was the attraction.

Edith's mother love suddenly fell below zero. She implored Ole to drop the little beast—he was now carrying it bodily by its neck and tail—and win the race to the propeller. But Ole's Norwegian perseverance was roused. Having begun the job he would finish it or bust.

Only an exceptionally strong man could have duplicated his feat. While with one hand he cranked the propeller he held the chick by its neck at arm's length with the other. The little beast had a wicked, raking kick with its feeble-looking legs. One rip with its claws might have taught Ole anatomy.

The bereaved family arrived in time to hear their darling's farewell wafted from above. It was dangling over the side of the plane, still kicking. Ole had not relaxed his stranglehold on its neck. With a deft swing he got it aboard and sat on its stomach. He still did not trust the chick with its own head. Consequently its last message to its mother was sufficiently like the skirl of a bagpipe to be distressing.

"Cuddle it up in the sealskins," Edith directed, "so it won't freeze on the way home."

Ole cuddled it. He was careful, however, not to let go of its neck.

"Won't father be delighted?" Edith resumed. "This is better than a whole continent of dead ones. I wonder what it eats?"

"Shall I let go of its neck and find out?"

"Not yet. Milk, I think, is probably the right diet for so tender an infant. Have we plenty of the canned variety aboard?"

"About a hundred cases, I suppose. They will last this little devil all of a week."

Their way home passed over a region which was new to them, some thirty miles west of the line which they had flown first. About ten miles beyond the blowholes they saw far beneath them a strange black lake.

"That looks interesting," Edith remarked, dipping down, "let's investigate. We can't be much later than we are already."

Nearing the surface of the lake they saw that it was in violent motion. Even by starlight Ole recognized the appearance of those huge bubbles instantly.

"Oil!" he shouted.

Oil was in fact bubbling up from hundreds of gushers at the bottom of the lake. The theory which Ole spontaneously brought forth was probably not far from the truth. The underground tides having risen to the rock roof above them were forcing the crude oil through a chain of blowholes. At this point some obstruction, possibly a heavy fall of rock from the roof, jarred loose by the violent earthquakes, had blocked the passageway damming back the tidal oil. Consequently it now spouted through the gas vents. The correspondingly slower motion of the heavy oil as it was forced upward had not generated sufficient friction to ignite the fluid. Such at any rate was Ole's theory.

As a first rough guess it may pass. Much further work, however, must be done before all the scientific puzzles raised by Lane's historic expedition are finally elucidated.

The practical question troubling Ole now was whether the oil would be sucked down with the receding subterranean tide. If so Anderson might find it difficult to form a stock company. For obviously it would be one thing to sell shares in a thirty by fifteen mile lake of oil and quite another to float stock on a dirty hole in the ground. He comforted himself with the reflection that more oil stock is sold on one smell of oil than on a thousand gushers. With a practically unlimited supply of smell in the hole even when empty they might easily make millionaires of themselves and the entire crew in a month.

The southern boundary of the lake gave Ole a qualm. On the south the oil was dammed back by a mere swell in the ice not fifty feet broad on top and less than twenty feet high. What if this slight wall should give way before the pressure of the oil? The millions of dollars in that beautiful lake would rush down the blowholes on the plain beyond. To the north, on the shore nearer the ship, conditions were more satisfactory. Here the wall of the long trough—fifteen miles broad by thirty long—was well over a hundred yards across the top. His calculations, of course, were only rough estimates based on their time of flight and their first observation from above that the lake was about twice as long as it was broad.

With a thousand fortunes in sight Ole forgot himself. A tentative nip on his leg reminded him of his infant charge. Once more he grasped it firmly by the neck.

The reception of the wanderers was cordial in the extreme. Edith had expected the very deuce from her father, but she was totally unprepared for Drake's attack. The devoted John tersely vented a longing to shake the tar out of her.

"Try it," Edith suggested. "You might find it profitable."

"What?" the Captain shouted. "Have you found oil?"

"Oceans of it."

The Captain forgave both her and Ole on the spot.

"Father," said Edith, uncovering the devil chick which till now they had kept concealed beneath the skins, "I have brought you a little playmate. Am I forgiven?"

Ole at that instant loosened his stranglehold on the chick's windpipe. A whooping squawk greeted the Doctor.

"Oh you beautiful child!" he exclaimed with wondering reverence. But whether he was referring to Edith or her peace offering she was unable to decide.

15 ANTICIPATIONS

"What do you expect to get out of all this, Doctor?" the Captain asked curiously.

They were sitting in the Captain's cabin. Eight days had elapsed since the advent of the devil chick. Tomorrow the explorers were to begin their first serious attack on the unknown. Everything was in readiness for a quick march to the heart of the mystery and for a safe return to the ship.

Lane parried the Captain's question.

"I may have come for my share of the oil stock. I'm a member of the crew, am I not?"

"You're no money grubber. Come on, tell us why you came. I've owned up to everything. A thousand acre orange grove in California with nothing to do but boss it drove me into this mess. After twenty years of whaling you might be just as ready as I am to sell your soul for a pint of dirty oil. I've had enough of the cold and the stink. Now I want sunshine and orange blossoms. What do you want? You have all the money you need. Now just why did you come?"

"Perhaps I came to collect all those magnificent specimens we have stowed away. The lively little devil chick alone is enough to make any lover of the beautiful happy for life. Perhaps that is what I expect in return for my money.

"I don't think so," said the Captain shrewdly.

"To change the subject for a moment," Lane rejoined after a pause, "have you any relatives who would miss you if you died?"

"Not one. Why?"

"Because we may never see the ship again after tomorrow."

"If these two," the Captain indicated Edith and Ole, "got through alive, why can't we? There is dynamite enough between here and the crater to blow up an army of two-legged reptiles. We shan't be taken by surprise."

"It isn't that. Yet if you were to ask me what I anticipate I should have to put you off. For I don't know myself. Only I have a feeling that we may blunder into more than we foresee. Don't you feel the same, Drake?"

"Yes," he admitted uneasily. "That's why I say Edith shouldn't go. Not on the first attack, anyway. If everything is all right she can come with us the second time."

"There may be no second attempt," Edith replied. "I'm coming, John. Now don't get fussy about it."

"All this may seem rather old womanish to you, Captain," the Doctor resumed. "Nevertheless that is how Drake and I feel. We have collaborated during the past seven or eight evenings and have now a fairly definite theory."

"As to feeling nervous," the Captain laughed, "I occasionally have an attack of nerves myself when I think of all that beautiful oil being sucked down the blowholes. It may at any time, you know. But you haven't told us yet why you want to go on."

"Drake really knows more about what may be ahead of us than I do." He grew strangely serious. "On the eve of what may be our last peaceful day on earth I think it only right to tell you everything I suspect. Drake can speak for himself later.

"This is no mere naturalist's holiday. The tons of specimens we have gathered are priceless beyond count, no doubt, compared to the oceans of oil which you expect to discover. Yet priceless as our collections are, and rich as your oil fields may prove, both together are not worth the fraction of a cent when balanced against the true purpose of this expedition."

Anderson gaped at him. "What under the sun did you come for?"

"As I have said, I don't really know. I can only guess. If my suspicion is right we shall save civilization from a horrible destruction."

The Captain looked incredulous. "You're pulling my leg for what Ole and I did to yours in San Francisco. When did you find out that we are a gang of anointed crusaders prancing forth to make the world safe for democracy?"

"We shall not make it safe for democracy, or for aristocracy, or for socialism, or for any other pet creed. What we shall make the world safe for is life itself. I am serious. This is the greatest adventure. It was on the slaughter beach that I first definitely recognized something fundamentally evil in all the strange things we have seen so far. The second definite hint came from that black rock over which Drake stumbled."

"The inscriptions on it?" Ole asked sagaciously.

"No. The rock itself gave the clue. Drake, have you a piece of the one you chipped yesterday?"

Drake produced a small fragment of the black rock. Lane handed it to the Captain.

"You were trained as a mining engineer, Anderson. Even twenty years of whales can't have made you forget all the simplest things in elementary geology. Take a good look at that chunk of rock and tell me what you think it is. Here's my magnifying glass."

The Captain studied the fragment long and curiously.

"I don't want to make a fool of myself," he said at last, handing back the glass and rock.

"Go ahead. What is the stuff? I'm not trying to trap you."

"Well, Doctor, either I have forgotten all I ever knew or that stuff isn't rock at all."

"If it isn't rock, what is it?"

"Manufactured, I should say—some artificial stone, if you like, or a queer sort of cement."

"Precisely."

"Well, what of it?"

"Doesn't it strike you as remarkable that millions upon millions of tons of artificial cement, scribbled over with inscriptions, should exist on a continent that died before America was born? The inscriptions alone would not be so mysterious. Races without number, I am convinced, have lived, died and been forgotten since the beginning of time. The archæan rocks are an unread history. But that any race should pave vast areas of its dwelling place with an unimaginable mass of artificial cement as hard as diamond, is a thing for which history has no parallel. It is unique."

"You are right," Ole agreed. "No race known ever paved more than ten acres in one place. The ancient Babylonians—"

"Shut up, Ole. Go on, Doctor."

"Well, that is about all. Drake can tell the rest better."

"But you haven't said yet what made you bite in San Francisco."

"Your pickled reptile."

"That won't go. You have just said that all your junk isn't worth half a cent compared to the real thing you are after."

"I am after my life's ambition. Does that satisfy you?"

"Perfectly. What is your life's ambition?"

The Doctor laughed. "You are a greater sea lawyer than Ole. I may as well give you the whole story and be done with it. Then Drake can tell you something worth hearing."

He paused for a moment, selecting the few facts necessary.

"It all began," he resumed, "when I was about ten years old. An aunt gave me for Christmas a copy of that remarkable scientific romance by Mary Shelley—the wife of the poet—based on the artificial creation of life."

"I've read it," Ole interrupted eagerly. "It's a peach. Just like a nightmare. 'Frankenstein' is the name of the book."

"Most readers with any brains at all enjoy the story. If nothing else it is imaginative, and that's a great deal in a world of prosy, oversexed bores. Well, that book determined the course of my life. You remember, Ole, how the hero of the story creates a living creature out of chemicals. This creature was no mere amœba, but a complex, highly organized, half-human monstrosity.

"It is nothing against Mrs. Shelley's fascinating tale to state that today we know definitely that such a thing is impossible. By merely mixing together chemicals as her hero did it is not feasible to create a complex, highly organized animal.

"On the other hand it may be possible to create out of chemicals a colloid—a sort of jelly or gluelike substance—having some of the essential properties of living matter. Although thus far no chemist or biologist has actually done this, it is not a sheer impossibility. If it could be done, and this is what I wish to emphasize, it would be an incomparably easier feat than the one which is the basis of Mrs. Shelley's story.

"We can see the relative difficulty of the two by an example from another field. The first savages killed one another by hurling stones with their bare hands. We destroy one another wholesale by—among other ingenious and devilish ways—exceedingly complicated machines. There is a vastly greater gap between a glue-like substance having some resemblance to living matter, and the simplest organized living creature, than exists between a lump of stone hurtling through the air and a torpedo directed by wireless.

"All this by the way. The significant thing for me in Mrs. Shelley's book is that it awoke my imagination when I was ten years old. I determined to become a scientist. The creation of life was to be my life's ambition. This, I believe, is the greatest adventure.

"Then later, learning something of science while picking up an education in odd hours, I saw clearly that I was a million miles from my goal. And still later, digging deeper into the natural sciences, I realized that my ambition was a fantastic dream.

"I saw then, and I see now, that if life is to be created by human beings using purely artificial means it will not be in our generation, nor in our century, nor perhaps in the next two centuries. That it will be done eventually I have not the slightest doubt. But thus far we have not succeeded even in stating the problem precisely.

"When we come to know exactly what it is that we are seeking we shall find it. At present we lack even a definition of life that is scientific and more than a scholastic jumble of words. Consequently, although many of us may feel that we know what we are looking for, few indeed have the training, the ability and the scientific tact to seek it intelligently. Men who today search for the origin of life are hopeless cranks in a class with circle squarers and inventors of perpetual motion.

"Having realized early that my first ambition was a chimera, I turned to more natural and far more useful investigations. I do not regret the time lost in the vain pursuit of unattainable knowledge. It was not indeed lost, for it was my apprenticeship to true science. Most of my work since has been in the laws governing the growth and decay of animals, and, as a by-product, the study of such diseases as depend upon abnormal growth. I need not bore you with any of this.

"I said that I abandoned my quest for life. That is not strictly true. It is impossible to eradicate from the mind the hopes, desires and fears of childhood and adolescence. Although in maturity I put away all thought of ever directly attacking the problem of life, my subconscious habits of thought were unalterably fixed in my youth. My psychology is what it was and I yet am driven against my will, for the most part subconsciously, to think incessantly of the problem of life.

"All my work, I sometimes think, has been aimed at my first ambition. It frequently gives me a shock to discover that what I am truly interested in doing is not the artificial duplication of cancerous growths, but the out and out creation of living cells. It is almost as if some familiar spirit keeps whispering 'do this, and in spite of yourself you will find what you are looking for,' and I, not consciously hearing the whisper do as I am directed. This of course is merely my own repressed desire taking its revenge.

"Again I do not regret. For my work has led to at least three positive facts recognized by competent authorities as contributions of real value to our knowledge and control of certain diseases.

"Now, Anderson, you will ask what all this has to do with our expedition. In one word, everything. But for my repressed ambition you would never have obtained one cent toward expenses. I am not interested in oil or in any other form of wealth. I would not walk across this cabin to make a million dollars. For I have all the money that is good for myself and Edith. More would be a nuisance. Had you come to me without that pickled reptile I should have shown you the door at once.

"You remember how at first I mistook your find for a young specimen of a known prehistoric animal. It is true that no fossil yet discovered has both scales and feathers.

There is a 'missing link' in the chain from reptiles to birds no less than in that from anthropoids to men. But for all that your monster did not at first look wholly anomalous. It might, in short, have been a natural animal. And that is what I at first thought it was.

"Then, while you were talking of your adventures, I began to think. If you were an ex-zoölogist instead of an ex-mining engineer, I could make my next point—the crux of the whole story—much clearer.

"Thinking over your specimen and looking more closely at it, I recognized that the monster was indeed a monster, a thing never created and evolved by nature. There were certain astounding differences between the obvious anatomy of the creature and any conceivable product of orderly evolution.

"A frog will not evolve into a horse no matter how much time you give him. From now to the end of eternity all the descendants of frogs will retain certain specific peculiarities of structure which will easily differentiate them from horses. At no point of the story will the two become confused. It will be possible a million years hence for any trained scientist to say at a glance that the descendants of our frogs and of our horses living in his day, or fossilized in the rocks of his time, never had a common ancestor.

"And so it was with your monster. At first it might have been a missing link between the birds and the reptiles. Closer inspection showed that none of its ancestors were related to reptiles and that none of its descendants would ever evolve into birds. And it fitted nowhere else into the scheme of evolution.

"Nor was it a deformity. A kitten with three eyes is still a young cat for all its eyes. A man with six fingers on his right hand still belongs to the family of men. Mere abnormality does not exclude a freak from the family to which it otherwise would belong. Your queer find, Anderson, was no deformed reptile, nor was it a freak bird, 'thrust into the world before its time but half made up.'

"There remained but one rational conclusion. The thing was no creation of nature but the result of a conscious attempt to imitate nature. Either that monster had been created whole and alive by intelligent beings, or it was the descendant of remote ancestors so created.

"The first possibility was out of the question. Had the monster been recently created we should have had another Frankenstein. I know enough of the present state of biology to be certain that such a complete creation of a highly complex organism today is impossible.

"There remained the alternative. Your monster was the descendant of inconceivably remote ancestors, and those ancestors, incomparably simpler in structure, had been created by conscious, intelligent beings.

"Evolution had done the rest. Shaping the initial, simple organism through millions of years, time and evolution had gradually complicated its simplicity into a highly developed organism.

"The first creation probably was a mere speck of living matter, perhaps a single cell, and this full-blown monster of yours was the slow flower of ages blooming from that first almost formless seed.

"Such was my guess while you sat talking of the monsters boiling up in oil from the floor of the ocean. I decided to chance your veracity and see for myself.

"On the slaughter beach, you remember, I pointed out how all those dead monsters differed radically, in spite of superficial resemblances, from their nearest types in the fossil beds. The number and arrangement of one monster's teeth I emphasized as particularly significant. Nature does not cram one man's mouth full with eighty teeth and give his neighbor only sixteen. She does nothing by violent jumps that can be seen by a blind man. Her changes are minute. That is my second point.

"On that beach another thought disturbed me greatly. All those monsters gave me the impression of being badly botched jobs. Suppose you were aiming to create a harmless toad and achieved a deadly rattlesnake. You wouldn't consider yourself a master of the technique of life, would you? Well, neither can the beings whose scientific blundering millions of years ago started the evolution of all those hideous monsters on the beach.

"What those misguided experimenters intended to do I don't know. What they did start, I do know, and I pronounce its fruit an obscene abomination. Not one of those huge creatures had intelligence above a worm's, and not one of them ever could be of any possible value to the world. They are merely gigantic feeding, breeding and fighting machines with just a spark of intelligence—enough to make them exceedingly dangerous and no more.

"I suspect that all those huge brutes are, as I have tried to make clear, the result of minute seeds first created and sown millions of years ago. Further, I believe that nature, taking the artificially created seeds, has grown from them, through countless mutations, the changing shapes whose perfected, dangerous uselessness infests the secret places of this continent. The beginning was unnatural, the development and its conclusion are the work of natural laws.

"Finally I believe that the original creators of those monstrosities realized when it was too late what they were doing, foresaw its consequences, became terrified, tried to undo their blundering work and perished in a war to destroy their own creations. This, however, belongs to Drake's part of the investigation. He can tell it better than I.

"Now last, let me say exactly what I expect to get from this expedition. I hope from close study of the anatomy, habits and environment of these strange creatures to rediscover their origin. See what this implies. If I am successful I shall be able to create artificially a true living seed of life. Whether or not I shall wish to do so depends upon what we discover in the next few days.

"Mind, I am not expecting to make a gigantic lizard out of dead slime or anything of that fantastic sort. But I do hope to rediscover the lost secret which started all those monstrosities. A mere speck of living matter, a single cell visible only under a high power microscope is all that I shall achieve, if anything. For I am convinced that the originators of that aborted creation on the beach achieved no more. One spark starts the forest fire; their invisible specks of artificial living matter started the self-imposed catastrophe that wiped them out."

"But Doctor," Ole objected, "if they only made those very small specks of living matter how were they wiped out? You say it took millions of years to evolve dangerous animals out of those bad beginnings. The things were too small, according to you, to bother a flea. If I get your meaning they were nothing better than pieces of jelly invisible to the naked eye. How could such things fight anybody?"

"That is what I hope to find out, definitely and in detail. Drake and I already have a rational theory."

"Is it your theory that they were disease germs when first created?"

"No, Ole, nothing so romantic. As I tried to make plain a robin's egg will never hatch crocodiles. Nor will a disease germ ever evolve into a three-hundred foot brute with a head and body like a bad dream."

"Then what is your theory?"

"On that point, if I understand your question, I have none. Before indulging in hypotheses on the origin of life I shall find out the facts."

"Listen, Doctor. I have a theory. Those things were first created—"

"Oh, pipe down, Ole." The Captain was back on the job. "Now Drake, let us have your side of it."

"It is so late," Drake yawned, "that I shall have to beg off this time. We start at five in the morning. Good-night, everybody."

16 ATTACK

By forced marches the party reached the north shore of the oil lake early the third morning after leaving the ship. Lane, Anderson, Ole and Drake had gone by land. Edith was to arrive at the base by air. While the men marched she flew back and forth to the ship for last minute supplies which she dropped conveniently near the southern boundary of the oil lake.

No detail that might increase the safety of the expedition had been neglected. Between the ship and the north shore of the lake a chain of provision caches made starvation impossible no matter what might happen. The party of five might all have hung onto the plane somehow, and so have reached their goal more quickly. But for several reasons they decided to march, carrying with them the essentials of a light prospecting outfit. Anderson half expected to find indications of oil by zigzagging slightly across the line of caches. He was nothing if not optimistic.

In case of an accident to the ship, Bronson's men had deposited provisions in caches parallel to the inlet north a distance of forty miles. As a final measure of safety they had landed every gallon of petrol, storing it a mile inland in a deep dugout. Even if forced to flee on foot the expedition would have sufficient provisions. Each man could pack on his back a sleeping bag and short rations enough from the northerly caches to last him to the coast. Should no whaling vessel appear within two weeks to take them off, Edith or Ole was to fly northeast to the nearest whaling station for help. No member of the party expected the worst to happen. But Anderson disbelieved in luck, preferring arduous certainty to easy going chance.

At this moment the Captain, speechless with cupidity, was gazing over the thirty-mile expanse of bubbling black oil. With a hundred huge fortunes before his eyes he was beginning to regret that Ole and the crew had been promised a share of the profits. More potential gold bubbled and swirled in that vast bowl than the most ingeniously dissolute debauchee could squander in fifty lifetimes. Yet the Captain wished that Ole and the crew were in Halifax. Such is human nature.

The men were waiting for Edith. She was to transport them and their packs comfortably one at a time to the south shore of the lake. They were then to march at once for the blowholes where Edith and Ole had seen the monsters warming themselves. Lane's objective was the ruined crater. He and Drake were determined to inspect the black rocks at first hand. The shattered floor being his ultimate goal, the Doctor hoped also to penetrate the black smoke at the bottom and search for further animal remains.

An immediate assault on the crater would, of course, be suicide. The famished monsters would consider the party as a trifling hors d'oeuvre vouchsafed by the generosity of Heaven for the great feast to come.

How then were the explorers to traverse the region of blowholes, scale the crater lip, and reach the Doctor's objective? This puzzle had exercised the wits of the party for the first two days after the return of Edith and Ole with the devil chick. Between the oil lake and the black rocks lay the blowholes, and 'round these the sociable monsters might gather at just the most embarrassing moment.

The puzzle had indeed seemed unsolvable. Of all unpracticable beings it was Drake who solved the problem by a brilliant flash of imagination. And of all things that might have inspired him it actually was the last that might occur to a practical man. Who but Drake would have turned for inspiration to the memory of his sufferings in a dentist's chair? Having sat for several hours with the glass hook of a long rubber siphon under his tongue, he now remembered his discomfort with advantage.

As a consequence Edith and Ole during the six days following had transported every foot of hose—fire hose and other—on the ship to the south shore of the oil lake. All the iron pipe that could be spared also was taken to the same depot. To both ends of each section of hose the men had tied heavy iron slugs, and the end of each pipe they bent into a short L. This inefficient looking junk, a tangle of doubly weighted hoses and bent pipes, constituted the entire arsenal of the attacking party. With this alone they must overcome the army of huge lizards. Otherwise they must turn back, provided they were not eaten first.

"There she comes," the Doctor announced, pointing to a tiny speck against the blue far to the north. "Ole, you fly over first and take our packs. Hang them on somehow."

Ole seemed nervous at the prospect of being left alone with the packs on the south shore while Edith returned for the next passenger.

"What if those brutes come out to get warm while the plane is over on this side?"

"But you said the blowholes end quite a distance south of the lake," the Doctor replied. "They won't come several miles from the heat just to say hello to you."

"They will if they smell me."

"Cheer up, Ole," said Drake; "we will see you avenged."

"Lot of good that will do me. You go over first."

"I'm not fat enough."

The dispute was cut short by the landing of Edith.

"Captain Anderson," she began at once, "Bronson asked me to tell you that he may be forced to steam down the inlet at any minute. A wave of warm water came down again early this morning."

"Boiling?"

"No, just warm enough to raise a thick fog over the inlet."

"There is no great danger, I guess. If he has to run he can make it. And we are safe with all the supplies cached and the plane. What did he want me to do?"

"To send back word by me if he is to move at once. If he doesn't hear from you by night he will stay where he is."

"What about it, Lane?"

"I see no immediate danger. There has been no violent earthquake."

"That's my best judgment too. He is safe enough where he is. All right, Ole, hop in. Miss Lane will waft you over for lunch."

"For lunch?"

"Yes, idiot. Not yours, theirs."

With a fat groan Ole obeyed orders.

Arrived at the south shore of the lake they noted with alarm that the oil had risen since their visit the previous week. The black waves were crawling slowly up the narrow rise separating the lake from the chain of blowholes. Should the wall of rock and ice give way under the steadily increasing pressure, Anderson's fortune would vanish down the blowholes in a week. The thought that even if the wall held yet a flow of oil over the top might overspread the plain and catch fire from the blowholes, setting the entire lake aflame, was anything but reassuring. Leaving Ole to his dismal theories Edith skimmed back for the next passenger.

Shortly after one o'clock the party assembled on the south shore with their packs, ready for the opening move of their offensive. The blowholes were still quiescent. This favoring the strategy of the proposed attack the party decided to take advantage of it immediately.

Their first question was, who is to bell the cat? More definitely, which members of the party should risk their lives to carry out Drake's ingenious plan? The scheme demanded half an hour's work around the blowholes. The workers, if seen by the reptiles, certainly would be welcomed by the whole rookery. And no pair of human legs was a match for the slowest of the huge lizards. Again, if the work party proceeded on foot by daylight to the blowholes they were sure to be seen. If they waited till dark the blowholes might flare up just at the wrong time, and refreshments would enliven an otherwise dull gathering round the home fires. It was clear that the party must go by airplane.

The landing on a plain spotted with bottomless wells would be difficult enough, but the quick escape, if necessary, would be a feat for the most expert aviator. A landing at night obviously was out of the question.

Edith was elected pilot by the simple process of elimination. Who should be her helper? An active, practical man was needed for the job. Although Drake pleaded for the honor of carrying his scheme into effect, he was rejected on the first ballot. His forte was brains, not beef. Lane followed him on the second. It was between Ole and the Captain. Anderson being ignorant of aviation, Ole won the honor which only Drake coveted.

Having loaded the plane with all the bent pipe and weighted hose it could lift, Ole took his place behind Edith. They were off.

In all they made ten trips. Their work, they hoped, had converted a hundred and eight of the blowholes nearest the ruined crater into deadly engines of destruction. They had worked unmolested. The rookery either was asleep or all except the babies were away for the week-end foraging under the black smoke of the crater.

"Well, Drake," the Doctor asked, "have you the courage of your invention?"

"Absolutely. It would wipe out an army."

"That may be just the optimism of the inventor. What about it, Anderson? Do you feel like marching forward to await developments? Or shall we camp here until after the blow is over?"

"To stay here would be the sane thing, I suppose. Still, I want to see the show. I vote for marching."

"So do I. Unless we sit on him Drake of course won't miss seeing his idea in action. How about you, Ole?"

"Miss Lane and I will take care of the plane."

"All right, go ahead with our packs and wait for us on this side just before the beginning of the blowholes. If the reptiles see you before the blow, don't bother about our packs. Leave them and fly due east to confuse the brutes. Then they won't blunder into us."

Two hours after sundown Edith heard the far off crunching of the men's boots in the frozen snow.

"There they are," she said. "Ole, meet them and show them the way here."

A hot drink all round from the thermos bottles and a full meal cheered the tedium of the early watch. Deciding at eleven o'clock that the blowholes probably would not spout that night, all but the first watchman turned into their sleeping bags. The temperature being several degrees above zero they were quite comfortable.

In the brilliantly clear starlight the black barrier of the crater lip seemed ominously near. Yet, conscious as they were of what the rocks hid, all but the sentry slept like stones. The rookery also was fast asleep or numbed by the cold, for no drowsy squawks floated over the silence of no man's land.

It was the calm sleep before battle. Should Drake's strategy prove inadequate the attackers would not see the sunrise. If on the other hand Drake's invention was all that he hoped, those huge two legged reptiles would never again visit the black ruins of their shattered paradise. Their next gathering round the cheerful fires would be their last. They would die happy, poor brutes. Better one last hour of comfort and then oblivion forever, than the slow death of years of recurrent cold and increasing starvation. Left to themselves they might starve and fight and freeze and cling with all their brute instinct to life for half a century. It was more humane to destroy them outright.

Midnight passed without a tremor. Anderson relieved Lane. Two o'clock uneventfully came and went, and Drake relieved Anderson.

For the first half hour of Drake's watch all remained quiet with the stillness of a dead world. Then he became aware of a faint stirring among the infested rocks. Huge creatures not yet awake were moving uneasily in their sleep. Something had disturbed them.

In a few moments they might awake fully and scour the plain. For all Drake or the others knew the creatures might be nocturnal in their habits, prowling for their food only in the darkest hours of the early morning. He had not anticipated this. Should the monsters emerge before the blowholes spouted his stratagem was worthless. It took him but a second to make up his mind. He instantly roused the sleepers.

"Get out of here at once. They're coming."

Not stopping to argue, the men shook themselves together. They were still half-dazed by sleep. Drake's news falling on befogged brains completed their befuddlement. It did not occur to one of them that all five might easily climb onto the plane and reach safety in ten minutes. The unpractical Drake, being the only member of the party with all his wits, of course did not think of anything so simple and obvious.

"Take your father north ten miles, leave him, and come back for one of us," he ordered Edith. "Ole, crank up."

Ole was about to obey when a sleepy chorus of clattering squawks drifted over the ice of no man's land. It occurred to him that probably the reptiles had been away from home, foraging, while he and Edith were preparing the attack that afternoon. This, in Ole's opinion, accounted for their good luck.

"If I start the motor," he said in a hoarse whisper, "those brutes will hear it. In five minutes we shall be smothered."

"They are awake anyway," Drake whispered back. "If they come out they will see the plane against the snow."

Still hesitating Ole regarded Drake curiously in the dark.

"I can't see your face, String Bean," he said, still whispering hoarsely, "but I can guess its color. What are you going to do if those brutes race out before Miss Lane comes back to fetch you? She will take you next."

"Don't stand there whispering and shaking like a blasted jelly. Crank that motor! She could have been there and back by now."

"All right, General," Ole whispered. "One second. Now before I obey orders I'll tell you what I'm going to do next. The instant this propeller hums you'll see me making tracks for the nearest blowhole. If I beat the brutes to it, I dive. It won't be suicide because there is no way out. I had rather smash or drown in oil than die the other way. Take my tip and follow me. I've seen the brutes; you haven't. And I've had one race. Miss Lane will tell you about it in Heaven. I don't want another. All right, General, here goes."

He braced himself to spin the blades.

"Wait," Lane whispered tensely. "I felt it coming."

His more sensitive nervous system had detected the true cause of the reptiles' awakening. Scarcely breathing the others stood rigid in an agony of hoping. Did the ice sway beneath their feet ever so gently? Or was it merely the wish rocking their imaginations? Seconds passed without a recurrence of the sensation. Then, with infinite relief they heard, miles beneath them and far to the north, the faint, muffled buffeting of subterranean thunder. The jarring became unmistakable. In a moment the icebound plain was vibrating like a steel plate beneath the impact of a trip-hammer.

Half a mile to the south they heard the swish of air being sucked down the blowholes. Then while the ice heaved like a wave of the sea, they saw the black skyline of the ruined paradise boiling with gigantic shapes that inked out the low stars for an instant and vanished.

A moment later a thudding in the upper air announced the kindling of the innumerable flame cones, the ice for twenty miles around leapt into dull crimson, and they saw the whole herd of gigantic monsters racing with incredible speed directly toward them.

Ten minutes would decide whether Drake's invention meant victory or death. The flame cones descended, hovered a second in mid air, lengthened downward with a reverberant roar and became pillars of fire.

Once more the sociable monsters forgot the miseries of their frozen existence. Gathering round the comforting flames with ludicrous yet touching exclamations of delight they surrendered themselves to the gracious warmth. Around many of the roaring fires a dozen or more snuggled at a safe distance in rings of blissful enjoyment. Thawing rapidly in the fierce heat they licked their flanks, rolled over on their backs and pawed luxuriously at the warm air.

The sounds of their pleasure, the inarticulate noises of their gratitude, would have softened the most calloused heart to pity. There was an appeal in the playful antics of the colossal beasts that was irresistible. Huge tails that might have buckled steel plates in the full viciousness of their cut slapped harmlessly against lean sides whose ribs stuck out like the timbers of an unfinished hull. They were starving; yet for this hour they frolicked in the enjoyment of their other great need, heat.

Their slow brains neither speculated nor dreamed. When once more the flames vanished into the bowels of the earth they would crawl back to their frozen caves. Waking or sleeping they would remember nothing of their transient happiness. Only at the distant thunder of the next subterranean tide would their instincts urge them to break anew the iron spell of their misery. Without memory each pain was a miracle, each pleasure an accident without cause or consequence. Without consciousness of the past their future was a blank, their existence a void. With no pleasure remembered they could look forward to none.

They were damned with life. Would it not be a gentle act of mercy to bless them with death?

Watching their happiness the author of their destruction felt no regret. They would be killed painlessly at the high tide of their pleasure.

"Look," he said, pointing to a blowhole where four of the great lizards basked in the heat. "Those have it already."

They saw the four huge bodies roll over as if to sleep. The monsters shuffled on their sides and lay still, their great tails listlessly curved on the ice, and their long necks resting on one another's flanks.

One by one others of the friendly rings fell asleep. Then, in fifteen minutes, all were locked fast in death.

Still the cheerful flames thundered up undiminished. The late comers, the babies of the sleeping monsters, began to arrive. Hopping feebly they joined their mothers and nestled down in the genial glow. Soon they too were asleep forever.

Suddenly the air about the sleepers burst with a dull explosion into a sheet of fire. The instant flame lived but a second. Only the cheery fires rustled and glowed above the dead.

17   AT CLOSE QUARTERS

An hour before sunrise the ice again began to shake. They heard the returning subterranean wave bursting through the underground corridors. The pillared flames, struggling an instant, plunged down the blowholes. Only the morning star shed its chilly ray on the sleeping monsters, cold now as the barren ice they cumbered. Obliterating the very memory of their last happiness the passing wave, with a whistling reverberation, sucked down the warm air about the sleeping forms.

The party waited until two hours after sunrise before venturing among the dead. There remained one simple task before proceeding to the ruined paradise, lest on their return they meet the same fate as the monsters.

To save time the men loaded their packs before starting. On the previous afternoon Edith and Ole had transported four fifty-pound cases of dynamite from the caches on the south shore of the oil lake. Each of the men now loaded one of the fifty-pound cases on his back with his sleeping bag and enough food to last two days, or on short rations, four. In addition Ole packed a five-foot steel drill and a heavy sledge-hammer.

Edith was to have charge of the plane. A landing in the ruined crater being out of the question she was to circle above the men in their descent, mark their route, and watch until they emerged from the smoke. Should they not reappear by dark she was to fly to a safe place, camp, and return at daylight to watch for them. If they appeared she was to observe the easiest route up the rocks of the crater side, and by flying toward it, direct them. But if by noon they did not come out of the smoke she was to fly straight back to the ship and guide Bronson's search party.

The men planned to descend the crater only far enough to learn what they wished to know, Anderson and Ole whether oil was to be found, Lane and Drake the appearance of the black cement in situ.

Edith accompanied the men on foot to the blowholes. Threading their way between the huge carcasses the party methodically undid Ole's and Edith's work of the previous afternoon. There being no further use for the weighted hose and bent pipes they threw the sections down the blowholes. No echoes rose.

"How on earth did you ever think of it?" Anderson asked Drake as he heaved down the last bent pipe.

"As I told you," Drake answered modestly. "That siphon arrangement the dentist puts into your mouth to keep it dry while he works gave me the idea. If we could stick one leg of a pipe bent into a right angle down a blowhole, laying the other flush along the surface of the ice, some of the gas being forced up the hole would spray out over the surrounding ice. From watching those flames the first day we saw them I knew that the gas ignites only when it meets the air. The columns of gas caught at the top. The flame only travelled down the column as the upward pressure of the gas diminished. For this and other obvious reasons it was clear that the flames did not start down in the blow-holes, at least not until after the pressure had decreased markedly and the flames were about to be sucked down and extinguished. A considerable volume of gas therefore would be blown out through the pipes and hose over the ice before the flames descended low enough to ignite the mixture of air and gas near the surface.

"As for the rest, I trusted to nature. The gas, I knew from my school chemistry, must be rich in carbon monoxide. Now carbon monoxide is deadly in even minute quantities to all animal life. Less than a minute under that enormous pressure would suffice to spray out enough of the gas to asphyxiate an army of monsters. Long before it became rich enough in carbon monoxide to explode the mixture of gas and air would reach the point fatal to animal life. You saw what happened."

"The monsters probably did not actually die," Lane added, "until some time after the flash. The gas they had inhaled took some minutes to do its work thoroughly."

"Well," said Edith, sadly regarding the pathetic groups, "I am glad it was painless. They just fell asleep."

"I shouldn't have cried if they had kicked a bit," Ole remarked viciously.

"I'll never call you unpractical again," Edith said to Drake. "Merely in putting these poor things out of their misery you have justified your existence."

Drake shouldered his heavy pack and strode off after the others.

"Because a man prefers to use his head instead of his feet like a baboon," he flung back, "you call him unpractical.

You're as short-sighted as the pick and shovel men in the street."

"Now don't get a swelled head over your smartness," she called after him, "or you'll rise and burst like a toy balloon. Good-bye. I'll come and fetch you when you stub your toe."

The men fully realized the danger of their undertaking. Although they probably had exterminated one rookery of the huge monsters there must be hundreds more infesting the ruined crater. They accordingly chose a route down the steep side as nearly as possible in line with the destroyed rookery. The scramble down over the chaotic fragments of rock alone was no easy undertaking, nor was its safety increased by the two hundred pounds of dynamite which the men carried. A slip on the treacherous rocks might set off a private eruption. There was one comforting thought, however, which gave them courage. Should one of them stumble and explode his charge neither he nor the rest would ever know it.

By noon they had safely descended about a thousand feet. Another thousand feet would take them down to the rolling black billows. Already the reek of burning petroleum was acrid in their nostrils. Ole and the Captain, breathing deeply, filled their lungs with the odor of wealth.

"Here you are, Anderson," said the Doctor. "Strike the rock and see the oil gush forth." They were resting on a ledge of blocks at the base of a two hundred foot cliff in the face of the crater wall. On either side of the unbroken expanse of cement great void pockets and tunnels gaped in the shattered wall of what, before the explosion which destroyed it, had been a green paradise such as that of Edith's and Ole's discovery. The whole wall probably was honeycombed with galleries, tunnels and vast chambers which, until the eruption, had been sealed over by thick masses of cement. The explanation of these which Lane gave later is reasonable and probably correct.

"Where is my oil?" Anderson demanded.

"Almost anywhere behind those rocks if you go far enough, I should say. For some time past I have noticed indications. See that stain up there?" The Captain nodded. "That's oil. It is probably oozing along a fissure through the rocks. Find the other end of the fissure and you tap your first oil tank."

"But you said the other day that oil in this kind of rock—or cement—is impossible."

"And I meant it. Since then I have done some thinking. The oil is seeping through defects in the ruins of this artificial wall. I have good reasons for supposing that this wall was built ages ago partly to keep out the raw material that ultimately became oil."

"How thick is this cement?"

"I haven't the least idea. It may be a foot or a hundred miles. I should chance a shot if I were you."

The Captain was already busy with his dynamite.

"Better stand aside when you do," Lane advised. "The oil may shoot you into the middle of eternity."

Ole's steady swing soon drilled a hole for the stick of dynamite. He stood back on the ledge a few feet wiping the sweat from his face while Anderson placed the charge and laid out the three minute fuse. He moved forward to watch the Captain just in time. A fifty-ton block of the black cement hurtled down from the brow of the cliff, shot directly through the place where he had been standing, ricocheted on the lip of the ledge and shattered itself to bits all down the steep slope to the smoke.

"Who in hell did that?" Ole shouted, white with rage.

"Not guilty," said Drake, flattening himself against the wall just as the next huge missile crashed clear of the ledge. Smaller fragments showered down spattering the ledge with energetic chunks of cement that stung and bruised the would be dynamiters.

"I have a theory," the Doctor announced with a wry smile when the pelting finally ceased. "Pardon me, Ole, for taking it out of your mouth. There is something alive up there moving about and dislodging the loose blocks. Of course that first fifty-ton brick may have been very nicely balanced, needing only a slight push to send it over. The alternative is that our friend up there weighs two or three hundred tons. Take your choice."

"What shall we do?" Anderson asked, going white.

"Go ahead with our work. If the brute comes down after us we can crawl along the base of the cliff and get into one of those empty pockets. The ledge peters out nicely over there to the right. That beast, if it is the size I estimate, can't get a foothold on anything narrower than a city highway."

"Yes," said Drake, "and this ledge right here is just broad enough for the brute's rump. It will camp here for a week if necessary waiting for us to come out to dinner."

"Would you prefer to race it to the bottom? The smoke down there, I suspect, covers a multitude of prowlers feasting on the dead."

"It isn't so bad," the Captain said hopefully. "We can set off dynamite sticks to scare the brute away."

"Our popgun won't annoy it after the explosions it must have heard in the neighborhood of this exciting hole," Drake objected. "But your idea is good. Edith will hear our efforts and bring help."

"Dessert, you mean," Lane dryly corrected him. "Go ahead, Captain, touch it off. We might as well find out all there is to be known about the place if we've got to die in it."

"If I strike oil," the Captain grimly rejoined, "I'll sell stock to the devil himself."

He lit the fuse and followed the others to a safe place against the wall.

The explosion flaked off a thick slab of the cement, revealing a deep pocket, or possibly the entrance to a tunnel, similar to the others in the face of the cliff. Not a drop of oil issued.

"Sold." The Captain swore heartily.

They followed him to the hole. The entrance was just high enough for a tall man to walk through without bending his neck. Anderson entered. His feet raised a cloud of greenish gray dust.

"Empty," he said to those without.

He was about to continue his disgruntled observations when a cascade of rubble plunged over the top of the cliff. Not waiting for an invitation the others joined him in the dark pocket. Their haste raised the pungent, suffocating greenish gray dust in clouds.

"It's coming," said the Doctor. "Down the slope to the left as fast as its tonnage will let it. Our fireworks attracted its attention."

"I hope it slips and breaks its beastly neck," Drake remarked viciously.

"Oh," the Doctor replied, "since the big blow up here it probably has acquired a sure foot in scrambling about this hole. Most likely it does all its heavier feeding in Ole's tunnel restaurant, coming out here merely for exercise and lighter refreshments. We're just in time for lunch."

"I don't believe you give a damn whether you live or die," the Captain snapped.

"Except for Edith's sake I don't. I would give a great deal to see one of those brutes alive and at close quarters."

"You'll shake hands with it in five minutes."

"If it becomes too sociable I shall take a short cut out of my troubles. Fit up one of your sticks with a cap and give it about a ten-second fuse."

"Do you mean it?"

"Certainly. If I must die I see neither virtue nor courage in deliberately choosing a hideous death. I shall not kiss death till hell stares me in the face."

The Captain handed him the prepared stick of dynamite.

"If you go that way," he said, "the rest of us must follow, you know."

"Not necessarily. This pocket is almost a tunnel, I'm sure. It certainly is long enough for you to get your packs out of danger of detonation from my explosion."

"I'm for the shortcut," said Drake.

"So am I." It was Anderson.

"Then I must," said Ole. "In my case it won't be suicide. I do it against my will."

Unstrapping his pack he knelt down and prayed, silently. The others respectfully turned their backs, listening to the crash of falling rocks heralding the approach of the monster. Anderson began to grow nervous.

"We might as well go farther back," he suggested.

"All right," Lane replied. "You men leave your packs and go clear to the back of the cave. I'll take three sticks together so as to be sure of setting off the lot. It will be over before you know anything."

"What about you?"

"I'm going to see it. Don't be afraid. I shall take no chance of being caught before my time."

Ole rose from his knees. Their gigantic enemy, to judge by the sounds, was now lumbering its slow way along the ledge. Ole spoke.

"The Lord has answered."

"Let us hear what He said." The Captain was sarcastic. He disbelieved in Ole's private conversations with headquarters. "Most likely it will be your last message."

"That beast may be too big to get in through the hole."

"Then it will sit down outside and wait for us."

"I see your idea," Drake exclaimed. "When the brute squats we can tickle its rump and make it move on. Captain, fit up a punk with a three-minute fuse."

Anderson did the quickest job of his life. Fantastic visions of euthanasia vanished like the fumes of a sickly dream. The men once more were what nature intended them to be, resourceful, self-reliant, and instinctively determined to fight to the last breath.

"I'll never sneer at you again, Ole," the Captain promised solemnly. "You put guts into us. Take your dynamite clear to the back of the tunnel—mine too. Hurry! Drake, lug back yours and Lane's."

Drake and Ole rejoined the others just as the vast bulk of the monster blacked out the opening. Still lumbering stupidly forward it passed the entrance. Daylight again entering the pocket the four crept to the opening.

Lane peered out. The brainless monster had reached the end of its path. Further progress along the narrowing ledge being impossible the brute squatted. In its stupidity it had gone so far that now it could not turn with safety. A cat in a similar predicament would have backed instantly. Apparently the solution of its problem was beyond the monster's infinitesimal intelligence. It just squatted.

The Doctor was entranced. He saw only the creature's mountainous back, one enormous hind foot with its fifty-inch talons, and the gross, forty-foot tail tapering out to a blunt nub. But even this much with the close view of the monster's irregular ridge of fleshy humps and its blotched hide—it had no armor of horny scales, merely a thick skin like an elephant's—rotten with festering colonies of parasites, was a feast to the eyes. He longed to scrape off a specimen of those living diseases devouring the monster from the nub of its tail to the limit of visibility. And he did.

Emptying his tobacco box he stepped softly through the entrance. Going noiselessly up to the nearest patch of disease on the brute's tail he scraped it with the sharp edge of the open box. The huge beast gave no sign of feeling. Closing the box carefully Lane estimated the distance to the entrance to the cave. Then with all his force he kicked the sorest looking spot on the tail and bolted. He regained the cave just as the tail struck the cliff like a broadside from a battleship.

"Why the devil did you do that?" Anderson demanded. "Are you crazy?"

"We planned to make it move on, didn't we?" the Doctor asked innocently.

"Not that way. But for your damn foolishness we might have got out of here unnoticed."

"To tell the truth I wanted to see how long it would take a nervous impulse to travel the distance from the brute's tail to its head."

"Well, you saw, confound it. Now you've started the machinery. Go out and stop it."

"I have made a most interesting discovery," the Doctor rhapsodized. "Zoologists have long suspected that the biggest of the prehistoric monsters had two main nervous centres, one in the head, the other somewhere in the rear. One paleontologist of note even went so far as to assert that reptiles roughly like this one could reason simultaneously à priori and à posteriori. His theory is brilliantly confirmed. That brainless lout registered my kick in its tail. It would have taken a week to get the news up in its head."

"Oh blast your theories!"

The Captain had good grounds for his impatience. Lane's energetic kick had solved the monster's problem. The whole stupid mass was slowly backing. In a few moments the brute's brainless head would be opposite the entrance.

"Draw farther back," Lane advised. "It will probably want to look in. Sort of reverse reflex action, you know. Where the tail went the head will follow."

He was right. The last few yards of the bony neck passed, and the flat, reptilian head blocked the entrance. By tilting it sideways the monster managed to insinuate its head. The thirty-foot neck followed slowly, with ample leeway on either side of the entrance.

Just as they became aware of its heavy, slow breathing the monster saw them in the dim light. In a flash the lethargy of the brute vanished. The straining neck, lashing from side to side, cut the air like a whip. The whole vast bulk of the giant hurled itself furiously against the jarring cliff in an endeavor to follow the head.

Great flakes of the black cement crumbled from the rapidly widening entrance as the balked hunger of the monster rose to a screaming fury.

Its deafening screeches, like the shrilling of a herd of wild camels, shook the cave with a terrific din, and its panting breath raised the gray green dust in stifling clouds.

It was now or never. While Drake struck matches, Anderson rapidly but coolly prepared two more sticks of dynamite. Then, watching his chance, he lit all three fuses at once and deftly rolled the sticks over the floor of the cave so that one lay in the middle and one at either end of the arc threshed out by the huge serpent head. He overtook the others before they reached the end of the cave.

When the terrific thunder finally ceased, and the men realized that their two hundreds had not exploded, they stumbled back through the dark in a daze to the entrance. In their confusion they blundered directly into the headless stump of neck-gushing blood like a hydrant.

18 THE ENEMY

They blasted their way out. When the gory job was done they were scarlet from boots to hair. Crawling out under the smoking shoulders of the butchered giant they saw Edith circling dangerously near the rocks, risking herself and the plane in her eagerness to help should her chance come. They signalled that all was well, and she wheeled farther from the shattered wall.

During their long descent Edith had lost sight of the men among the huge blocks littering the sides of the crater. She rediscovered them a second after she observed the monster starting to back in response to her father's kick. With her binoculars she made out her father peering through the entrance to the cave. Until that moment she had not seen the monster. From her height it was as inconspicuous as an ant crawling about among the jumbled blocks. Unless one knew exactly where to look it was safe from detection.

Her feelings as she watched the gigantic brute trying to break its way into the cave may be imagined. The three muffled detonations in rapid succession, the third of which blew off the monster's head, reassured her. Someone's brain was still working in that cave. She saw the entire carcass of the brute bound from the ledge as if in astonished pain. Descending with a dead slap that echoed round the crater, the massive body struck the ledge, the enormous hind legs kicked convulsively, the powerful tail thrashed the flying blocks of cement, and with a last shudder from shoulder to rump the monster became still. The neck was not withdrawn. Guessing what had happened Edith sighed her thankfulness and stood by to help.

"Well," said Anderson, "is that a day's work? Does anyone want to go farther down?"

"Let us go down another hundred feet," Drake proposed. "So far we have passed only half a dozen blocks showing traces of inscriptions. I should like if possible to photograph one unbroken record. Ole has a pocket camera."

"Very well," the Captain agreed. "You and Ole keep in sight of this ledge while Lane and I take a look round the cave. There may be an ooze of oil at the back. Didn't you smell petroleum, Doctor, when we were waiting for that shot to go off?"

"I can't say that I did, but then I was so busy waiting. Drake, why don't you try that other unbroken bluff over to the left? If our theory is right you should find inscriptions, if anywhere, either on what was the surface of the cement before the explosion or on a concealed layer some inches deeper into the cement. If you can find an unbroken stretch you will have the revised version of the prehistoric fight. What we want is the original history. Look for a place where only a few inches of the outer surface have been flaked off by the explosion."

While Lane and Anderson explored the cave, Drake and Ole descended in quest of inscriptions. Edith hovered above the climbers like an anxious robin over her fledglings.

"That's for you," Ole remarked with a grin.

"Mind your own business," Drake snapped.

Reaching the unbroken cliff which Lane had pointed out they found it blank.

"There's another over there," Ole observed hopefully, indicating a smooth vertical expanse about a thousand yards to their left.

"Yes, but if we go there we shall be out of sight of the ledge."

"It's safe enough." He glanced up at the circling airplane. "Take my tip and don't let her see you running away."

With a muttered comment on Ole's meddlesome stupidity Drake started over the intervening blocks like an excited crab. His impetuosity was rewarded.

"Hurry up with your camera," he shouted. "This is just what we want."

They regretted keenly that Ole had not packed a hundred pounds of films instead of his dynamite. Five or six acres of cliff was covered with representations of monsters in every conceivable posture. Evidently this was a record of importance.

Both strata of inscriptions were represented on the cliff. In several places the impact of the bombarding blocks from the eruption had flaked off great scales from the outer layer of cement, baring the original inscriptions. The unscarred surface bore the revised version. After deliberating they decided to photograph the entire cliff in three dozen sections—the limit of Ole's films. This seemed better than concentrating on individual inscriptions. Drake hoped from enlargement of the three dozen pictures to obtain a complete record of everything on the cliff.

Anderson and Lane meanwhile were busy in the cave. To the Captain's disappointment they found no trace of oil.

"You have that lake beyond the blowholes," Lane expostulated. "Isn't that enough?"

"No. I want to endow a school of whales."

"For that rotten pun you deserve to lose everything from your shirt to your soul. Let us get into the fresh air. This vile dust is choking me."

"It has a mouldy smell, hasn't it?"

"You're right," the Doctor agreed. "I wonder what it is." His interest was aroused.

"Take some out to the daylight and see. These matches were made by the devil only to burn my fingers."

Lane scooped up a double handful of the dust and hurried to the entrance.

"Spores," he announced excitedly.

Although he did not recognize it he had met the enemy.

"I'm no wiser," the Captain remarked.

"These are masses of seeds from some fernlike plant. Lord! I wish I had a microscope. Haven't you ever seen the underside of a fern frond?" The Captain nodded. "Well, all that brown stuff on it is millions of fern seeds finer than dust."

"But this stuff is grayish green."

"That makes it all the more interesting. These are the spores, the life germs, of some unknown plant. I am sure of it. We must take back all we can carry. Cram your pockets."

Lane dived into the cave and set the example. Reluctantly enough Anderson followed suit.

"Over by the wall where we haven't trampled the stuff should be a good place," Lane continued. "Sift it through your fingers and save anything not finer than dust."

Presently Lane rose to his feet with an exclamation of delight.

"Look what I've found!"

Anderson followed him to the light. The Doctor was lost in the contemplation of a tiny desiccated frond of some plant that resembled a fern yet most decidedly was not a fern. The dried foliage, more like a rank mould than a decent plant, was of hair-like fineness.

"Where have I seen something like this before?" Lane muttered to himself. "It was alive. Where the deuce was it?"

"In Heaven, before you were born," the Captain suggested. He also was an admirer of Maeterlinck, having read Ole's bedraggled *Bluebird*.

"Rot," said the Doctor. He was not an admirer of the romantic Belgian. "But your suggestion, by the law that action and reaction are equal and opposite, recalls the place where I did see this plant growing. It was next door to hell."

"San Francisco?" the Captain hazarded.

"No. On that beach of monsters. Ole blew the stomach out of one and in the process ripped the lining. Some of this plant, as fresh as newly cut lettuce, dropped out of the rent. I remember now. We planned to collect some on our way back to the ship. When we returned we were too heavily loaded to take on more. Also it was getting dark.

So we had to leave it till next day. By morning the oil and slush oozing into the hole in the ice where the plant lay had made soup of everything. Well, this more than makes up for our loss. I shall have a chance to settle whether life remains dormant under the right conditions, practically indefinitely."

"Ah, your theory of immortal whales?"

"The laugh will be on you when I make this greenish dust grow. The chances are infinity to nothing that the living plant disappeared from the earth millions of years ago."

Lane was wrong in his first statement. Less than twenty-four hours later he found that the laugh was on him. And a nasty, sardonic laugh it was at that. He spoke from insufficient knowledge.

Between them he and Drake had reconstructed the history of the perished race whose records the rigors of the Antarctic solitudes had preserved unviolated. Drake as decipherer, and Lane as scientist, working together imagined themselves in possession of all the essential details of the catastrophe which had swept intelligence from the Earth when the poles were regions of perpetual summer. In the light of what happened less than twenty-four hours after Lane's discovery of the greenish spores, neither he nor Drake is now willing to claim finality for their conclusions. Before the struggle in which they all but perished, both were confident of their theory. It explained all the facts in their possession and it was rational.

Their desperate fight for life showed them that they had not visualized one half of the truth. What they had guessed was the obvious part. Their failure to reconstruct a single less obvious detail has taught them modesty. Neither Drake nor Lane will now admit that he knows more than a small fraction of that obliterated history.

Lane moreover for the present is disinclined to speculate on the obscure science behind the history. He prefers to leave fundamental theories and explanations to Ole. And it may be said in passing that Ole's most ambitious theory has already attracted numerous followers. His fame, however, is rather mixed. His following is as large as Lane's is select. For the notorious conservatism of professional scientists holds them back in following Ole in regions where the more adventurous layman rushes in whooping.

Lane had been so absorbed in his greenish spores that he failed to note the disappearance of Ole and Drake. They came into sight just as Anderson began to swear. Joining the others they voted it a day's work, firmly strapped on their packs, and started up the thousand foot scramble to the skyline. Topping it shortly before sunset they marched fast and reached the site of their last night's camp before dusk. Edith joined them presently.

"Shall we camp here?" she asked.

"We might as well," Anderson replied. "It is convenient to the crater. Have you any reason for wishing to go farther back toward the oil lake?"

"Perhaps not. You can decide best. The wind seems to be rising. Up on the three thousand foot level it is blowing half a gale—thirty miles an hour from the north. Camped here in the open we shall have trouble with the plane if the current descends during the night."

"There is only a four or five mile breeze blowing from the southeast down here at present," the Captain pointed out. "So far as I can see the weather is exactly what it has been the past nine days."

"All right. If you are satisfied I am. Only I thought if there is any danger of the wind rising in the night it would be easier to manage the plane in the shelter of the south bank of the oil lake."

"There is no danger, I am sure. This breeze won't go to more than six miles an hour at any time during the night. Your speaking of the lake reminds me of something. Will you take Ole and fly to the cache on the south shore for more matches? He can dig them out."

"Of course. We shall be back in half an hour."

"And while you are there," her father begged, "dig up some sort of a tin can for me. Bring one with a lid. I want to pack these precious spores safely away."

"Very well. I shall bring a fresh tin of ship bread and we can have a real feast. I know how to make a heavenly hoosh with hardtack and corned beef. You may have the tin."

"And the rest of you the stew, I suppose?"

"If you go shares on your blessed spores," she laughed, "we'll do likewise on the banquet."

When she returned Anderson thankfully emptied his pockets of the greenish gray mess.

"Be careful," Lane admonished, hopping about excitedly on the frozen snow. "You're losing half of the stuff. The breeze carries it off like smoke."

The Captain did indeed lose about a pound and three-quarters. Finally turning his pockets inside out he gave them a thorough dusting in the breeze. Although Lane was more careful he also lost half a pound to the wind.

"Well," he said, "I have enough anyway." He slapped down the lid. "With this I should be able to prove whether or not the life principle can remain indefinitely in abeyance."

"The great Swedish chemist Arrhenius almost says it can," Ole informed them. "He has a theory that life originates on planets by the life seeds from another planet. The seeds drift across empty spaces for ages till they strike a planet cool enough for life. When the life seeds drift too close to the sun or some other star the heat destroys them."

Lane received Arrhenius' famous theory with the silence of disrespect. He was already familiar with it as a speculation of the well known physicists Tait and Stewart. To him it had always been the example par excellence of the incompetence of the average scientist to reason straight about another man's specialty. The Captain thought he saw the point.

"The hen and the egg over again, isn't it? What starts life on the first planet? How do your precious life seeds begin in the first place?"

"They're not mine," Ole retorted indignantly. "Arrhenius invented them. The life came to the first planet from another planet."

"Exactly," the Captain sneered. "And when the chain is complete you have perpetual motion. Go and patent it."

The dispute becoming personal, the pacific Drake intervened.

"Both of you are right. Ole can't be held responsible for any foolishness but his own. Nor can you, Captain, be blamed for criticizing a scientific theory. The ones that I have looked into are all like that. They assume the egg in order to produce the hen to explain the egg."

"And you," the Doctor hotly interposed, "being a bat-eyed archæologist, are a competent critic of science. You may be able to read prehistoric picture books but you couldn't tell the difference between evolution and relativity. Just because you mess about with fossilized opinions you set yourself up as a judge of modern science."

"Not at all," Drake retorted. "I only say that my training in antiquities enables me to tell fresh eggs from Chinese. And if Arrhenius' perpetual motion theory of the origin of life isn't a scientific bad egg I have no nose. One doesn't need a brain to test things as far gone as that."

"Now you two," said Edith, giving each of them a shake, "eat your hoosh before it freezes. You can fight afterwards."

"We won't want to," Drake grinned, "with a gallon of food under our belts."

"True," the Doctor agreed. "If those poor monsters over there had been properly fed they might have made great pets. The struggle for subsistence ruined their tempers."

"I wonder if the blowholes will perform tonight?" Edith asked.

"No," Ole confidently asserted. "By my theory they should not go off till early tomorrow forenoon."

"Your theory be blowed," the Captain growled. He was jealous. "You're always theorizing and always wrong."

But Ole was right. There was no flareup till nine o'clock the next morning.

19 ATTACKED

After the meal they luxuriously crawled into their warm sleeping bags and lay talking for an hour. Having exterminated the adjacent rookery of monsters they saw no necessity for setting a watch. The chances of any adventurous prowlers from the interior of the crater foraging the icy wilderness were negligible.

They decided to have a good night's sleep and be fresh in the morning for a deeper descent into the crater, The day following Edith had reserved to take her father to the unruined paradise which she and Ole had discovered. The others were to march to the oil lake and wait there for Edith to take them across. They were then to return to the ship for a second attempt to reach the black barrier of Anderson's first objective. Although they had not yet devised a means for traversing the dangerous trough of blowholes which they had blundered on in their first expedition, nevertheless they felt confident that necessity would stimulate their inventiveness to a safe plan.

Anderson was more determined than ever to reach his first goal. There was no doubt that the black rock barrier beyond the trough was the wall of another vast ruined paradise. Therefore, he argued, there must be oil in its vicinity. What was true of one hole in the ice, he said, must be true of another just like it. Lane had considerably modified his veto of the possibility of finding oil in such a formation. And the deciding factor in his change of opinion was his discovery that the black cement was not of natural origin.

"What do you make of it all, Lane?" the Captain asked from his sleeping bag.

"I told you the other day. We have discovered the final product of an intelligence that vanished from the earth before America was a continent. That intelligence, I believe, either deliberately or accidentally solved the problem of life. For some reasons I think it more probable that the initial discovery was a blunder.

"The authors of the mistake were impotent to control it. Everything we have discovered points to their inability to direct their creation. As I said the other day they realized what they had done only when it was too late, foresaw its probable consequences, and destroyed their entire civilization in the attempt to nullify their blunder. That they failed to carry out their destructive purpose completely is self-evident. Had they succeeded not one of those dead monsters over there would ever have come into existence."

"If they knew enough to create life," Ole objected, "they must have known how to destroy it."

"Not necessarily. An idiot with a test tube of the right sort of germs might start a plague that not all the doctors of the world could control. And so with this thing. The minute specks of living matter which they created—I am assuming the process for the sake of illustration only— multiplied like bacteria. Now what is the last remedy for a plague infested village? Why, to burn it to the ground. So possibly those rash experimenters learned. But the seeds of life—again I am merely guessing—had been scattered broadcast over the country by the winds.

"What was to be done? Fire the whole country? That would have been useless. For it is impossible to bake the soil over thousands of square miles to a depth of several feet. I am assuming from tangible evidence that the plague of life had passed so far beyond control that the very soil was impregnated with its germs.

"What would they do? What could they do but seal every mile of the infected soil? No air must reach the life spores. Light must be excluded. They systematically set about burying the fertility of their continent under millions of tons of air tight cement."

"But why should they bring slow starvation on themselves," Edith objected, "if, as you say, they had not created any dangerous animals to prey on them, but only the merest beginnings of life?"

"For one very good reason, my darling angel child. We may assume that their intelligence was higher than ours. Otherwise they could not have created life. Knowing enough even to blunder onto the secret of life they certainly would be competent to decide whether their creation was in line with orderly, normal evolution. Finding that their artificial life spores all were but the potential ancestors of abominations to be evolved to maturity millions of years in the future, they looked forward to the probable state of the world as a result of their mistake. They foresaw hell on earth.

"There was no immediate danger. There was not even the possibility of slight discomfort for millions upon millions of years. But there was the absolute certainty at the end of ages of a world that a decent beast wouldn't live in. They weighed one against the other—the certainty of continued happiness for their race for a few million years longer against the equal certainty of hell on earth forever thereafter. And they decided that their protracted happiness, even their continued existence, was not worth its deferred cost.

"I have said that they were intelligent. The deliberate sacrifice of their own happiness for a future that would never dream of their existence, proves my assertion. It is your stupid man who has the soul of a hog. Drake, you go on."

"Let me first knock the stuffing out of one of Ole's numerous theories," Drake began. "Then I can go on where the Doctor stopped. Ole maintains that the intelligent beings—I won't call them human, for they were too unselfish to deserve the epithet—who depicted all those acres of fantastic monsters actually saw the creatures whose outlines they pressed into the wet cement. He contends that the artists drew from living models. That I flatly deny. I admit that they saw the models which inspired them. But they saw with the mind's eye only. Lane, I believe, is right. They actually created nothing more terrifying to behold than tiny specks of jelly."

"You must prove your theory," Ole exploded, rising bodily in his sleeping bag to defend his offspring.

"It proved itself the first time I saw your precious photographs. Of all those thousands of different monsters represented in your pictures, not one was in a posture that by any stretch of the imagination could be called natural. Every last one of them is drawn in some grotesque attitude that would set an Apache artist's teeth on edge. There has been a deliberate and successful attempt to make each posture unnatural in at least one detail. The variations are not mere conventions. They are systematic, infinitely various, and exceedingly ingenious.

"That gave me my first clue. Whatever race designed those inscriptions had done its best to convey the information that the beasts were in a definite sense, imaginary. They were not imaginary in the sense that a fire breathing dragon is fictitious. By the help of half a ton of books I learned that such creatures were not flesh and bone impossibilities. They might have come into being if natural evolution had started from different beginnings. Lane helped me a lot on this. My own first guess was merely a jump in the dark.

"Being ideal representations of non-existent but possible creatures, what could they signify? The answer was immediate: the results of an elaborate scientific prophecy.

"Even I, unscientific antiquarian as I am, have heard of those astronomers who predicted the exact spot in the heavens in which a planet—Neptune—that no human eye had ever seen, would be found at a definite time on a certain night. And in spite of Lane's harsh estimate of my scientific incompetence, I have also admired that splendid discovery by the Scotch mathematician who foresaw from his equations our wireless waves and described their behavior a generation before wireless became practical.

"Knowing these antiquarian scraps of scientific history I let my imagination loose. If it is possible for us to predict unseen planets and foretell in detail great scientific advances, why should not a more intelligent race beat us at our own game? We predict only physical things. Why shouldn't Lane, if he had brains enough, predict the future course of a hen's life from an examination of the unhatched egg?"

"No reason at all," Lane laughed. "Some day they will do better than that. You should let your imagination go."

"It might never come back to earth if I let loose altogether. Well, I made my working guess. I supposed that the authors of those inscriptions were predicting the distant evolution of some form of life. Taking that as a foundation I tried what I could build.

"You remember my remarking the entire absence of human figures from the inscriptions. Not one of those thousands of creatures represented could by any flight of the imagination be considered above brute intelligence. The artists had taken great trouble to depict in each instance a savage, almost brainless stupidity.

"Now I had also noticed immediately the vivid and lifelike pictograms of sanguinary battles. Putting these two facts together, the total absence of all higher intelligence and the repeated depiction of terrible conflicts, I reached what seemed an obvious conclusion.

"The authors of the inscriptions, I inferred, were predicting their own annihilation by an enemy as yet not fully created. Further they predicted the subsequent reign of brutal anarchy and unintelligence. The inscriptions were a forecast of what was to happen in the course of evolution. Intelligence, they predicted, was to disappear from the earth. Brute force, nature gone mad, and a chaos of living things were to rule in the place of dethroned order.

"So much for the prophecy. Now for the recorded history. Almost at the first glance I recognized that two distinct periods of art, separated by a vast interval of time, were represented in the inscriptions. Between the earlier and the later the technique of pictorial design had changed fundamentally. The art of both periods is developed almost to perfection. Nevertheless, ages separate the two schools, and they belong to the same race. I need not bore you with the evidence. It is of the same sort as that which enables archæologists to say at a glance whether a sculpture is Greek or Egyptian and further to fix its date relatively to some standard object.

"Notice now the extraordinary and significant detail. The two periods of art, although widely separated in time, were of equal brilliance. During the ages between the first and second there had been no decline. We have no parallel to this in recorded history. A few centuries, or at most two or three thousand years, sees the rise to approximate perfection and the sure descent to mediocrity.

"This fact puzzled me more than all the other difficulties together, and it still is baffling although to a lesser degree. I was totally unable to decide which inscriptions were the earlier. The inscriptions of both periods depicted struggles and, so far as I could see for a long time, struggles of almost identical character. What was the obvious conclusion? The earlier inscriptions prophesied the ghastly conflict, the later recorded its occurrence. I became convinced that the forgotten race early foresaw its extinction in the shadowy future, lived for ages in undiminished vigor anticipating destruction, and finally was overwhelmed in the height of its power, surviving only long enough to leave a record of impending and absolute defeat.

"I then tried on this hypothesis to decide which set of inscriptions was the earlier. The net result was nil. Either the problem was beyond me or I had gone stale.

"The intense scrutiny was not however a dead waste. A suspicion which had long been germinating in my subconscious mind struggled up to certainty. One set of inscriptions undoubtedly and possibly the other also, was in cipher. The actual conflict depicted was merely the symbol of a deeper war. It was not beast against beast, but beast against intelligence. Unmistakably the battles of one set of inscriptions were symbols of a conflict that was not material. What then could have been its nature?

"By a process of exclusion I decided that the only rational guess was a struggle against natural laws. The conflict was not material; it could not be against spirits. It therefore most probably was intellect against brute nature, the endless struggle of intelligence to be master of itself and creator of its own fate. The symbolic set of inscriptions, I decided, must record the struggles of the long extinct race to subdue nature. In short the inscription must be a summary of the more important scientific discoveries and technical achievements of the race.

"The next question was, why should they wish to conceal their scientific knowledge? My answer was immediate. It was also, I am now convinced, inadequate. The scientific knowledge of the race, I reasoned, must have been entrusted to a particular cult whose business it was to increase and apply the store of wisdom. To prevent disasters this cult by means of hieroglyphics and symbolic language would conceal from the uninitiated all dangerous discoveries. Only a history of the severe struggle to master the secrets of life and the material universe would be recorded, so that later generations of seekers should not repeat the experiments and encounter the same dangers.

"It was now natural to ascribe the purely symbolic, or scientific, writings to the earlier period. The later inscriptions I took to be a record of the destruction of the race by the creations of its own science. The ruin which their scientists early predicted overtook them, and the perishing race left a warning to intelligent life, should such ever again inhabit the world, not to repeat the uncontrollable blunder which had destroyed its first perpetrators.

"This hypothesis received a startling confirmation when we discovered that lump of black cement with the embedded inscriptions. The interior inscriptions, those which had been cemented over, belonged to what I had decided was the earlier period; those on the face of the fragment to the latter. Evidently the attempt at concealment had been much more thorough than I dreamed. The race not only disguised their dangerous scientific knowledge in ambiguous symbolism; it actually buried the obnoxious wisdom beneath several inches of a cement as hard as diamond.

"What could have driven them to such drastic caution? Only the desperate determination to obliterate the last traces of their scientific knowledge. And why? Because in the final conflict they had found its consequences terrible beyond belief.

"As to the nature of their dangerous knowledge and the aspect of the monstrous catastrophe which it engendered, I can only follow Lane in his speculations. That race blundered onto the secret of life. Creating it, they fashioned the seeds of abominations. This they realized. And they foresaw that with the lapse of ages evolution would breed from their beginnings, innocuous enough at the time and for millions of years to come, a swarming, uncontrollable multitude of monstrosities without intelligence.

"Lane has outlined their probable motives in choosing for themselves wholesale destruction. Until we shall have spent several years on the inscriptions we can venture no theory as to how they created life."

"I have a theory!" Ole exploded. He had been suffering for twenty minutes.

"Pipe down," the Captain ordered. "Lane, how do you account for all those dead monsters over there by the blowholes? And for the thousands on the beach, to say nothing of the half million I saw boiling up from the bottom of the ocean?"

"Easily. Those originators of life destroyed their creation, I pointed out, by burying the fertile soil of their continent under millions of tons of air-tight cement. A job like that takes time. The longer they worked at it the slower became their rate of progress. And for a very simple reason. As the cemented region grew the food supply diminished. They took care, of course, to cement over the most dangerous places first, leaving the lighter work for the last few survivors of the race.

"Now where did they get the rock and other material for making their untold millions of tons of the hardest cement?"

"Out of the ground, of course. Mines."

"Exactly. That crater we were in today is the ruin of one of their mines. The vast circular depression that Ole and Edith visited is another. It fortunately is still undestroyed. That black barrier you are so determined to explore is the ruined floor of another, heaved up by the explosion of vast quantities of oil and natural gas. How many more there may be dotted about this frozen continent I hope some day to discover.

"Well, as I see it, they mined out those enormous holes to get material for their cement. The execution of so vast a project as theirs demanded the highest intelligence and extraordinary engineering skill. I suspect that they sunk those pits so deep in order to utilize the internal heat of the earth. In their day, millions of years ago, the heat at comparatively shallow depths must have been much greater than it is today in our deepest mines. For the same purpose, and also perhaps in the search for rarer minerals required in making their time-outlasting cement, they drove enormous tunnels, galleries and vast pockets far into the rocks at every stage of their work. We have heard the tides of oil and water surging along them under our feet.

"Now for your animals. The race in its prime having cemented all the most dangerous regions, the diminishing survivors had only to complete the project by cementing the easier places. Their task was to seal the mines and subterranean chambers. The mines are these vast holes in this forsaken wilderness. The one we explored this morning certainly has been plastered with cement. They did a thorough job. That black wall must have been yards thick before the gas explosion blew the whole interior to bits.

"The first engineers, foreseeing that the last survivors must perish of starvation before the completion of their work, took the precaution of making the sides of their mines perpendicular. It was extremely improbable that every square yard of the floors, walls and roofs of the open mines and subterranean galleries would be safely cemented over before the last worker perished. Hundreds, perhaps thousands, of acres of free soil would be left exposed to the light, air and moisture. The dangerous life seeds polluting these extensive uncemented areas would live and develop, and with the lapse of ages evolve into abominations. That is why they made those pits, three miles deep, with perpendicular walls as smooth as glass. Whatever bred in those mines and galleries would live and die there. Soil and heat alike eventually becoming exhausted, the last vestiges of life in the mines and tunnels would perish. We happen to have arrived before the natural end, which may not come for millions of years yet.

"Why don't we find the mighty engines which those great workers must have used? Those which they left exposed to the air were rust a million years ago. Stone will outlast iron, and this cement, hard as diamond, would outlast the finest steel. As for such of their machines as they used in their tunnels and caves, I confidently expect to find traces, perhaps even one or two complete engines. For I intend to explore thoroughly every mile of those subterranean galleries from here to the South Pole if necessary, and from there to far under the floor of the Antarctic ocean.

"I am convinced that the agelong action of heat and water has slowly widened the tunnels and extended them far out under the ocean. The roof of one of these, weakening under the same course, gave way, letting in the ocean. You saw the backwash of oil and dead beasts blown up by the steam when the returning wave burst through to the subterranean fires. The monsters, I suspect, came from another such paradise as the one Ole and Edith discovered. I shouldn't wonder if it turned out to be the one you are set on visiting.

"I have also a theory, as Ole might say, concerning the origin of your oil. These monsters have been living, evolving, multiplying and dying in the galleries and uncemented mines for millions of years, literally for ages of geologic time. Their constantly decomposing carcasses are responsible for the lakes and oceans of oil which, I feel confident, swing their black tides deep down under this polar ice cap.

"Now, one last thing, and I shall have done. We've been talking an hour and it's time we all went to sleep. I am willing to bet my specimens, including the incomparable devil chick, against your oil lake, that when we visit the unruined mine the day after tomorrow, Edith and I shan't find a single inscription on its walls. No other pit besides the one we explored today, I am convinced, will show the trace of an inscription. One record, the authors of the inscriptions rightly surmised, would be sufficient. So why waste their labor in leaving a score? The first record, the one which they later cemented over, was inscribed near the beginning of their gigantic labor. They were just about to cement over the walls of the first vast mine, now grown so unwieldy as to be unmanageable. They decided to leave a record of the harsh science which was driving them to suicide.

"Accordingly, as they worked, they pressed into the unset cement the secret symbolism of their fatal discoveries. This record they intended as a warning to their successors should intelligence ever again visit the earth. Thousands of years later, still toiling at their stupendous task, they realized fully its crushing magnitude and the horror of the doom which they labored to nullify. While their own end still was thousands of years in the future they decided to obliterate forever the record of the knowledge which had driven their race down the long, slow way to death. Returning to their first mine they cemented over the dangerous science which was their ruin. Now let us go to sleep."

"Not yet," Ole expostulated. "You have no theory of how they created life. Your science comes to a dead halt. Now I have a theory—"

"Shut up, Ole!" the Captain roared. "We want to sleep."

"Shut up yourself!" Ole bellowed, struggling to his feet, sleeping bag and all. "It is always 'shut up Ole.' The rest of you gab all day and rave all night. I never get a chance to say anything. Now you are going to listen to me and learn something for once. I have a theory," he shouted, "and you've got to accept it because it is common-sense and the only true theory of life." They were sound asleep already.

Ole however was not to be balked. He talked to the bags and, having delivered himself, joined his audience in slumber.

Edith was the first to awake. She first noticed an oppressive warmth. Not yet fully aroused she turned over on her side for a last nap. The sense of discomfort increased. Her hair, she imagined, had fallen over her face as she turned. Some strands evidently had got into her mouth.

Still lazy, she tried to eject the supposed hair with her tongue. Failing, she used her fingers. The suspected hair having an unusual feel she held it before her eyes for examination. In the semi-darkness she saw that it was green. Startled, she looked more attentively. What she saw was a mass of fern-like foliage of hair-like fineness.

It was the enemy.

20 DESPERATE

Edith's cries brought the others, unable to get out of their sleeping bags, struggling to their feet. The mouths of the bags were choked with thick masses of the hair-like vegetation.

Freeing their heads from the entangling meshes they stared out over a dense, matted jungle of green hair five feet high. To the south numerous vivid mounds marked the thickly overgrown carcasses of the asphyxiated monsters. To the north stretched a dense mat of impenetrable vegetation disappearing in a dark green cloud on the horizon.

A hundred yards beyond the mounded monsters the tangled green mass ended abruptly, save for a single band a hundred yards broad reaching to the base of the black rocks. There the band stopped. It marked the course which the men had taken across the ice on their return from the crater.

Were their ears deceived? They stood motionless, five blunted pillars festooned with great streamers and wreaths of the rank, fungus like green weed, listening in fear to the rustling crepitation. The whole mass was growing audibly.

Then they noticed a deep green discoloration of the ice on the west side of the broad band between the blowholes and the rocks. The edges of the band were not sharp, like the edge of a cornfield. The green mass, tapering down at the boundaries, merged with the ice and snow. That green tinge on the ice far beyond the limit of growing vegetation was the dust of innumerable spores blown from the living plants by the East wind which rose with the dawn.

Attempting to move they found themselves bound from feet to armpits by living ropes woven from thousands of growing, hairlike strands. They fully realized their desperate situation only when Edith with a frightened cry called attention to the airplane. It had disappeared beneath a tangled mound of green ropes. Even if they could extricate the machine it would be impossible to rise. That matted vegetation would stop a thousand horsepower tractor in less than a hundred yards.

"It is those infernal spores," the Doctor said quietly. "See how our track from the rocks to the blowholes is marked by the filthy weeds. All that started from the dust Anderson and I shed from our boots and our clothes as we marched. The sea of green rope between us and the horizon grew up in the night from the spores we lost to the wind. Evidently this stuff grows very slowly at first, then like a fire, or we should have noticed it before we went to sleep. So much for theory. Has anyone a plan for getting out of this? Don't get panicky. Take your time."

"We might try to break our way through to the clean ice east of the band," the Captain suggested, "and march round the stuff."

"Not much chance of beating it to the ship, I'm afraid. Still, that's one plan. Any more?"

There was no response.

"Well," said Lane, "I suppose it is forward march. Not that I am particularly anxious to return to civilization with this blunder on my head. My stupidity has let loose one of the enemies which that forgotten race gave its life to chain. Having done the asinine thing I now see how it could have been avoided. Evidently these spores require cold and moisture in order to grow like this. Possibly a low temperature actually forces the growth beyond all nature. In the dry, warm pockets in the cement, sealed from light and moisture, the spores would lie dormant indefinitely.

"Probably what we found is the mass of spores from a growth which started from a few dusted off the bodies of the last workers. When the vegetation had exhausted the soil and moisture in the pocket it ceased to grow. In the warmth, I imagine, the growth was slow and natural. The spores have retained their life all these millions of years, waiting for a fool like me to broadcast them over the ideal medium for their luxuriant growth and propagation. Did those dead workers foresee the ice ages ahead? Did they seal the caves against the escape of this fiend to its stimulating cold? I don't know. Such is my theory, and it is my last. Which way, Anderson?"

"Head northeast. Ole, you're the strongest. Go first till you give in. We must head off the stuff before it grows over that bay against the rocks to the left. Then we can climb along the rocks and beat it to the east—if we can. It is an inch higher than it was when we began talking."

Ole made about twenty feet. Panting and sweating he stopped for breath. He made another two feet and collapsed in the green slush.

"All right, Ole," the Captain said, taking his place. "Fall behind while I have a go."

Anderson gave out at the third yard.

"Drake, you're next."

Drake made less than a yard. Lane followed with a yard and a half. Edith shoved. And so it went until complete exhaustion overtook them less than a hundred feet from their starting place. By now the green mass grew high above their heads when they stood erect.

"I can do no more," Anderson panted. "We might as well give up."

Saying nothing they flung themselves down on the green mess they had trampled. Presently Edith got to her feet and beckoned to Drake. He followed her back along the green tunnel. The hair-like mass at the farther end was already a foot high. This was a second growth springing rankly up from the trampled slush of the first.

"I wish you to know," Edith began when they reached the end, "that I have always loved you. We shall not get out of here. I feel no shame in telling you."

"Why didn't you tell me before," he said, touched to the heart. "I never knew you cared that way for me, although I hoped that some day you might, darling. We shall die here. Let us forget the past and not think of the cold eternity before us. The present is enough."

And they spent their priceless moments as only lovers know how. Death might strangle them before night, certainly before morning. These few moments were their eternity.

Years later, it seemed to them, they heard someone ripping through the young growth in the tunnel. It was Ole.

"The Doctor sent me to fetch some grub," he apologized guiltily.

Edith's heart gave a great leap. While there is appetite there is hope. Her father's head had started working again.

"Come on," she said to Drake, "we shall be married after all."

They found Lane and the Captain sitting in silence. Anderson's face was expressionless. The Doctor glanced up at Edith's happy face, and a spasm of pain contracted his own. For he had sent Ole to fetch, not food, but a hundred pounds of dynamite. He had hoped to end the misery of all of them painlessly and instantaneously without Edith's foreknowledge.

"Have you thought of a way out?" she asked hopefully.

"Yes," he said. "But seeing you I haven't the courage to take it."

She guessed.

"John and I," she said, laying her hand on Drake's arm, "will go back again to the end of the tunnel where you can't see us. I'm not afraid."

"But I am," he said.

She stood looking down at him, all the love and affection of her past happy life in her eyes.

"You needn't be afraid. I never was frightened of the dark."

Ole joined them, dragging his mossgrown pack. Anderson glared at him.

"Why didn't you do it back there instead of coming here to scare the girl to death?"

"I'm not going to do it. You are. Suicide and murder are against my religion."

"Blowing you to hell is the only good thing about this whole business. Hand me a cap and cut off a three-inch fuse."

In spite of himself Ole began to fumble. His half-frozen fingers refused to pick out the cap. Then searching for his knife to cut the fuse he remembered what had become of it. He looked at Edith.

"You couldn't fetch my knife, could you?"

"No, stupid," she laughed. "How could I fly back to the tunnel?"

"Here," the Captain exclaimed, impatiently brushing him aside, "I'll do it if you haven't brains enough to use your teeth."

Drawing out his knife he opened the blade and gave Ole a sour look.

"I've a good mind to cut your fat throat," he said. "They can't hang me."

"Then you will go to hell for sure," Ole asserted with certain confidence.

Working in silence Anderson methodically set about his business. Lane still sat in the green slush, trying not to think of Edith. Presently he rose to his feet.

"The blowholes will spout in a moment," he said. "I just felt the suspicion of a tremor."

Involuntarily Anderson paused in his work.

"You're right. Well, we shall add to the general celebration in a minute or two."

The violent shaking began and ended with unexpected suddenness, throwing them down in the slush. A dull thudding in the air announced the kindling of the flame cones.

"Gas, oil!" Lane shouted.

In his excitement he was incapable of giving coherent expression to the association of ideas which flashed across his memory. The others started away from him. Even Edith drew back in alarm. Although they were about to die it seemed a terrible thing that one of their number should go out of life mad.

"Don't you remember, Ole?" he continued, barely able to utter the words for emotion. "The oil from the shale on the beach oozed down into the hole where that green stuff lay. That plant was the same as this. What destroyed it? Oil! The whole mass was dissolved, a mess of brown sludge when we saw it next. Oil is its natural enemy! Those gas flames made me think of oil. Thank God for memory!"

They still thought him demented.

"Nitric acid might as well be its natural enemy," Drake remarked, "for all the good it will do us. Where are we to get oil?"

Drake had not yet learned that genius is the gift for making the most of circumstances.

"Where?" the Doctor shouted. "From the tank of the airplane of course. Edith, can you spare two hundred gallons and still have enough petrol to take us to the south shore of the oil lake?"

"Yes. It is less than a ten-minute fly. I can spare three hundred gallons if you need that much and have plenty to fly to the cache by the ship."

But Lane had not yet thought that far. Neither his own possible escape from death nor that of the party had yet come above his horizon. He was planning greater deliverance.

"Break through to the plane, Ole," he ordered, "while I get the can."

The twelve feet to the oil tank took only half an hour. Hope had trebled their strength. The first petrol drawn was used to soak the spores in the can. These were then thrown away in the tunnel and the can washed clean.

"Strip that green devil off the plane somehow, the rest of you," Lane directed, "while I spread the petrol in the tunnel."

They went at the job like tigers.

"Look," Lane cried from the tunnel. "See what the soaked spores did."

Hurrying back they found him standing in a pool of brown muck. Like a field of dry flax before a fire the eight-foot wall of green hair was dissolving round the edges of the pool. The almost instantaneous decay ate like a flame into the impenetrable thicket. Lane carefully spread his can of oil against the matted roots along the left side of the tunnel. When he returned with the second can a band of brown slush two feet broad marked the destruction wrought by the first.

Four hours later they had cleared the plane and opened up a straight alleyway through the matted tangle sufficiently broad and long enough for the plane to run along and take the air.

"Hang on all your dynamite," Lane ordered. "I'll bring the can. Leave everything else."

Ole and Edith climbed into their places, Drake sat on the back of the seat clutching Ole round the neck, while Lane and the Captain disposing themselves on either side of Drake clung to him and to one another. The load, although considerable, was far below the plane's lifting capacity. Edith ran it down the long alleyway and lifted from the brown sludge with thirty feet to spare.

Their last look at the blowholes showed the green mounds all about them lit up by the cheery fires.

Rising to the thousand foot level they saw beneath them a vivid green band twelve miles broad winding like a river due north toward the oil lake.

"That's what the wind did with the spores we lost last night. The stuff multiplies on itself like compound interest at ten thousand per cent. Unless we stop its growth now this whole continent will be matted thick in a month."

"And then it will blow across the ocean to South America."

"Not if I can help it. We don't know yet whether it can multiply like this in a warmer climate. Freezing temperature seems to act on it like a violent stimulant. For all we know it might be controllable at ten degrees and perish at fifty. But I'm not going to find out. This plague will never get farther than that lake. Land near the cache, Edith. We shall need all the dynamite we have."

Anderson guessing the Doctor's purpose made no remonstrance. The oil had risen higher in the lake during the night. Six inches more and it would begin spilling over the south barrier of the lake. But they could not wait for nature. The green plague river was broadening before their eyes. In half a day it would have streamed up the intervening three miles to the oil lake, surrounded it, and swept onto the desolate plain beyond in its ever swifter rush to the ocean.

Ole unearthed the pick and began digging furiously into the ice under the narrowest point of the barrier.

"How long will it take to fly across the lake, Edith?" Lane asked.

"Twenty minutes at the most."

"Then give your shots a twenty-minute fuse," Lane directed. "We shan't stay to see the show. The oil may catch when the dynamite explodes. All hands soak themselves in crude oil. We can't risk starting those infernal spores in a new place."

Setting the example Lane baled up several canfulls of the black oil and drenched himself from head to feet. Then he soused the plane. Having finished he passed the can to Drake and stood watching Anderson at his work. The Captain was saying nothing in the presence of his tragedy.

"Look here, Captain," Lane said, "all this is due to my stupidity alone. I have lost your oil for you. In slight return I shall make you a present of the finest thousand-acre orange grove in California."

The proud temptation to refuse gave way to the memory of twenty years of cold and stink.

"I accept the sunshine and orange blossoms with all my thanks," the Captain replied.

"And while you are about that job," Lane continued, "put this in with the dynamite too." He handed the Captain his tobacco box containing the parasites which he had scraped from the monster's tail. "I shall not take another chance with any of the infernal diseases of the archæan age," he said.

Having planted the last charge Anderson soaked his clothing in oil before lighting all four fuses. He then clambered up on the plane with the others. They were off as fast as they could fly.

Twenty minutes passed, twenty-five, and they were well beyond the north shore of the lake speeding toward the ship.

"Are you sure those fuses were dry?" Lane shouted above the roar of the propeller.

Anderson nodded. They flew another three minutes before hearing in rapid succession the four dull explosions which announced the release of the oil flood.

Nearing the ship they saw Bronson and the men on the ice near the petrol cache loafing about, exercising the dogs and the now sturdy devil chick.

"Out of here at once," Anderson ordered. "Is steam up?"

"Yes sir."

"Send four of the men to the petrol cache to fill the tank of the plane to capacity. Order the rest to get the sledges and their packs in shape for an immediate march to the coast. Hell's going to break loose."

Bronson obeyed orders on the run.

"Now Edith," Anderson continued, "you and Hansen stand by ready to follow the ship down the channel. If mud comes down and mires us fly as fast as you can to the nearest whaling station and send help. Ole will do the navigating. We shall pack to the coast and wait there for relief."

"Can I take the devil chick?" she pleaded.

"That brute? It's as big as a cow."

"The plane can lift it easily."

"Nothing doing. But," he added, seeing the tears in her eyes, "we'll herd the ugly beast along with us to the coast if we have to hike."

Bronson rejoined them to say that the plane was now ready for a thousand mile flight.

"Very well. Get the ship out of here. Have the men ready to leave her at the first sign of trouble."

The men were already stowing their effects, including the obstinate devil chick, aboard the ship.

Bronson had gone but four steps when the ice leapt into a crimson glow.

"Get the men on the ice and run for the coast," Anderson shouted.

The men needed no orders. They were swarming out as fast as they could. The appalling concussion swept over them just as they reached the ice. Looking south they saw the roof of the continent hurtling skyward. A vast gush of red flames surging up overtook the black mass, flattened along its underside in curling billows of crimson, and for an instant pressed the millions of tons of suspended rock and cement hard against the sky. Then it fell.

The fliers were already headed for the coast. Edith's last vision of the ship revealed one of the crew tugging desperately at the devil chick's head in a final attempt to get it ashore again. Failing, the man abandoned the wretched creature and jumped to save his own life.

The falling of the suspended rock had set up a choppy land tide of waves twenty feet high. Like a thunderclap the walls of the inlet met, parted, and met again. The ship was matches.

Explosion after explosion rolled the fleeing machine over and over in the turbulent air like a feather. But it was a well built plane, and nothing of consequence snapped.

The fliers, better than the men far behind reeling over the heaving ice, knew what might come at any instant. The oil which had gushed over the plain from the lake, to plunge down the flaming blowholes and generate vast quantities of gas, must still be rushing in a river of fire toward the subterranean reservoirs beneath the unruined paradise. That the two chains of underground lakes were connected they had good grounds for believing.

Their expectations were realized late that afternoon as they sped northeast in their flight toward the nearest whaling station. Neither has any memory of how they weathered the unimaginable tempest of detonations which shook the upper air from the Antarctic to Rio. The unruined paradise was ruined.

Four weeks later the whaling vessel *Orion* of Boston rescued a party of stunned and half-starved men shivering on the ice at the mouth of what had been the inlet. They were unable to give any coherent account of their experiences. Not a member of the crew had been lost. The expedition had returned with its life.

Eric Temple Bell (1883–1960) was a mathematician who taught at the California Institute of Technology. The eponym of Bell polynomials and Bell numbers of combinatorics, his 1937 book *Men of Mathematics* would help to inspire Julia Robinson, John Forbes Nash Jr., Andrew Wiles, and other future mathematicians. Writing as John Taine, he published many proto-sf novels, several of which—including 1929's *The Greatest Adventure*—involve scientifically precipitated, yet out-of-control evolution.

S. L. Huang is a Hugo-winning, bestselling author who justifies an MIT degree by using it to write eccentric mathematical superhero fiction. Huang is the author of the Cas Russell novels from Tor Books, including *Zero Sum Game*, *Null Set*, and *Critical Point*, as well as the new fantasies *Burning Roses* and *The Water Outlaws*. Huang's stories have appeared in *Analog*, *F&SF*, *Nature*, and elsewhere. Huang is also a Hollywood stunt performer and firearms expert, with credits including *Battlestar Galactica* and *Top Shot*.